PRAISE FOR

If You Find This

A Booklist Top Ten 2015 Debut Novel
An Edgar Award Nominee for
Best Juvenile Mystery

"This unique book is both **a ripping adventure** and a piercing portrait of an extraordinary boy. **You've never heard a tale told like this**.... For that, and many other reasons, **it demands to be read** and discussed."
—Adam Gidwitz, *New York Times* bestselling and Newbery Honor author of *A Tale Dark and Grimm* and *The Inquisitor's Tale*

"An **intriguing** treasure hunt of a book that will be **forever treasured**." —Vince Vawter, Newbery Honor author of *Paperboy*

"*If You Find This* is a seriously **offbeat**, ambitious, and ultimately charming tale, witty and eloquent, with surprising moments of beauty—to say nothing of the **rollicking** treasure hunt at its heart. **Three cheers to Matthew Baker for writing us a twenty-first-century *Tom Sawyer*!**" —Tony Abbott, author of *Firegirl* and *The Postcard*

IF YOU FIND THIS

by

MATTHEW BAKER

LITTLE, BROWN AND COMPANY
New York Boston

Text copyright © 2015 by Matthew Baker
Illustrations copyright © 2015 by Iacopo Bruno

Cover art by Iacopo Bruno. Background map by Matthew Baker.
Cover copyright © 2015 by Hachette Book Group, Inc.

Little, Brown and Company
Hachette Book Group
1290 Avenue of the Americas, New York, NY 10104
Visit us at LBYR.com

Originally published in hardcover and ebook by
Little, Brown and Company in March 2015
First Trade Paperback Edition: October 2017

Little, Brown and Company is a division of Hachette Book Group, Inc. The Little, Brown name and logo are trademarks of Hachette Book Group, Inc.

The publisher is not responsible for websites (or their content) that are not owned by the publisher.

The Library of Congress has cataloged the hardcover edition as follows:

Baker, Matthew, 1985–
    If you find this / by Matthew Baker.
        pages cm
    Summary: When the grandfather he never knew is released from prison suffering from dementia, eleven-year-old Nicholas, a mathematical and musical genius, tries to save the family's home by helping search for heirlooms Grandpa claims to have buried.
    ISBN 978-0-316-24008-6 (hardcover)—ISBN 978-0-316-24010-9 (ebook)—ISBN 978-0-316-24014-7 (library edition ebook)
    [1. Grandfathers—Fiction.   2. Old age—Fiction.   3. Lost and found possessions— Fiction.   4. Heirlooms—Fiction.   5. Friendship—Fiction.]   I. Title.
    PZ7.B174729If 2015
    [Fic]—dc23

                                                    2013044749

ISBNs: 978-0-316-24009-3 (pbk.), 978-0-316-24010-9 (ebook)
Printed in the United States of America
LSC-C
10 9 8 7 6 5 4 3 2 1

Robert Rowe, I'll plant you here
Also the one who went unnamed

Peter was alone on the lagoon. The rock was very small now; soon it would be submerged...Peter was not quite like other boys; but he was afraid at last. A tremour ran through him, like a shudder passing over the sea; but on the sea one shudder follows another till there are hundreds of them, and Peter felt just the one. Next moment he was standing erect on the rock again, with that smile on his face and a drum beating within him. It was saying, "To die will be an awfully big adventure."

—JAMES MATTHEW BARRIE, Peter Pan

IF YOU FIND THIS

If I die, or get kidnapped by the Isaacs, someone needs to know the truth about what happened to my grandfather. About where my grandfather is. That's why I'm writing all of this down. I'm going to keep these notes under the clothes in my dresser, so if I'm dead, if you're reading this, that must mean you were cleaning the dresser out to throw my clothes away. Which means you found the hatchet too—I didn't steal it, Zeke stole it, to break through the cellar door—and you found the earring, so I did steal that, but I was only keeping it to remember what the homeschooler said to Jordan. I'm going to write down exactly how everything happened. I'm not going to lie to make myself seem braver or smarter than I actually was, because I wasn't brave, I wasn't smart, I was afraid, and even if I got all A's and had square roots memorized like the square root of 537,289, there were problems I couldn't solve alone. If I'm dead, I'm sorry, I had to risk everything. We were trying to find the heirlooms. That's what this is about. Buried heirlooms. A map made of letters and numbers. A revolver, a clock, a hammer, a box. This is about my grandfather, my father, my brother. This is about trying to save someone you love.

This is what I'm saying. I need you to understand how everything happened. I need you to understand that none of it was my fault. When you're eleven, you don't always get to choose between good and bad. Sometimes you have to choose between bad and bad. Sometimes you have to choose between worse and worst.

IN THE YEARS OF TREES

My brother is a tree. He wasn't always a tree. When I was seven, my mom was pregnant and my brother was inside her. I had been asking for a brother for years and years and years, and now I was finally going to have one. But the night before my eighth birthday, my brother came out too soon. He was half-grown, unfinished. There was nothing the doctors could do. He was already dead. We hadn't even named him yet.

I should have known my brother would be born too soon, because a brother being born is a Big Event. The doctors had predicted my brother wouldn't be born until months after my eighth birthday, but that never could have happened. Big Events only happen on years that you're a prime. A prime is a number that's divisible only by one and itself—the primes I've been are two, three, five, seven, and eleven. When I was two, our dog got hit by a truck. When I was three, our kitchen caught on fire. When I was five, I broke my leg, I skipped a grade, and our dog got pregnant and we had to give away the puppies. When I was seven, my mom got pregnant and my brother was born and died. When I turned eleven, my dad got fired from the factory where he built cars and moved to the Upper Peninsula to work at my uncle's repair shop and was never home and we had to give away our dog because we couldn't afford to feed her. Nothing like that happens years that I'm not a prime. That year that my brother died I was seven and my mom was forty-one and my dad was forty-three. All of us were primes. My brother never had a chance.

After my brother died, my parents said we would plant a tree so we would remember him always, and they drove away (like they had before, to the hospital, when everything had gone wrong) and drove back again with a tree roped to the car—a pine, a sapling, just barely younger than me in the years of trees. After we had buried my brother in the dirt at the edge of our backyard, beyond the swing set he could not climb on and the sandbox he could not play in, we sat on the deck drinking lemonade. I was so happy to have a brother again. My parents never talked about him after that, but I understood that he wasn't dead anymore—that instead he had become this other thing.

During the years that followed, a dog snapped at me in the woods and I got a white scar on my hand, and my dad tripped into me in the garage and I got a white scar on my knee, and birds pecked at my brother with their beaks and scarred my brother's branches, and my dad bumped into my brother with a wheelbarrow and scarred my brother's trunk, and my brother kept my knife in the crook of his branches and my socks sometimes hanging from his twigs and my shoes at his roots, and I kept his pinecones on my windowsill and fistfuls of his needles on my dresser and his sap in a jar in my room in the house where he could not go, and in this way we grew together. I told him everything.

THE PRISONER LIVES

Everything started when I got home from school and my mom shouted, "Nicholas, come into the kitchen, there's something you need to know." Actually, everything started when the Isaacs found me at school and said, "Meet us tonight, the graveyard at sunset, and don't even think about not coming." Or, actually, everything started with locker partners.

Seventh grade means riding a different bus, means having a new building, means sharing lockers with locker partners. Everyone else in my grade was thirteen or twelve, but because I skipped kindergarten, I was still only eleven. Seventh graders are in their own building across from the high school. Everyone had to choose a locker partner. No one wanted Zeke Song, so we were assigned to each other, because no one wanted me either. Zeke is a thief. He steals high-tops from the locker room, backpacks from the choir room, and instruments from the band room. Then he sells everything for money. He keeps the money in a gold backpack on the floor of our locker.

It's not because he's a thief that everyone avoids him. Everyone avoids him because he draws mermaids on his arms in silver marker and because sometimes he barks at teachers like he's a dog. Actually, he probably still would have friends, even with the mermaid drawings and the dog barking, except for that once in fifth grade he kissed Little Isaac on the lips. That's why everyone avoids him. You can't cross Little Isaac like that and still have any friends.

I never saw Zeke at our locker normally—during school he was always sneaking around, stealing. So a few days ago I was unlocking our locker to get my sack lunch (my parents couldn't afford to buy me cafeteria lunch any-more) when I decided to unzip the gold backpack. Just to count the money. Everyone was already in the cafeteria. The hallway was empty. As per usual, the gold backpack was on the floor of our locker, and Zeke's dictionary—a thick one, with a stained cover—sat on the shelf above.

I unzipped the gold backpack halfway. Then I spotted Little Isaac and Big Isaac walking down the hallway. The Isaacs aren't brothers—they're just both named Isaac. Little Isaac is the one who dribbles the ball down the court. Big Isaac is the one who stands under the basket.

"There you are," Little Isaac said.

In band class everyone had learned new terms. *Forte* means "play loudly." *Piano* means "play softly." *Da capo* means "return to the beginning," means "play the song again." In band class I play the violin. I already knew about forte and piano and da capo from taking violin lessons, but some kids learned just that morning.

I rezipped the backpack, shut the locker, spun the combination.

Big Isaac poked the locker with a thumb.

"Unlock it," Big Isaac said.

"But I'm going to lunch," I said.
forte

"He told you to unlock it," Little Isaac said.
forte

Sometimes when people talk piano, that means they're
piano
afraid of you. Sometimes piano means that only you're
supposed to hear what they're saying. Sometimes piano
just means that they're tired. But when Little Isaac talks
piano, that means he's giving you a warning.

The choir teacher came around the corner carrying a
stack of songbooks, glancing at us.

The Isaacs raised their eyebrows, and shifted their
eyes.

"Never mind the locker, Isaac," Big Isaac said.

"Isaac, you're right, never mind the locker," Little
forte
Isaac said.

Little Isaac smiled a fake smile. Big Isaac smiled a fake
forte
smile. I tried slipping past them. They grabbed me. I'm
abnormally skinny, which makes me easy to grab.

"But you," Little Isaac said, frowning now. "Meet us
tonight, the graveyard at sunset, and don't even think
piano
about not coming."

9

Why did they want me to meet them? After school, on the bus, I tried calculating an answer to that question. I live in a village on the shore of Lake Michigan, in the Lower Peninsula, obviously. The lake is the size of a sea, takes a whole day to cross in a sailboat. When our bus passes the wharf, you can see the lake through the trees, just more and more and more water that never ends. Michigan has 64,969 bodies of water (prime). You're never more than seven miles away from a body of water (prime). Anything that isn't water, it's trees. I realized suddenly that maybe the Isaacs were going to ask me to check their math homework. Sometimes kids ask that, because they know my brain is like a calculator. I decided to hope that's what the Isaacs wanted. I was staring through the window with my nose pressed against the glass.

Just then, a fight erupted in the seat across from mine. I didn't know then this fight was noteworthy, but it's noteworthy, 100%. The fight started between a pair of kids in my grade, Jordan Odom and Mark "Flatface" Huff. In sixth grade, Jordan had been friends with Mark Huff. In sixth grade, Jordan had been friends with everyone. But on the bus that afternoon Mark Huff suddenly vaulted over his seat into Jordan's. They wrapped around each other like they were hugging, except they were punching each other's ribs. The Geluso twins vaulted over their seat, and then they were punching Jordan too. One Geluso head-butted Jordan's chin. One Geluso bit Jordan's ear. By now, everyone was cheering, all rooting for Jordan to

forte

lose.

Mr. Carl, our driver, yanked the bus over to the side of the road.

"Knock that off!" Mr. Carl shouted.

forte

The bus had stopped on the empty stretch of road across from the ghosthouse. From the road, all you can see of the ghosthouse is its roof poking above the trees, half of the shingles missing, half of the shingles bleached white by the sun. Kids used to explore the ghosthouse on dares, but no one's dared to go there since a ghost tripped Mark Huff out the attic window.

"Hey, I said, knock that off!" Mr. Carl shouted, getting

forte

angry now.

Everyone quit cheering. The Geluso twins scrambled to their seat. Mark Huff limped to his. Jordan has messy red hair and a gap in his teeth. Now he had a bloody ear, a split lip, and a cut under his chin too.

"You're dead," Mark Huff muttered.

Jordan didn't say anything—just stared at his shoes *piano* on the floor.

●

At home, I gathered the mail from the mailbox, ran up the driveway, then gathered the newspaper from the stoop. My mom's car was parked in the driveway instead of the garage, which meant she must have gone somewhere earlier and was leaving again soon. There were acorns, dark green and pale brown, that had fallen from the trees above the car and gotten caught in its hood.

I knew this was going to be a year of Big Events. I was eleven years old (prime). Plus I was in seventh grade (prime). Plus I was taking an eleventh-grade math class (prime). Plus the year was 1999 (prime). After my dad lost his job and had to move to the Upper Peninsula, the next Big Event of the year was when my mom planted a

FOR SALE sign in our yard. My parents said we weren't making the money we needed to keep our house anymore. I had been afraid of this. Lots of people in our village had been losing their jobs, had been losing their houses to the banks. The houses sat empty, waiting for someone with the money to buy them. No one had the money to buy them. I liked our house, but I could have been happy living anywhere. That wasn't the problem. The problem was that my brother the tree was buried in the backyard, and we couldn't take him with us.

I was avoiding looking at the FOR SALE sign, because seeing it there in our yard always made me feel helpless, and doomed, and kind of dizzy. But I could hear it anyway, swaying in the breeze, creaking, like it wasn't going to let me forget that my days here *piano* were numbered. I slipped into the house, as the door thunked shut behind me.

Inside, I slid onto the piano *forte* bench, I was dying to play a song, but before I could even get my fingers onto the keys I heard my mom shouting, "Nicholas, come into the kitchen, there's something *forte* you need to know."

Our kitchen smelled like cinnamon, as per usual, plus

cigarettes, which was new. Mom smokes now? I thought, but I didn't say anything. Parents have all sorts of secrets. When you live with them you're always finding out new things about them. I piled stamped envelopes on the counter, alongside the newspaper.

"Dad call today?" I said.

forte

"He'll call his next day off," my mom said. "The usual schedule." She was chopping green tomatoes on the cut-

forte

ting board. She doesn't normally make me a sandwich after school, but it looked like she was making me a sand-wich. She was wearing her uniform, plus her name tag, which says BEA. She works at the rest home, changing sheets and sweeping floors. We both have tangled hair and upturned noses. "Nicholas, your grandfather is here."

I shoved a lock of hair out of my eyes.

"Grandfather? What grandfather? I thought he was dead?" I said.

forte

"Grandpa Funes is dead. This is Grandpa Rose," my mom said.

forte

"Your father?" I said.

forte

"Yes," my mom said.

forte

14

"You said he was dead," I said.

"I never said he was dead," my mom said.
forte

"You definitely said he was dead," I said.
forte

"He wasn't," my mom said.
forte

"Where has he been?" I said.
forte

"Prison," my mom said.
piano

My dad's nickname for Grandpa Rose was The Prisoner. I had never understood the nickname until now.

"Prison? Since when? This whole time?" I said.
forte

"Twice. Once before I was born. And once since I was fifteen," my mom said. She nicked a finger with the knife. She gasped, like THAT HURT. She cranked the faucet and held the finger under the water. "And if I told you
forte
piano
he was dead, that's because everybody said that this time he would die before his sentence ended, and I thought it would be better for me and for you and for everybody to pretend that he was dead already, than to talk about him being in prison." She wiped her hands with a faded towel. "But he didn't die. He had cancer but survived it. He had a stroke but survived it. He had another stroke but survived it. He somehow survived everything, and his sentence

ended, and today he called me from the train station to tell me that he was home."

My mom hardly ever talked about Grandpa Rose. And she never had said anything about him being a criminal. Or about him being in prison. Or about him being alive.

"Now he lives here?" I said.

"He's eighty-nine, Nicholas. *forte* Sometimes he gets confused. He can have problems remembering where he is, or what he's doing, or who he's talking to," my mom said. "When I drove to the train station, Grandpa Rose *forte* wasn't there anymore. I searched the phone booths. I searched the ticket counters. I searched the train platforms. I begged a worker to search the bathrooms. He wasn't anywhere. I drove home again, worried sick something had happened. Then I saw him. Walking along the road, covered with dust, dragging a suitcase. Headed the completely wrong direction. It took me an hour to get him into the car. He didn't remember calling me. He didn't even remember who I was." She laid the tomatoes on the sandwich. "He can't live here. We can't take care of him. Especially with your dad gone." She handed me the plate. "I'm late already. I can't miss work. I need you to watch him. Tonight I'll ask about getting a room at the rest home. The sandwich is for him. There are leftovers if you're hungry."

I wanted to say, "I can't watch Grandpa Rose because I have to meet the Isaacs at the graveyard and if I don't then they'll hurt me," but I couldn't tell her that.

"If he offers you a cigarette, say no. If he offers to teach you how to steal a car, say no. He might get confused, but if he tries to leave, just sit him down again and turn on the television," my mom said. "He can sleep on the couch, okay? Call me if you have questions. Do your homework, brush your teeth." She kissed my head, which I don't allow unless we're alone. Then she threw open the door and sent me scooting onto the deck.

Grandpa Rose was sitting on a chair there with a cigarette pinched between a pair of fingers. He had a thick gnarled beard, white with streaks of gray, twisted into snarls across his cheeks, curled over his lips, in knots under his jaw. He was wearing gray pants, a leather belt, and a bluish shirt with the shirtsleeves rolled to the elbows. Beyond him the wind was tearing gold leaves from the oak trees, floating the leaves off into the woods. My mom shut the door without saying goodbye.

I brought him the sandwich.

"I hear you're a whiz with numbers," Grandpa Rose said. He bit into the sandwich and stared at me as he chewed. Everyone says my eyes are the color of limes, but my dad has brown eyes and my mom has brown eyes, so I always thought that my green eyes hadn't come from anyone. But Grandpa Rose's eyes were that exact same green as mine. He was huge and skinny, and his skin was wrinkled and veiny, and his face was freckled with white sunspots. He was the best grandfather I ever could have imagined. I was too afraid of him to speak or even breathe. "A math whiz. Like Grandma Rose. Your Grandma Rose was a whiz with numbers too. Bring me my cane, would you, kid?"

He was scratching at the beard like it was a sweater he wasn't used to wearing. I brought him the cane that was leaning against the house.

"Naptime for this grandpa," Grandpa Rose said. "I have a big trip to make later, so I'm going to need my energy."

18

He swallowed the rest of the sandwich and hobbled into the house. I wanted to know if he had ever killed anyone. I wanted to know if he remembered my name.

Grandpa Rose was snoring already on the couch. I took my violin from my backpack and hopped the railing and ran to the woods to talk to my brother the tree. We talk with music. Whenever I have a question, I ask my brother. My brother always has an answer. When I'm not home my brother talks to the birds, who have been everywhere and seen everything, and to the older trees, who are majorly wise.

I sawed my bow across my violin, making notes that meant, BROTHER OUR GRANDPA ROSE IS ALIVE SOMEHOW AND AT OUR HOUSE. I AM SUPPOSED TO WATCH HIM BUT I AM SUPPOSED TO MEET THE ISAACS AT THE GRAVEYARD TOO. SO NOW WHAT?

My brother uses the wind to make music with his branches. Also sometimes the birds help him with his songs.

My brother's song said, MEET THE ISAACS. BUT TAKE YOUR KNIFE. I WILL WATCH OUR GRANDFATHER FROM HERE.

My knife was back in the house, in my bedroom, in my closet somewhere. I didn't have time to get it. The sun was setting. The Isaacs were probably already waiting. I hid my violin under the deck and ran down the driveway.

●

Our road runs from the wharf, past the ghosthouse, through our neighborhood, into town. I was heading toward town, obviously. I crossed the stone bridge over the creek, where the woods finally die off into lampposts and sidewalks, and kept running. Downtown in our village is just one strip, lined by shops with square signs and diamond windows. Just before the shops is the grave-yard, with hundreds and hundreds of tilting gravestones and crumbling monuments, sprawling over hills over-grown with weeds. The rest home sits across the street from the graveyard, its door facing its gate. I've never had a grandparent who lived at the rest home, only a mom who works there. I clattered into the graveyard over its *forte* spiked fence.

Gold clouds were drifting above the graveyard. Below, Little Isaac and Big Isaac were leaning against a tomb topped with a stone boy. The stone boy was naked except for some stone leaves. Beyond the tomb sat a chained mausoleum, the sort of building where whole families were buried, that said XAVIER 1847–1913.

"Hi," I said.

forte

"Consider yourself tardy," Little Isaac said.

forte

Big Isaac grabbed me and dragged me behind the tomb and shoved me against the stone boy, while Little Isaac stooped in the weeds for a wound coil of moldy rope. I shouted for help as the Isaacs tied me to the stone legs.

forte

Big Isaac hit me in the ribs.

"Stop screaming," Little Isaac said.

"You're acting like a kindergartner," Big Isaac said.

forte

"All we want is the combination to your locker," Little Isaac said.

forte

forte

The Isaacs peeked around the tomb as a truck sputtered past the graveyard. The Isaacs were wearing black basketball hoodies. Basketball hoodies have names and numbers printed on the back. Little Isaac's said ISAAC 17. Big Isaac's said ISAAC 19. Little Isaac's pouch was bulging with something that had edges like a knife's.

"Now there aren't any teachers around, let's try this again," Little Isaac said.

"Are you going to take Zeke's money?" I said.
forte

"You think we need Zeke's money?" Little Isaac said.
forte

"We don't need anybody's money. Our parents give us anything we want. No, your locker partner stole something from us, something we need."

"You're going to take Zeke's money," I said.
forte

Big Isaac hit me again. I made myself think about music so I wouldn't have to think about hurting. I thought, forte means loud. I thought, piano means soft. I thought, da capo means return to the beginning, means play the song again. Big Isaac hit me again. Kids love the Isaacs. The Isaacs are as mean as Jordan Odom, but he's mean to everyone, which is why everyone hates him. The Isaacs are only mean to kids like me, kids who don't have any friends. Every year the Isaacs have to buy extra yearbooks, because so many kids sign their original yearbooks that there isn't any room for more signatures. Big Isaac hit me again. I didn't want to give the combination to the Isaacs. I was trying to protect Zeke.

Little Isaac unlaced my high-tops and twisted them off and tossed them behind a tomb, as Big Isaac lifted a boot to stomp my toes, and I braced myself against the stone boy, already wincing.

"Just say the combination," Little Isaac said.

piano

Then I thought of a way to tell them the combination without telling them. I shouted the combination, but in a language they didn't speak. I shouted the combination in square roots.

"The square root of 529! The square root of 49! The square root of 2,209! That's the combination!" I shouted.

forte

Big Isaac stomped my toes anyway. I shouted the square roots again. Little Isaac reached into the pouch of his hoodie.

forte

"Saw that coming," Little Isaac said, taking a calcu-lator from the pouch. "I might not be a genius, but that doesn't mean I don't know how to use a calculator." He punched different numbers into the keys of the calculator. "23. 7. 47. That's the combination? 23. 7. 47." He snorted. "Thanks, sucker."

forte

piano

The Isaacs stalked into the graveyard, vanishing beyond some mossy tombs.

I jerked against the rope until I could wriggle loose. Then I sat against the XAVIER mausoleum, peeking under my shirt. My ribs were marked with newborn bruises. I knew what this was for the Isaacs. This wasn't the end of anything. This was the da capo. I was a song they would want to keep singing.

I found my high-tops behind an urn of flowers. I limped home carrying a high-top in each hand.

I picked my way through scattered rocks, fallen acorns, rosy shards of glass, in my socks. Trees swayed above the road, as squirrels leapt between branches. I was crossing the stone bridge, back over the creek again, when I spotted something flickering through the woods. A glint of jean, a wink of shirt. Someone creeping through the trees. It was my locker partner.

Zeke slipped from the trees into the road. His dogs were there too, three wolfdogs with bright eyes and thick tongues. Zeke has dark hair like mine, but buzzed to the

scalp. His arms, as per usual, were scrawled with drawings of mermaids.

"Did you give them the combination?" Zeke said.
forte

"I didn't mean to," I said.
forte

"Coward," Zeke said.
forte

He had never spoken to me before. His voice was
reedy, sort of growly. One of his wolfdogs huffed.
piano

"What did you steal from them?" I said, but Zeke
forte

and his wolfdogs had trotted into the trees, had splashed
piano

across the creek, had vanished already. Now he hated me
too.

And when I got home, Grandpa Rose wasn't napping
on the couch, wasn't sitting on the deck, wasn't anywhere.
His cane was gone. He was gone. Gold leaves had blown
into the house through the door he hadn't shut.

I had lost him.

I didn't even know where to start looking.

A WARNING

Everyone is afraid of me because of my theories. I have too many of them. I talk about them when I shouldn't. The problem is that I'm always thinking and that I can't stop thinking. Like one morning when I was in first grade, I thought of something I hadn't thought of before. I woke, I blinked a few times, I saw the ceiling above my bed—and then I realized that I was in the same body that I had been in when I had fallen asleep. And it surprised me. It seemed odd to me. That I would never be in another body. That I always would be stuck in my own body. That every morning I would be waking to that same ceiling. I don't know why, but it made me sad. Even more than sad. Sad^{sad}—sad to the power of sad—sad multiplied by itself a sad number of times. That I would never know what it was like to be anyone other than me—what chocolate tasted like to their tongue, what the color green looked like to them, what it felt like to have their feet.

On the playground that afternoon, I was drawing a forest with chalk I had brought from home. Mark Huff and the Geluso twins had borrowed some of the chalk to draw pirates fighting on a ghost ship. I stopped drawing.

"Want to know something that, once you start thinking about it, you'll never stop thinking about it, and then you'll lose your mind?" I said.

Mark Huff said *forte* yes. The Geluso twins didn't say *piano* anything.

"Every morning you're going to wake in the same body. You'll only ever be in one body. You'll only ever be yourself," I said.

None of *forte* them said anything. They gave me back my chalk. Then they ran away toward the soccer field. Before that they had asked to borrow my chalk almost every day. After that they never asked to borrow my chalk again.

I'm telling you this as a warning. Kids at school don't talk to me because they think that I have Dangerous Ideas. And I can't explain everything that's happened without Dangerous Ideas. So if you found these, I can't stop you from reading them. But you might want to stop yourself.

THE GHOSTHOUSE

I started to panic. I ran to my bedroom and cupped brittle brown pine needles between my hands and made myself breathe. The needles smell like my brother, which helps calm me down. I breathed through the needles, crisp tart air. I needed to think.

Grandpa Rose was missing. That was a fact. My mom worked the night shift and wouldn't get home until almost morning. That was a fact. If I called my mom and said that I had lost Grandpa Rose, I would be grounded for the rest of my life, or at least until eighth grade. That was a fact. I would have to find Grandpa Rose myself.

I didn't have any facts about where Grandpa Rose might have gone. To answer the question, I needed additional information. In my parents' bedroom I found Grandpa Rose's luggage, a leather suitcase with metal hinges. In the suitcase there were,

1. A broken music box, dark wood with gold swirls on the lid
2. A passport, with stamps on every page, plus a photo of MONTE ROSE
3. A couple of letters written in a language I couldn't understand (Italian?)
4. Underwear (boxers with green stripes)
5. Socks (the kind with gold toes)

I memorized the information. I kicked into my high-tops. Then I dug through my closet for my knife. The knife has a cracking leather sheath, a cracking leather handle, and a blunt chipped blade the length of a geometry compass. I belted it to my leg, where it would be hidden under my jeans, and went looking for Grandpa Rose.

●

By now dinnertime had come and gone, and all the neighborhood regulars were out, enjoying what remained of the daylight before the twilight went to dusk. Mark Huff, kicking a soccer ball around his yard. The Geluso
piano
twins, careening around on bicycles, shouting some-
forte
thing about zombies. Emma Dirge and her sisters floating up and down on their trampoline, their dresses snapping against their legs as they floated up, puffing out again as they floated down. Leah Keen sprawled on the grass underneath, watching the feet slamming against the trampoline. Everyone ignored me, as per usual.

The Geluso twins cranked past me on their bicycles.
piano
"Have you seen my grandfather?" I shouted.
forte
They looped around, skidding to a stop where I was
piano
standing.

"What did you say?" Crooked Teeth said.
forte
"Have you seen my grandfather?" I said.
forte
"We don't pay attention to old people," The Unibrow said.
forte

31

They hopped onto their bicycles and cranked away
piano
again.

●

Zeke and his wolfdogs were sprawled across the wildflowers along the creek. Zeke had his jeans rolled to the knees,
was feeding his wolfdogs biscuits from the pocket of his
shirt. I peeked over the railing of the stone bridge.

"My grandfather ran away while I was getting tor-
tured by kids who hate you," I shouted.
forte

Zeke didn't say anything.

"It's your fault he's missing, so you're going to help me
find him," I shouted.
forte

A wolfdog raised its head and growled.
piano

"You can't make me," Zeke said.
forte

It was true, which was frustrating, so I kicked the
bridge, which hurt. Zeke laughed. I shoved a lock of hair
forte
out of my eyes and kept walking.

As I was crossing the bridge, though, Zeke and his
wolfdogs scrambled from the trees into the road.

"If I help you, you have to swear that next time you
won't give the Isaacs even a single number," Zeke said.
forte

"They already know our combination," I said.

forte

"I'll fix that," Zeke said.

forte

"How?" I said.

forte

"Also, if you're trying to find your grandfather, you're going the wrong way. He wasn't headed into town. He was headed toward the wharf," Zeke said.

forte

"You saw him?" I said.

forte

"He had your same eyes," Zeke said.

forte

●

The wolfdogs needed Grandpa Rose's scent, so we headed toward my house.

Something I think is odd is that we'll give a person a name, but we won't give a group of people a name too. Like how my name is Nicholas, and my mom's name is Beatrice, but when we're together, Nicholas + Beatrice, we're something different. When I'm part of Nicholas + Beatrice, I'm different from when I'm only Nicholas. Or when Little Isaac is only Little Isaac, he's nice, and when Big Isaac is only Big Isaac, he's nice, but Little Isaac + Big Isaac is something mean, but then Little Isaac + Big Isaac + Mark Huff is something nice again.

Nicholas + Zeke was a sort of equation no one had ever had to solve before. Emma Dirge and Leah Keen were perched in the gnarled branches of a beech tree, watching us through the leaves as we flew past. For them, Nicholas + Zeke = ? They didn't know whether Nicholas + Zeke was something they should want to talk to or something they shouldn't.

As we ran up my driveway, Emma and Leah dropped from the beech tree, brushed some bark mulch from their knees, then hurried off toward Mark Huff's, to gossip, probably. I dug my key out of my pocket, and let us in.

The house was quiet. The furniture was turning bluish in the dying light. The wolfdogs sniffed the couch's cushions, the piano's keys, the oven. Zeke barked at them, and they trotted after us down the hallway, sniffing the carpet.

forte

Grandpa Rose's suitcase was still in my parents' bedroom. My mom probably wouldn't have wanted me bringing someone from school in there—especially when the bed hadn't been made, and dirty pajamas were hanging from a lampshade—but this was an emergency, obviously. Beyond the dusty glass of the windowpane, our backyard was visible—my brother was upset, trembling in the wind, worried about Grandpa Rose being missing.

I unlatched the suitcase. Zeke lifted out the music box, touching a finger to its gold crank, its gold clasp, the gold pattern twisting in swirls across the dark wood of its lid.

"Where did your grandfather get something as old as this?" Zeke said.

forte

"How do you know it's old?" I said.

forte

Zeke chewed a lip. He tucked the music box back into the suitcase. Then he plucked a handful of dirty socks from the suitcase for the wolfdogs to sniff.

"You have that scent?" Zeke murmured, nuzzling his

piano

head against theirs.

●

I didn't know if we were friends now, or just locker partners searching for a missing grandfather. I wanted to be friends, because I thought having a friend would be like having a brother. It's not that I didn't love my brother. It's that sometimes I would have liked having a human brother too.

The wolfdogs were trotting ahead, sniffing the gravel for some scent of Grandpa Rose.

"What's your grandfather after?" Zeke said.

forte

"I don't think he's after anything. He gets confused sometimes," I said.

forte

"He didn't look confused. He looked like he was after something," Zeke said.

forte

We were to the wharf almost. We rounded the bend in the road, passing onto the empty stretch where the ghosthouse sat perched on its hill. Its winding dirt driveway, like the rest of the hill, was buried under dying leaves. The mailbox had missing numbers.

The wolfdogs stopped, raising their heads, their snouts pointing at where the roof of the ghosthouse was poking above the trees.

I didn't like where this was headed. Even just looking at the ghosthouse made me feel at risk of getting haunted. I didn't want to go anywhere near that hill.

Zeke sniffed the air.

piano

"He was smoking before," Zeke said. "Do you smell that?"

forte

I sniffed the air. I couldn't smell anything except rotting leaves, rotting pine, and the wind from the lake.

Zeke sniffed again, scowling.

forte

"We're not far now," Zeke said. "I smell cigarette."

forte

●

I kept begging the trail to change direction, but instead the wolfdogs slipped into the underbrush and scrambled over a toppled wooden fence and then galloped straight *piano* up the hill, sniffing at leaves and twigs and dirt, until the scent had led us all the way to the ghosthouse.

"Have you ever been here?" I whispered.

"Not since that ghost tripped Mark Huff out the attic *piano* window," Zeke whispered.

The sky was going dark, and getting starry, and every-*piano* thing was transforming into silhouettes. The ghosthouse loomed above the yard. Tattered curtains flapped beyond shattered windows. A dead walnut tree was hunched next to the porch. Weeds had grown through fallen shutters. A bucket swung creaking from a rope above a stone well. I was freezing, suddenly, and had frozen—was too afraid *piano* to get any closer—stood shivering with my knife clutched between both hands.

"Grandpa Rose?" I whispered.

piano

Zeke crept up the steps, squatted on the porch, then turned and waved a stomped cigarette.

"He must be here," Zeke hissed.

I crept up the steps. The wolfdogs prowled below, *piano* sniffing the roots of the walnut tree, the raspberries growing along the cellar, a bird's nest that had fallen from the roof. I kept imagining that any moment a pale dead face was going to appear in a window, shrieking something at us, which was only making things worse.

"You think he went inside?" I whispered.

"Maybe let's try looking through the window," Zeke *piano* whispered.

The wolfdogs had vanished. We crept across the *piano* porch, past the door, toward the window. I wasn't sure if a knife could do anything against a ghost, but I kept my knife out anyway. I was sweating. I was hardly breathing. I couldn't stop imagining those shrieking faces. We crouched beneath the windowsill, then peeked into the ghosthouse.

Dead leaves littered the floor. White ash littered the fireplace. Jags of glass hung from the frame of the window.

Nothing seemed to be moving, except for the flapping^{piano} curtains.

Suddenly from the backyard we heard a banging^{forte} sound.

Zeke looked afraid^{afraid}.

"What was that?" Zeke said.^{forte}

We hopped the railing from the porch onto the grass, peered around a drainpipe into the backyard. The wolf-dogs were circling a lopsided wooden shed, huffing at a smell in the dirt.^{piano} Past the shed sprawled a grassy meadow of milkweed and thistles, and then woods. Bats flitted over the meadow. Normally, in my neighborhood, by this time of night you would see the lit-up windows of houses everywhere. But here there weren't any lit-up windows— like the ghosthouse didn't just scare away people, but even other houses.

All that dark past the shed only made the light that was coming from the shed even freakier. Something was glowing in the shed—a ghostly golden glimmer, stream-ing through the slats between the wooden planks, burn-ing the dirt around the shed white.

We crept across the backyard, pressed our faces to the slats, squinting into the light.

In the shed, Grandpa Rose was rooting around a cluttered workbench, lit by a rusty metal lantern.

"That's him!" I whispered.

Grandpa Rose was mumbling, *piano* "Then key, then trunk, then cog." Then shouting, *piano* "No! Sinbad, Clemens! No no no!" Then mumbling, *forte* "Then key, then trunk, then cog." He didn't sound anything like the Grandpa Rose I had *piano* met before. He sounded like a different Grandpa Rose altogether. As confused as my mom had warned me.

"I've got to go," Zeke whispered.
piano

"But—" I said.
piano

"I did my part," Zeke whispered.
piano

Zeke backed away. He barked at his wolfdogs, then ran into the trees, his wolfdogs trailing him. He was gone.
forte

●

I stuffed my knife into its sheath, then knocked on the shed and cracked open the door. Grandpa Rose stumbled *piano* against the workbench, dropping his cane.

"It's me," I said.
_{forte}

Grandpa Rose frowned.

"Who?" Grandpa Rose said.
_{forte}

"Please, Grandpa Rose, we have to get home," I said.
_{forte}

"But I'm looking for something," Grandpa Rose said.
_{forte}

"Looking for what?" I said.
_{forte}

Grandpa Rose looked at the rusted tools hanging from the workbench. He touched a crowbar, a hammer, a saw. He scratched at his beard with both hands. "I can't remember," he muttered. Then he slapped the shed. He
_{piano} _{forte}
shouted, "I can't remember!"
_{forte}

I tried to pretend I wasn't afraid of him.

"You're confused, Grandpa Rose. Take my hand. I'll walk you home, and you can watch television, and everything will be okay," I said.
_{forte}

I held his arm. He may have been huge, but he was majorly weak. If you shut your eyes, it was like holding the arm of a kindergartner. That's how weak he was. I snuffed the lantern, then led Grandpa Rose out from the shed, into the dusk.

Back at the house, I got Grandpa Rose onto the couch and made another sandwich. He bit in, staring at me as he chewed. Pulpy tomato juice dripped between his fingers to the plate. The ragged blanket my mom keeps on the couch was draped over his body. He had barely lasted the walk home—I'd had to help him the whole way.

"I need you to take me back there," Grandpa Rose said.
forte

"That's the ghosthouse," I said.
forte

"That's my house," Grandpa Rose said.
forte

"Your house?" I said.
forte

I didn't know if this was the confused Grandpa Rose still or if this was the actual Grandpa Rose.

"Mom never said she lived at the ghosthouse," I said.
forte

"She didn't. I did," Grandpa Rose said.
forte

"When?" I said.
forte

"I have things buried," Grandpa Rose said.
forte

I stared through the window above the couch at the silhouettes of the trees in the backyard.

"I'm like that too. My brother's buried back there. If we have to sell our house, I'll never see him again," I said.
forte

"Brother?" Grandpa Rose said.

forte

I told Grandpa Rose about my brother the tree.

He stopped chewing. He swallowed, squinting. He stared through the window at the trees.

"I don't know how to be a grandfather," Grandpa Rose muttered.

piano

"I don't know how to be a grandfather either," I said.

forte

He wasn't blinking. Normally when someone doesn't know something, I try to help, but this was not my area of expertise.

"It's probably the same as being a father," I said.

forte

"Well, I never got that either," Grandpa Rose muttered.

piano

He wiped some tomato seeds from the snarls of hair around his mouth, then bit into the sandwich.

"Help me find what I buried, and you won't lose anything," Grandpa Rose said, chewing.

forte

"Find what?" I said.

forte

"Heirlooms," Grandpa Rose said, swallowing. "Your

forte

family heirlooms. For twenty-nine years they've been buried in the same place. Hidden where they were when I was arrested."

43

"Hidden where?" I said.

forte

"I was in prison, this time, for twenty-nine years," Grandpa Rose said. "Some of those years were for things I actually did. Most of those years were for things I actually

forte

didn't. But, for twenty-nine years, the only thing I lived for was the thought that if I survived that I could give the heirlooms to your mother." He handed me the plate. "I had a few other scores to settle after prison. But those are settled now. The heirlooms are my final job." He wrapped himself into the blanket. "I thought she would understand. But she doesn't understand. She keeps talking about making me live in a rest home." He sank into the couch. "I don't care where you keep me after we've found the heirlooms. Put me in the rest home if you want. But not yet." The blanket rose and fell with his chest. "I wasted my life. Doing wrong, making trouble. I've always been selfish. Before I die I want to do one good thing."

"How much are they worth?" I said.

forte

He was breathing like someone about to sink underwater.

"I made a map to the heirlooms," Grandpa Rose said.

forte

44

He clutched my elbow with a weak twitching grip.

"So I would remember," Grandpa Rose said.

forte

His blinks were changing tempo.

"My tattoos," Grandpa Rose muttered, and then his

piano

eyes shut, and his jaw sank, and his head rolled into the pillow. His face was pale. He wasn't moving. I was almost sure that he was dead.

"Grandpa Rose?" I whispered.

piano

I bent over his face. I held an ear to his lips. I couldn't hear anything.

Then a breath whistled from his chest, like wind whis-

piano

tling from a cave.

He wasn't dead. He was only sleeping.

DEAD MAN'S ROOM

I wasn't sure if the heirlooms existed, but if a map existed, the heirlooms might. And if the heirlooms existed, we could sell the heirlooms, and keep our house, and save my brother.

But what about tattoos?

What tattoos?

Grandpa Rose was already snoring. I took his hands. *forte* His hands had white sunspots but zero tattoos. I flipped his hands. His palms had thick wrinkles but zero tattoos. I rolled his shirtsleeves to the elbows. His arms had black hair but zero tattoos. I rolled his pants to the knees. His legs had black hair but zero tattoos. I unlaced his shoes, scuffed loafers with brown laces. I tossed his socks onto the rug. I crouched. His feet had overgrown toenails but zero tattoos. I flipped his feet. His soles had a black stain, a white scar, and a monster wart, but zero tattoos. I stood. His neck had a birthmark the shape of a whirlpool. His neck had zero tattoos.

If the tattoos were somewhere abnormal, like his butt or something, I wasn't looking there.

I found Grandpa Rose another blanket, and washed the plates in the sink, and brought my violin in *piano* from under the deck. I fell asleep doing homework at the table.

●

When my mom got home, she sat me up and peeled the homework from my face and led me to the bathroom half-asleep, my forehead smeared with backward numbers.

"If we had the money to keep the house, would we keep it?" I mumbled.

piano
She washed the numbers from my face.

"We would keep it. But we'll never have that kind of

money again. Not unless your dad got his job back at the factory," my mom murmured.

piano
She dabbed my face dry with a rough blue towel.

"I'm going to save the house, and every tree in that backyard," I mumbled.

piano
She paused, then set the towel aside, and kissed my head.

"Sorry, but that's impossible," my mom murmured.

piano
She led me to my bedroom. Grandpa Rose was still snoring. I crawled into bed and fell asleep again.
piano

●

Before breakfast in the morning, I kicked into my high-tops and grabbed my violin and ran outside to talk to my brother the tree.

On the deck, I paused. A deer with a crown of antlers was standing alongside my brother.

The deer stared at me. The door slammed shut behind me. *forte* The deer sprang into the woods.

WHO WAS THAT? my song said.

JUST A FRIEND, my brother's song said.

The dirt had paled. The grass had yellowed. We hadn't had a storm in weeks. When there wasn't rain, my brother couldn't drink. I plucked more notes into my violin.

HOW DO YOU FEEL? my song said.

MY ROOTS ARE ACHING, my brother's song said.

WHEN YOU'RE THIRSTY TELL ME, my song said.

I ran to the garage and rooted around for a bucket. My dad kept a photograph tacked to the pegboard in the garage of my mom pushing me on the swing set, which was majorly embarrassing, because back then my head had been way too big for my body. Actually, my head sort of still was. I filled a bucket at the spigot and poured water around my brother until everything there was muddy and swirling with gray and brown.

SO MUCH BETTER, my brother's song said.

My brother went quiet then, just gulping the water.

The heirlooms might not exist. But the heirlooms might exist. And if there was a chance I could save my brother, I had to try.

Before yesterday, my chances hadn't even been 1%.

WHY ARE YOU SMILING? my brother's song said, but I was already running back toward the house.

●

For breakfast I ate oatmeal. Grandpa Rose was awake but confused again. From my first to last bite of oatmeal, he just stared through the windows at the birdhouse, his eyes empty.

I had already searched through his suitcase—he hadn't brought a map with him, at least not a map on paper. But that night before it had almost sounded like he was saying the map and the tattoos were the same thing.

My mom was frying sizzling eggs at the stove.

forte
"Are the tattoos the map?" I whispered.
piano
Grandpa Rose blinked. My mom shook pepper into the pan. I took a bite of oatmeal, hunched low over the bowl, staring at Grandpa Rose.

"Are the tattoos the map?" I whispered.
piano
My mom's slippers scuffed against the floor as she car-
piano
ried her eggs to the table. I pretended to count the cracks in the bowl. Grandpa Rose was staring at nothing.

I decided just to ask my mom what she knew.

"Hey, Mom, do we have family heirlooms?" I said.

My mom frowned, raising her plate and tucking her
forte
shirt against her stomach as she slid into her chair.

"Did Grandpa Rose say something about that to you?"
my mom said, glancing at Grandpa Rose. "He kept going
forte
on about all of that in the car yesterday. Sorry, kiddo, but
there aren't any heirlooms. I tried to tell you, sometimes
he gets confused."

It wasn't impossible for parents to be wrong. For now,
I decided to ignore her theory about the heirlooms. Basically because I didn't like it.

My mom blew some hair out of her eyes, reaching for
a napkin.

"This afternoon I'm bringing him to the rest home,"
my mom said.
forte

"Can't he just live here?" I said.
forte

"He'll be safest living at the rest home. He needs to
live somewhere where he'll have constant supervision.
Even if that means that we have to take out more loans,"
my mom said.
forte

51

I had seen how grandparents lived there. Woken at dawn. Pills with every meal. Nightly scrubbings in showers the size of coffins. Grandpa Rose wouldn't be happy there. No one was.

Pulpy orange juice sloshed from a jug into a cup.

piano

Then, chewing some oatmeal, I suddenly thought of a genius plan.

"I'll come too," I said.

forte

"You want to come?" my mom said, surprised.

forte

"Yes," I said.

forte

He had said not to bring him to the rest home until we had found the heirlooms. But the rest home was maybe the only place I could learn the truth about the tattoos. During showers, the grandparents had to be completely naked—wherever those tattoos were, the nurse there that night for Grandpa Rose's shower was going to see everything.

"Then we'll pick you up on the way," my mom said.

forte

●

At school, in the parking lot, Zeke was selling stolen high-tops to a kid with lip piercings. Zeke always wore a plain

gray shirt with extra dark jeans, but every day wore completely different high-tops. Today's high-tops were bright
white, with silver laces. Whatever high-tops Zeke was
wearing were always up for sale, like an advertisement. If
you wanted, he would sell you the high-tops straight off of
his feet, then change into another pair.

As I thumped out of the bus, Zeke trotted over from
the garbage bin and shoved a scrap of paper into my hands.

forte

"Our new numbers," Zeke murmured.

piano

He ran into school, his dictionary tucked under his
arms like a football.

I unfolded the paper. The paper said 08—27—16 in silver
letters. The same color silver as the mermaid drawings on
Zeke's arms.

Mr. Tim, the janitor, was doing something to the door
of our locker. Little Isaac and Big Isaac were huddled in
the doorway of the bathroom, watching Mr. Tim from
the hoods of their hoodies. Mr. Tim wasn't very old but
already was bald about 83%.

"This your locker?" Mr. Tim said.

forte

I nodded.

"Ezekiel told me everything," Mr. Tim said. "Here's
forte
my question. For weeks neither of you have been able to
remember the combo? For weeks you've been afraid to
tell me that you forgot the combo? For weeks you've been
carrying your books around everywhere instead of asking me to reset the combo? Why's everybody afraid of
me? That's my question."

I didn't know the answer.

"You got the new combo?" Mr. Tim said.
forte

I nodded.

Mr. Tim grunted, like THIS TIME DON'T FORGET, then
piano
wheeled a garbage can toward the choir room. The Isaacs
kept huddling in the bathroom doorway. I spun our new
piano
numbers into our locker. I hated our new numbers. Our
original combination had been all primes, but our new
combination had zero primes, plus only one of the numbers was odd. As I walked to gym class, I tore the combination into shreds. I was afraid the Isaacs would follow
me, looking for our new combination, so I threw half of
the shreds into a garbage can in the hallway and half of
the shreds into a garbage can in the cafeteria.

•

My mom's car was parked at the curb after school. Grandpa Rose was in the backseat, wearing gray pants, a leather belt, and a bluish shirt, as per usual, and hugging his suitcase to his chest. I hopped into the car. We drove to the bank, then to the grocer, then past the graveyard with its mossy tombs and its chained mausoleums and on to the rest home.

A mustached guard supervised the door from a booth, sipping steaming coffee. Grandparents gaped from the *piano* doorways of numbered rooms, slouched across wheel-chairs, hunched over walkers. My mom spoke their *piano* names, smiling at a balding woman with flapping hands, touching the neck of a blind man with a stammering voice. *forte* The rest home smelled like hair spray, shaving cream, and whatever chemicals my mom used for mopping. We sat on rickety plastic chairs in the cafeteria. My mom vanished into the office. It was five, but dinner here was over already, and the cafeteria was empty.

Grandpa Rose stared at the wall, where a menu had been chalked onto a chalkboard.

- BREAKFAST: FRUIT YOGURT SCRAMBLED EGGS
- LUNCH: HAM SANDWICHES SOUP
- DINNER: TURKEY PEAS CARROTS

A nurse walked through and changed the menu from today's to tomorrow's. He only needed to erase three words to change it.

- BREAKFAST: FRUIT YOGURT BOILED EGGS
- LUNCH: TURKEY SANDWICHES SOUP
- DINNER: BEEF PEAS CARROTS

Grandpa Rose blinked. The nurse left again. The meals here sounded rotten.

"When you realize where you are, you're going to be mad, sorry. But there's something we need to do here. And my mom was bringing you either way," I said.

glissando

In band class, everyone had learned mezzo means "medium." So mezzo-forte means "play sort of loudly" and mezzo-piano means "play sort of softly." So from loudest to softest it's forte, mezzo-forte, mezzo-piano, piano. Everyone learned about glissandos too. A glissando is when you suddenly leap between two notes—like when a boy is talking and his voice cracks. At school kids perform glissandos constantly—some boy will be talking, trying to speak normally, when suddenly, on a random word like "milk," his voice will leap a whole octave. I can't stand anywhere near Emma Dirge and Leah Keen without glissandoing. When you glissando, your only move is to pretend that you didn't, praying that no one noticed. But, obviously, everyone noticed.

Sitting there with Grandpa Rose, I heard a voice, suddenly—a brassy jarring muddy lilt, the sound bouncing *piano* along the hallway and into the cafeteria. I leaned toward the sound, listening.

"I recognize that voice from somewhere," I said. *forte*

The voice was someone's from school. A kid's voice. You never heard that here.

"If I leave you alone, you're not going to run away again, are you?" I said. *forte*

Grandpa Rose sat clutching his cane, blinking at the chalkboard, quiet[braindead]. Trying to get him to answer questions when he was like this was pointless.

"Just don't move," I said. *forte*

I snuck off into the hallway.

Jordan Odom was sitting cross-legged on the floor of room #37 (prime). His hands were splayed across the linoleum, stubby fingers that never could have reached an octave on a keyboard. His high-tops had cracking leather, and his jeans were so worn the color had faded almost totally, and his sweatshirt looked like someone's castoff. He had black scabs under his chin and on his ears from the fight on the bus with Mark "Flatface" Huff. Jordan's the one who gave Mark Huff the nickname Flatface. Jordan gave everyone their nicknames. That's half of why no one is friends with him anymore. Jordan was the one who gave the Geluso twins the nicknames Crooked Teeth and The Unibrow (one has crooked teeth but doesn't have a unibrow, one has a unibrow but doesn't have crooked teeth). Emma Dirge he nicknamed Gimpy. Leah Keen he nicknamed Smelly.

I thought about heading back to the cafeteria. The showers would start soon. Whatever happened, I couldn't miss Grandpa Rose's. But I had to eavesdrop, here. My curiosity was hitting peak levels.

I leaned sideways and peeked further into the room. A bald grandfather was sprawled across a bed, the stripes of light from the blinds perpendicular to the stripes of white on his pajamas. His head was spotted with moles, and he was as gap-toothed as Jordan. I didn't know then that this talk was noteworthy, but it's noteworthy, 100%.

"Then I'll find you a new home," Jordan said.

"I don't want a home. I want euthanasia," Jordan's grandfather said.

forte

"Euthanasia?" Jordan said.

forte

"A mercy killing. A coup de grace. Like when a dog has cancer, or gets so old that its body hurts all the time, so its owners do what's humane and just put the dog down," Jordan's grandfather said.

forte

"You mean kill it?" Jordan said.

forte

"I'm an old dog. I hurt all the time. I don't want to end up like Don Wilmore," Jordan's grandfather said. "Don Wilmore lived here for nineteen years, until he was so old that his memories rotted away. He couldn't remember anything. Not even the names of his children. Not even the name of his wife. He had heart attacks, pneumonia, bronchitis, he should have died any number of times, but the nurses wouldn't let him, they kept saving him, they kept bringing him back. Those last few years, he wasn't a person anymore. He was an empty shell."

Thinking about it made me feel nervous^{helpless}. Grandpa Rose's memories were rotting away too. I didn't know how long he had before his memories would rot away totally.

Jordan's grandfather fumbled for a pair of glasses.

"But let's talk about something nice. Tell me about school today! What did you learn?" Jordan's grandfather said.

forte

Jordan squinted, thinking.

"Well, I learned that if out of total boredom you flush a urinal very quickly over and over and over about a hundred times, the urinal will break and completely flood the bathroom floor," Jordan said.

forte

Jordan's grandfather pretended to be ashamed, or maybe wasn't pretending.

"I'm sorry, but that does not count as learning," Jordan's grandfather said.

forte

"The janitor about cried when he saw all of that water," Jordan said.

forte

Jordan leaned against the radiator. He spotted me in the hallway. He frowned.

"Hey, move along, Boyfriend Of Zeke," Jordan said.

mezzo-forte

"What's that supposed to mean?" I said.

forte

"It means move along, so why aren't you moving?" Jordan said.

mezzo-forte

"I meant what's 'Boyfriend Of Zeke' supposed to mean?" I said.

forte

"It means everybody says you've been running around together," Jordan said.

mezzo-forte

Jordan's original nickname for me had been Calculator. Boyfriend Of Zeke didn't seem any better.

"If you aren't careful, he'll try planting a kiss on your lips, like he did to Little Isaac," Jordan said.

mezzo-forte

"He was just helping me find my grandfather," I said.

forte

A woman in a gray papery gown wheeled past, going about half a mile per hour. Her hair was like the hair of someone recently electrocuted. She braked, sat there, made some hacking noises, then started pushing the *forte* wheels again. She seemed as confused as Grandpa Rose.

"Threnody, come down from that boat!" she shouted. *mezzo-forte*

Her wheelchair creaked away toward the cafeteria. *mezzo-piano* Jordan hunched over his knees, gripping his high-tops, glaring at me. Jordan's grandfather smiled and waved hi.

"Hey, Calculator, didn't I tell you to move along?" Jordan said. *glissando*

●

In the cafeteria, the woman in the gray papery gown had braked across from Grandpa Rose. Then she had puked onto his shoes. Now she was crying.

"Worse than prison," Grandpa Rose muttered. *piano*

"I'm sorry, Hunter, I'm sorry," the woman cried. Her *mezzo-piano* lips were wet. I wanted to help her, but I was afraid to touch her.

My mom walked past the cafeteria carrying a bent box and saw what had happened.

"You're okay, Ms. Wilmore," my mom said. She cleaned *mezzo-piano* the woman's lips with a napkin. "Let's get you changed." She wheeled the woman into the hallway.

I didn't say anything. I was sort of stunned.

"I used to be stronger," Grandpa Rose said. "I'm weak
mezzo-piano
now, weaker than a month ago even, the weakest ever."
He punched his legs, like someone stranded kicking
a dead horse. "I thought I could find them myself, but I
don't think I can find them alone anymore. If I'm going
to find them, I need your help. If things get much worse, I
may need you to find them yourself."

"The heirlooms?" I said.
forte
"I don't like to beg, but if that's what it takes, I'll beg,"
Grandpa Rose said. He clutched the hem of my shirt. "I
mezzo-piano
don't have much time. Sneak me away from here. Take me
back there. Please, kid."

"You can't live at the ghosthouse," I said, but I wasn't
forte
sure. I thought, when a grandfather and a mom want different things, how do you know who to listen to?

The memories emptied from his eyes, like waves
crashing onto shore slipping away again.

"What's the map?" I said.
forte
"I tattooed myself," Grandpa Rose mumbled.
mezzo-piano
"Where?" I said.
forte

"To remember," Grandpa Rose mumbled.

mezzo-piano

"Are the heirlooms in the ghosthouse?" I said.

forte

"Everything," Grandpa Rose mumbled.

mezzo-piano

"How much are the heirlooms worth? Are they worth enough that we could keep our house? Are they worth enough that we could save my brother?" I said.

forte

His eyes lit.

"Even more than—" Grandpa Rose said, but then my mom carried a mop and a bucket into the cafeteria.

forte

My mom plunked the bucket onto the floor, slopping some chemicals.

forte *piano*

"Ms. Wilmore's husband died last week. We're emptying his room now. Then we'll unpack Grandpa Rose," my mom said.

forte

"You're leaving me in a dead man's room?" Grandpa Rose said.

forte

I didn't want to point out that every room was a dead man's room, here. Kids avoided this place for the same reason kids avoided the ghosthouse. Because people had died there.

"That's why she was upset? Because her husband's dead?" I said.

forte

64

"No," my mom said. She dunked the mop into the
bucket. *forte* "Usually she doesn't even know where she is. Usu-*piano*
ally she doesn't even know that he's gone."

It was even worse here than I had thought.

●

Grandpa Rose had room #53 (prime), where Mr. Wilmore
had lived a week ago. I tried not to think about whether
his scent was still hanging in the air, whether his voice
was still echoing against the windows. As nurses walked
from room to room, the showers there cranked, on off, on
off, on off. My mom was signing paperwork in the office. *forte*
A nurse with curly hair and speckled glasses was unwrap-
ping a bar of soap for Grandpa Rose. Grandpa Rose didn't
want to shower. He kept rambling about "rumrunners."
He kept asking for the "warden." He kept asking where he
was. As the nurse helped him into the shower, I started
talking. It was time for my genius plan.

"It's a project for school about relatives with tattoos,"
I said.
forte
A faint whiff of lemony soap drifted across the room. The
nurse stood watching Grandpa Rose through the curtain.

"I'd like to avoid seeing him naked, because that's gross, obviously," I said. "But, you have to look at him naked, which solves my problem. So, the tattoos are some-
glissando
where on his body. Whenever you're ready, I need a list of every tattoo, plus detailed descriptions."

The nurse squatted to catch a bottle of shampoo that had rolled out of the shower. Water slushed. Something
mezzo-forte
clonked.
mezzo-piano

"Do you see them? Can you read them? If there are a lot of them, just take them one by one," I said.
forte

The nurse reached through the curtain to steady Grandpa Rose. I couldn't tell if the nurse was listening to me or not. I hadn't counted on the fact that the nurse might just ignore me.

"So?" I said.
forte

The water stopped. Grandpa Rose stopped mumbling. The nurse led him from the shower wrapped in a bathrobe. His beard was matted and dripping water. The nurse toweled his face.

"Sorry," the nurse said.
mezzo-forte

The nurse checked a box on the clipboard hanging from the wall, then looked at me, finally.

"But your grandfather doesn't have any tattoos," the nurse said, and smiled, and then whisked off toward the next room.

mezzo-forte

EVERYONE SHOUTED

I'm the worst at soccer. It's because of what happens when everyone's shouting. I'll get the ball, and I'll think, pass it!, and everyone shouts, "Shoot it!" but *forte* I pass it anyway. Then everyone's mad at me for doing the wrong thing. When everyone shouts at me, I want to listen to them, but I can't. The kids on my team shout, "Shoot it shoot it shoot it!" but I was already thinking, pass it!, *forte* and once I've thought something, I can't stop myself from doing it.

My brain shouts at me sometimes too, like it's kids on

my team. My mom will bake cherry scones for someone's birthday at the rest home, and I'll stand over them on their tray, and look at them, and sniff them, and the kids in my brain will shout, "Don't eat those scones, they're not
forte
for you, they're for someone's birthday!" but I'll eat some anyway, five or seven of them. I'll pack a snowball with ice and dirt and rocks, and I'll watch someone's grandmother drive past in a van, and the kids in my brain will shout, "Don't throw that snowball!" and I try to listen to
forte
them, I want to listen to them, but I throw it anyway, and the snowball thuds into the van's bumper as I run into the
forte
woods and the grandmother stomps on the van's brakes.

That night, at the rest home, the kids in my brain were shouting like never before. Grandpa Rose was sitting on his bed, wearing that bathrobe and borrowed slippers, begging me to sneak him away to the ghosthouse. My mom was still signing paperwork. He wanted me to lie to her. He wanted me to hide him. He didn't want me to tell her where he was, so we could look for the heirlooms together. I still hadn't found any tattoos, I didn't know where the map was, my plan had failed totally. I needed additional information—even if the only place to get that was in the ghosthouse. The kids in my brain shouted, *forte* "Don't listen to him, listen to your mom, she knows what she's doing!" but even while everyone shouted, I was thinking, I'll sneak you away, I know exactly how to do it.

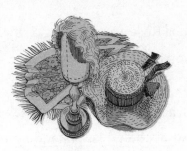

KIDNAPPERS

The next day, before band class started, kids tightened bows, greased cork, swabbed keys, squirted slide oil at each other, peered squinting through mouthpieces, tinkered with the cymbals and the xylophone and the tambourines. A pair of girls with trumpets were running through their parts, the counter-melody to the melody, their bells stuffed with rubber *mezzo-piano* mutes. I sat doing nothing, totally dazed.

People at the rest home were going to freak if Grandpa Rose escaped.

My mom especially.

But Grandpa Rose was counting on me.

I was so worried I could have puked.

●

Home after school, I packed a backpack for the break-out. Then I sat at the table, pretending to solve home-work equations, sketching the floor plan of the rest home instead. My mom was wearing some sweatshirt of my dad's, with an emblem of crossed hockey sticks.

"You aren't visiting Grandpa Rose today?" my mom called, plucking her keys from the counter, snatching her
mezzo-forte
purse from the armchair.

"Homework," I said.
mezzo-piano
She grabbed her uniform, kissed my head, and then flew out the door.

A spotted turtle was hanging around my brother. It still hadn't rained. I watered my brother, snatched my backpack, and ran to the graveyard.

●

I crouched against the XAVIER mausoleum. Brown geese lurched through the gravestones, braying. I eyed the rest
forte
home through the fence, watching the windows.

Jordan Odom shuffled alone into the rest home. His lip was split again. His wrists were bruised. Dead leaves were stuck to his sweatshirt, his backpack, his hair, like he had been fighting somewhere on the ground.

My mom was mopping the cafeteria.

The mustached guard was sipping a cup of coffee.

I broke into the rest home through the window of room #53.

●

The breakout ended up being more of a kidnapping. Grandpa Rose was confused again. He didn't remember me, was using words so bad that they can't be written, swearing^{unwritable}.

forte

"What's this you're plotting?" Grandpa Rose shouted.

forte

"Quiet, Grandpa Rose," I hissed.

piano

In the room next door, someone shouted something about sewers.

forte

I emptied my backpack, shaking out the disguise. A flowery shawl. A floppy straw hat. A wig of curly white hair that I had worn for a play, once, playing the part of a dead composer.

73

I yanked the wig over his hair, yanked the hat over his wig, wrapped him in the shawl.

"You devil," Grandpa Rose muttered.

"You agreed to this idea!" I hissed.

I tossed his suitcase out the window, boosted him through. He slipped, tripped, fell onto the concrete. His palms were scraped and bloody when I helped him stand.

Jordan Odom was gaping at us through the window of room #37.

I gathered the suitcase, then led Grandpa Rose off toward the ghosthouse.

●

We moved at about half a mile per hour. Grandpa Rose hunched over the cane, knuckles white, panting. He seemed < confused now. He yanked the hat lower onto the wig, as the shawl snapped about in the wind. I could smell cookouts—grilling meats—and someone burning leaves. The road wound through swaying maple trees, passing squat houses. High school kids loading the trunk of a car. Middle school kids teetering across a plank of wood, leaping from a treehouse into gold leaves piled

below. Elementary school kids sitting in a driveway, rip-ping heads from dolls, tossing the heads into the grass, singing a song about babies. No one's as weird as elemen-
mezzo-forte
tary schoolers.

"We're being tailed," Grandpa Rose muttered.
piano
"What?" I whispered.
piano
The suitcase whacked against my knees. I glanced
forte
backward. An old man was hobbling after us. It was Jor-dan's grandfather. Jordan was dragging him by his arms.

"Can we shake them?" Grandpa Rose muttered.
piano
"We'll cut through the woods," I whispered.
piano
Taking a corner in the road, we ducked into the trees. A branch hooked the shawl, snatching snarled strands of gold thread. Grandpa Rose wrenched the shawl from the branch. I glanced backward, but there was no one behind us, now.

"We lost them!" I whispered.
piano
Grandpa Rose grunted, nodding. Wind gusted through
piano   *forte*
and a flurry of maroon leaves tumbled whirling into the woods around us. We stumbled across the creek, scattering squawking herons.
forte

•

Standing on the porch of the ghosthouse, staring at the chipped paint and the busted knob of the door, I realized suddenly just what I had gotten myself into. This time I couldn't just peek in. This time I actually had to go inside.

The door creaked open. Grandpa Rose hobbled into the ghosthouse, leaving footprints in the dust. Dead leaves rasped against the floor. Tattered curtains fluttered in the wind. Grandpa Rose collapsed on the hearth of the fireplace, wiping sweat from his forehead with his sleeves.

I stepped into the ghosthouse. The door creaked shut. I had never been inside the ghosthouse before. But I had heard stories whispered, at the bus stop, in the locker room. Stories about floating jewelry, dancing mirrors. Stories about sinks of blood. Stories about ghosts like lightning blinding kids' eyes.

Grandpa Rose scratched at his beard with both hands, looking from staircase to fireplace, from fireplace to entryway.

"Will you be okay sleeping here?" I said.

"I've slept on floors before," Grandpa Rose said.

"I can bring you food," I said.

piano

"I'll drink the well's water," Grandpa Rose said.

forte

His volume was making me nervous. I felt like, if there were ghosts living here, we should be talking very quietly, or our voices might bring the ghosts out. There wasn't a room that didn't seem haunted. From the entryway, I could see halfway into the bathroom, where the faint shadow of something was flickering over the chipped basin of the sink. The wood floor in the kitchen was staggered with tilted floorboards, like something underground had tried to break through. A hooked chain dangled from the ceiling over the staircase, probably for a chandelier, maybe for a hanging. On the wall above the fireplace was a circle of paint a shade darker than the rest, like where once a portrait had hung, or where a ghost had sunk into the walls. Even the smell in here was freaky. My skin kept tingling, like something invisible was brushing against me.

"I need to get home right away, so that I'll have an alibi for when the nurses realize that you're gone, but after school tomorrow I'll be back so that we can start looking—" I said.

piano

I heard something murmuring.
piano

Suddenly Grandpa Rose was looking nervous too.

"Do you hear something?" Grandpa Rose whispered.
piano

I backpedaled into a wall. Grandpa Rose gripped the cane. Stories about vanishing doorways. Stories about ghosts like fog scorching kids' skin. Stories about voices shrieking in the fireplace. Something murmured again.
mezzo-piano
Something clanked. Something twanged. The door slammed
mezzo-forte   *mezzo-forte*   *forte*
open.

I dropped the suitcase, the latch snapped, socks
forte
spilled across the floor.

"Calculator?" someone said.
glissando

Jordan stepped into the ghosthouse, dust swirling at his high-tops.

"We didn't shake them, kid," Grandpa Rose muttered.
piano

●

Jordan pointed at me.

"What are you doing?" Jordan said.
forte

"Nothing," I said.
forte

"Didn't you hear what happened to Mark Huff?" Jordan said.
forte

"Ghost, attic window, tripped out," I said.

forte

"And you came here anyway?" Jordan said.

forte

"You have to leave," I said.

forte

Jordan wrapped an arm around my shoulders, like a coach about to teach a secret play to the star player.

"Listen, Calculator, I get what you're doing," Jordan whispered. "Your grandpa hated the rest home, so you found a different place for him to stay. But Grandpa Dykhouse, my grandpa, he hates the rest home too. He's miserable, living there. He can't eat, can't sleep. He's always depressed. I want a room for him here."

piano

Grandpa Dykhouse stepped into the doorway, wringing his hands. He was wearing faded jeans and a maroon sweater.

"Jordan?" Grandpa Dykhouse whispered.

piano

"There are other abandoned houses," I hissed.

piano

"This is the only haunted house," Jordan said.

piano

"This house is taken," I hissed.

piano

"I'll tell your parents where you're hiding your grandpa," Jordan said.

piano

"Mr. Rose?" Grandpa Dykhouse whispered.

piano

79

"King Gunga, everything's all set now, you can live here," Jordan called.

_{forte}

I had never heard Jordan use a nickname before that wasn't mean. I wanted a nickname like Grandpa Dykhouse's. I wanted a nickname like King Gunga.

"Jordan, I'm going back to the rest home, tonight. I agreed to come along only to make sure that Mr. Rose was going back to the rest home tonight too," Grandpa Dykhouse said.

_{forte}

"You aren't going back there. You hate the rest home. This house is yours now. Now you live here," Jordan said.

_{forte}

"Yes, I hate the rest home. This house, however, is filthy, in all likelihood is contaminated with asbestos, and looks about ready to collapse," Grandpa Dykhouse said.

_{forte}

"So? You can't count that stuff! You said you wanted to die! So then isn't an extremely dangerous house actually perfect?" Jordan said.

_{forte}

Grandpa Dykhouse ignored this.

"Mr. Rose, it's Mr. Dykhouse," Grandpa Dykhouse whispered. "Do you remember meeting earlier? At breakfast? Talking about boats?"

_{mezzo-piano}

Grandpa Rose was hunched on the hearth, muttering
piano
something about shells for cheap coffins.

Dogs were barking somewhere. The door creaked
mezzo-piano
mezzo-piano
shut. Grandpa Dykhouse hooked his glasses to his sweater,

shaking his head at me, like I had gotten a problem wrong.

"Nicholas, I'm sorry, but your grandfather can't stay

here," Grandpa Dykhouse said.
forte

"He has to," I said.
forte

"He can't be left alone, the state that he's in," Grandpa

Dykhouse said.
forte

"You can't take him back there!" I said. "Our family heir-
forte
looms are hidden somewhere, and we're losing our house, we

don't have the money we need to keep it, unless we find the

heirlooms! Grandpa Rose is the key! He hid them! He thinks

he can find them! He thinks we can find them together!"

"How do you know these heirlooms exist?" Grandpa

Dykhouse said.
forte

Dogs barked again. Beyond the broken window in the
mezzo-forte
kitchen, dusk had fallen across the meadow. I sat on the

staircase, burying my hands in my hair. I felt like I was

flunking the biggest exam of my life.

"I know there's a map, I don't know where. I know there are tattoos, I don't know whose. I know Grandpa Rose lived here, I don't know when," I said.

piano

"He lived in this house?" Grandpa Dykhouse said.

mezzo-piano

"If we lose our house, we lose my brother. My brother is buried in our backyard," I said.

piano

Grandpa Rose wiped ash from his hands onto his pants, leaving streaks of white across the gray, muttering

piano

something about prison hulks.

"He's confused now, but he made me swear to bring him here. You can't take him back to the rest home. The heirlooms could save our house. Please, Grandpa Dykhouse, just leave here, don't tell anyone where we are, forget you ever saw us," I said.

piano

Grandpa Dykhouse ran his hands across his cheeks, shaking his head again.

"He can't be left alone," Grandpa Dykhouse said.

forte

"If he's going to stay here, somebody needs to stay here with him." He raised a finger, like someone about to give a warning. "And—I can do that—but under certain conditions." He waved at all the empty rooms. "We'd need food. We'd need blankets. We'd need soap, jackets, silver-ware, pillows."

Jordan cheered. Something squealed in the kitchen.
forte   *mezzo-piano*
Mice, or maybe chipmunks.

"I don't know if he'll want a roommate," I said.
forte
"It's a roommate or the rest home," Grandpa Dyk-house said.
forte
"He gets confused sometimes. Plus he's been to prison. He won't be easy to live with," I said.
forte
"I was a school librarian for almost forty years," Grandpa Dykhouse said. He crossed his sneakers, lean-ing against the wallpaper. "There's nothing he can do I
forte
haven't already seen."

Grandpa Rose lay across the hearth, his wig's curls tangled, his face hidden under the brim of his hat.

"My father built this house," Grandpa Rose muttered.
piano
"I've done wrong my whole life. Been nothing but greedy. I don't care what happens to me after we've found them. After we've given them to your mother I'll live wherever you want. But until then I refuse to die, I refuse to quit, I will not stop looking. We can't leave them buried. The

heirlooms are worth a fortune. I want to do one good thing."

His chest rose and fell. White ash whirled. Dogs barked again. The porch creaked. A dog whined, claws
forte *piano* *forte*
clicking across the porch. Before I could shout, or scream,
piano
or warn anybody to hide, a silhouette appeared at the window.

Zeke peeked through. Zeke's eyes were > his normal eyes. Twice as big, maybe.

"Heirlooms?" Zeke said.
forte
As per usual, Grandpa Rose was snoring.
piano

WHICH UNDERWORLD

My mom didn't come home until dawn. I heard the door being eased shut, the patter of foot-*piano*steps, keys tinkling on the table. When I had *piano* kidnapped Grandpa Rose, I had felt = a hero, but now I felt < a hero. I pretended I was asleep. I didn't want to see her upset.

She had called earlier, just as I had come running through the door. Majorly frantic, she interrupted me to say that Grandpa Rose had wandered away from the rest home, and then asked whether Grandpa Rose had come back here. When I said he hadn't, she said to call the rest home if he did, that she had to go, and not to worry, and then she hung up.

Now she was in the doorway. Facing away, curled in my sheets, I saw her shadow glide across the wall. She knew I wasn't asleep somehow, but I kept pretending.

"We spent all night driving around, trying to find him," my mom said.

She sat on the bed. Bedsprings squeaked. I tried to *piano* breathe normally. *glissando*

"We didn't find him," my mom said.

The kids in my brain shouted, *piano* "Tell her where he's hiding!", shouted, *forte* "Say something, say anything, tell her the truth!" *forte*

She kissed my head.

"Don't worry, kiddo. He may be old, but he's tough. He'll be okay until we find him," my mom said.

Now I felt < a nothing. She was worried about me, she *piano* was worried about my feelings, and I was the one who knew where Grandpa Rose actually was.

When I woke again, my mom was asleep on the couch, clutching a faded photograph, her hair rayed around her head. In the photograph, a young Grandpa Rose was smoking a black cigarette under birch trees, alone, clean-shaven, wearing a buttoned shirt and tight suspenders. I had seen photographs of Grandpa Rose before. I had never seen a photograph of Grandma Rose though. My mom had said Grandma Rose had never let anyone take her picture.

I ate some toast. I grabbed my high-tops, my backpack, my violin. I ran through the fog and the dew and sat at the roots of my brother the tree.

I HAVE HIDDEN GRANDPA ROSE IN THE GHOSTHOUSE WHERE WE WILL HUNT FOR OUR FAMILY HEIRLOOMS, my song said.

FALL IS HERE. THE SNOWS ARE COMING. YOU CANNOT HIDE OUR GRANDFATHER FOREVER. HE CANNOT STAY WARM IN A HOUSE WITH NO WINDOWS, my brother's song said.

I was quiet^{thinking}.

IT'S TIME YOU KNEW THE TRUTH, my song said. OUR PARENTS ARE TRYING TO SELL OUR HOUSE. THEY SAID WE CAN'T TAKE YOU WITH US.

My brother's roots gripped the dirt.

IF WE CAN'T FIND OUR FAMILY HEIRLOOMS, WE'LL HAVE TO MOVE AWAY AND LEAVE YOU FOREVER, my song said. BUT KIDS HAVE BEEN TAKING THINGS FROM THE GHOSTHOUSE FOR YEARS AND YEARS AND YEARS, TAKEN EVEN THE DOORKNOBS FROM THE DOORS, TAKEN EVEN THE DOORS FROM THE CUPBOARDS, THEY'VE TAKEN ALL OF IT AWAY, AND WHAT IF OUR HEIRLOOMS WERE STOLEN BY KIDS YEARS AGO, OR WHAT IF THE HEIRLOOMS WERE NEVER HIDDEN IN THE GHOSTHOUSE, WHAT IF GRANDPA ROSE NEVER REMEMBERS WHERE THE MAP IS, WHAT IF THE TATTOOS DON'T EXIST, WHAT IF FOR ONCE I HAD A CHANCE TO FIX EVERYTHING AND I COULDN'T, WHAT IF I FAILED, WRECKED EVERYTHING, MADE EVERYTHING WORSE THAN BEFORE?

DO NOT FEAR THOSE THINGS, my brother's song said.

The dew on my brother's branches flashed in the sun.

My brother's song said, I BELIEVE THAT YOU CAN SAVE ME.

●

At school, I thumped off the bus, Mr. Carl bellowing
forte *forte*
goodbye.

In the parking lot, Little Isaac and Big Isaac were
banging on the garbage bin with sticks. Zeke's dictionary
forte
was on the pavement next to the garbage bin, like it had
been dropped there.

"Come out, come out, Freaky Zekey!" Little Isaac
shouted, stick clanging against the garbage bin.
forte *forte*
Zeke was crouched against a silver van, peeking at the
Isaacs. I crouched there too.

"Why are the Isaacs fighting that garbage bin?" I
whispered.
piano
"They think that I'm inside," Zeke whispered. "They
piano
were chasing me saying they were going to kill me, so I
jumped into the bin, and they were too grossed out to
jump in after me, so they shut the lid and ran away to get
some sticks. I snuck away again before they got back."

The Isaacs shouted Zeke's name again. Above the
forte
garbage bin, the school was scarred with initials kids had
carved into the brick. VF + BR floated there, my parents'
initials, wearing a lopsided heart. My dad had scratched

the same thing into the metal side of a drinking fountain, into the corner of a mirror in the cafeteria bathroom, into a sideline in the floor of the gym, back when this had been my parents' school.

"I'll help you find the heirlooms, but when we find them, I get half of them," Zeke said.

"Why would I want your help?" I said. *piano*

"I have a blueprint of the ghosthouse," Zeke said. *piano*

"Where did you find that?" I said. *piano*

"Borrowed it from some high schoolers," Zeke said. *piano*

"Does 'borrowed' mean 'stole'?" I said. *piano*

I didn't want to give away half of the heirlooms. But I didn't know if I could find the heirlooms alone. And half of everything was more than all of nothing.

"If the heirlooms are hidden in the ghosthouse, we'll need that blueprint," Zeke said.

"There's a map somewhere," I said. *piano*

"I don't have time to wait for your grandfather to remember where the map's at. And we don't need a map anyway. I'll bring a hatchet. We'll tear apart the ghosthouse. We'll find those heirlooms before sundown tonight," Zeke said.

piano

Mr. Tim jogged from the loading dock into the parking lot, shouting at the Isaacs to leave the garbage bin

forte

alone. Little Isaac's stick snapped. Little Isaac kicked the

piano   *forte*

garbage bin. Big Isaac swore^{unwritable}, and the Isaacs yanked

piano

their hoods over their heads and stalked into school.

●

I found Jordan at his locker, spinning the combination. Someone had written TRY BEING LOCKER PARTNERS WITH DAVY JONES on his locker in black marker.

"How old is your grandfather?" I said.

mezzo-forte

"Seventy-something? Seventy-one, seventy-three? What do you care?" Jordan said.

mezzo-piano

Seventy-three was a prime. Whatever age he was, though, he was almost young enough to be Grandpa Rose's son. Grandpa Rose was eighty-nine (prime). He wouldn't be a prime again until he was ninety-seven. He wouldn't have another year of Big Events for almost a decade.

"How'd he get the nickname King Gunga?" I said.
mezzo-forte

"Technically, it's short for King Gunga, The Viking Raider, Beloved By All Animals, And Feared Throughout The Seven Seas," Jordan said.
mezzo-piano

I was so jealous I could hardly stand. The nickname was even better than I had thought.

"Would you go away?" Jordan said.
mezzo-piano

He yanked on the handle. It stuck. He had spun in the wrong numbers.
piano

"Just don't tell anyone about the heirlooms," I said.
mezzo-forte

"Tell anyone?" Jordan said.
forte

He spun in the numbers again.
piano

"Sorry, Calculator, but that treasure of yours doesn't exist," Jordan said.
mezzo-forte

●

During band, the band director vanished into the office to dig for sheet music. Sheet music is like the bones of a song—music bars with notes marked between—that you bring to life with your instrument. The band director keeps boxes of it stacked in the office.

The second the band director shut the door, three of

the drummers started singing "The Ballad Of Dirge And Keen." *forte* Emma Dirge and Leah Keen don't take band, but kids think it's funny to sing even when Emma and Leah aren't around.

"The Ballad Of Dirge And Keen" is a song about Emma Dirge and Leah Keen and a pair of escaped circus monkeys. During the song Emma and Leah fall in love with the monkeys. Then other things happen that I probably shouldn't say.

It's the number one meanest song anyone's ever written. Which means that it was written, obviously, by Jordan. He wrote it during the winter of sixth grade, back when Emma Dirge was still his friend, and Leah Keen was still his friend, and Mark Huff, and the Geluso twins, and the Isaacs. Even more than the nicknames, that's why everyone hates him—everyone loves Emma and Leah, and whenever Emma and Leah hear someone singing the song, they run into the nearest bathroom together to cry about it.

Some of the tubas started singing along with the drummers, *forte* doing the motions that went with the song. Kids hate Jordan for writing the song, but they still like to sing it.

I was studying notecards during math when Jordan snuck over. This week I was learning about imaginary numbers, like "i," which is the square root of –1. "i" doesn't exist, but mathematicians use it anyway, because it's useful for solving certain problems.

"Did you ask Boylover to come to the ghosthouse again tonight?" Jordan muttered, crouching by my desk.

"Zeke's going to help *me* find the heirlooms," I said, still looking at the notecards.

"I don't trust that thief anywhere near the ghosthouse while my grandpa's there," Jordan muttered, pretending to fix a shoelace.

"Noted," I said.

The first few weeks of school, I took my eleventh-grade math class at the high school, with eleventh graders, obviously. But in the hallway after class, the eleventh graders would shove me, and throw bottles at me, and once locked me in a locker. So now instead once a week the eleventh-grade math teacher walks over and teaches me that week's concepts and leaves me that week's homework.

So during other school days I sit in a normal seventh-grade algebra class, and while Jordan and Leah Keen and the Geluso twins learn about graph trees and bound variables, I work through my homework at a desk in the back. No one is supposed to bother me. I'm supposed to concentrate on the calculus.

"I've always hated that kid," Jordan muttered, still fid-*piano*
dling with the shoelace.

Then the math teacher spotted him and called him to
forte
the chalkboard to solve a problem for the class.

●

My mom's car was parked at the curb, across from the buses. She was wearing hoop earrings and a gray sweatshirt. She had the day off.

"Let's grab groceries," my mom said.
forte
I didn't want to, but I couldn't say no. When my mom gets upset, she likes to buy green tea, dark chocolate, and yogurt, and then eat them all together. As upset as she was about Grandpa Rose, we were going to be buying a whole cartload of chocolate bars. I got into the car.

"Another man wandered away from the rest home

yesterday," my mom said. She dug through her purse.
forte
"His name is Edmond Dykhouse." She handed me a photograph of Grandpa Dykhouse. "If you see him anywhere, Nicholas, you need to tell someone."

I looked at the photograph. I sat very still. I handed her the photograph.

"I memorized his face," I said.
glissando
A fact is something that's the same at any age, but a belief is something different. That's the hardest thing about being eleven. Before you're eleven you'll believe whatever your parents tell you, but once you're eleven you have to start choosing what to believe, and sometimes that puts you at odds with your parents. My mom worked for the rest home. She loved it—she believed in it—but I had come to stand against it.

"They've been reported missing persons," my mom said.
forte
We drove to the grocer. The grocer is downtown, across from the arcade and exactly the same size. Some grandfathers in raincoats were perched on a bench there,

probably waiting for some grandmothers. The raincoats were majorly illogical. The sky had zero clouds.

My mom eyed the grandfathers through the window while we shopped, like she thought that if she kept staring one of them might transform into Grandpa Rose.

"I printed flyers with his picture, spent all day going from door to door, looking for somebody who had seen him," my mom said. "People hardly glanced at the flyer. Everybody was ^forte^ busy with their own problems. One woman, she wouldn't take the flyer of Grandpa Rose, but she made me take a flyer of her missing parrots."

My mom wheeled an empty cart. I realized suddenly that even if my mom didn't believe that the heirlooms existed, she still might remember something that could help us find them. But I knew I had to be careful what I asked about. If I asked the wrong question, or phrased a question the wrong way, or spoke in the wrong tone of voice, she might get suspicious. I would have to be sure never to ask too many at once.

I tried to keep my voice casual^chitchat^.

"Grandpa Rose was born here, in this town?" I said.
forte

"Yes," my mom said.
forte

"And grew up here?" I said.
forte

"In town somewhere," my mom said. "He never talked
forte
about his childhood." The cart's wheels rattled across the
mezzo-forte
tiles. "Neither did Grandma Rose. Grandpa Rose was
never home, and she wouldn't talk about him when he
was gone. It was like she would pretend he didn't exist."

"Why wasn't he ever home?" I said.
forte

"He didn't like being there," my mom said.
forte

"What was wrong with him?" I said.
forte

"I don't know," my mom said.
forte

My mom stopped the cart at a crate of acorn squash.
She rapped her knuckles on the skin of a squash, like ARE
piano
YOU RIPE? I had probably hit my limit for research questions. Also, the answers were making me sort of upset. I
moved on to the next job on my agenda, which was gathering provisions.

"Mom? Can we get some canned vegetables? Like
peas or yams or something?" I said.
forte

"Since when do you like canned vegetables?" my mom said.
forte

My mom wouldn't eat anything unhealthy anymore, after what had happened to my brother. The doctors had said what she had eaten during the pregnancy wouldn't have changed anything, but, still, now all she would buy were things like acorn squash and fiddlehead greens and heirloom tomatoes. We hadn't ordered a pizza in over three years.

"I'm really really really in the mood for peas. Can we get, like, fifty cans?" I said.
forte

●

I crossed the yard through warbling grasshoppers and
mezzo-forte
buzzing wasps with an armful of blankets and jackets and
mezzo-piano
canned vegetables. Sunlight spiked through the birch trees onto the brown grass. The leaves that had fallen onto the yard formed overlapping shapes of pale gold and dark gold and bright maroon. The ghosthouse sounded as empty as usual. The door creaked open. Grandpa Rose
piano
was eating raspberries on the staircase, with that rusty metal lantern from the shed sitting alongside him, unlit.

"Hey kid," Grandpa Rose said.

forte

"I'm mad at you," I said.

forte

"Me?" Grandpa Rose said.

forte

I dumped everything in the entryway.

"Why didn't you like being home when my mom was a kid?" I said.

forte

"I did," Grandpa Rose said.

forte

"You weren't," I said.

forte

"I wanted to be there. I wanted to be away," Grandpa Rose said.

forte

"That's impossible. Those are opposite. You can't have felt both," I said.

forte

"Don't you know about contradictions?" Grandpa Rose said.

forte

"I can't handle contradictions," I said.

forte

Grandpa Rose frowned.

"I've only ever felt contradictions," Grandpa Rose said.

forte

"Contradictions basically break my brain," I said.

forte

I turned away to stack canned peas against the fireplace, still kind of mad.

"Hey, I warned you, kid, I never tried being good

before," Grandpa Rose said.
forte

I lobbed a bar of soap into the sink, still not talking.

Grandpa Rose tilted his head, trying to catch my atten-

tion. I pitched a roll of toilet paper toward the bathtub,

still not talking. Grandpa Rose slid across the stair, trying

to sneak back into my line of sight. I rooted through the

crumpled blankets.

"Your Grandma Rose used to ignore me like that

sometimes, too, so I already know this can't last forever,"

Grandpa Rose said, laughing.
forte　　*piano*

I threw a jacket at Grandpa Rose.

"Don't get it dirty," I said.
mezzo-forte

"This is your father's?" Grandpa Rose said.
forte

"Correct," I said.
mezzo-forte

Grandpa Rose shrugged on the jacket. He buttoned

the buttons, touched the pockets, sniffed the collar. In
fermata

band class, everyone had learned new terms. Fortissimo

means "play very loudly" (even louder than forte). Pianis-

simo means "play very softly" (even softer than piano).

Fermata means "hold that note." So if you're playing a

song and you see a note with a fermata, you just blow and blow and blow the note until you run out of breath.

"What's your father like?" Grandpa Rose said.
mezzo-forte

"I don't know," I said.
mezzo-forte

"What's your mother say?" Grandpa Rose said.
mezzo-forte

"I don't know," I said.
mezzo-forte

"He treats her alright?" Grandpa Rose said.
mezzo-forte

"Like she's queen of everything," I said.
mezzo-forte

Grandpa Rose nodded, grunting, scratching at his
piano
beard with both hands.

"He would rather sleep on a couch in the Upper Peninsula than disappoint her," I said.
mezzo-forte

I wasn't mad anymore, already. Grandpa Rose was freakishly good at that. His eyes had this way of sucking any mad straight out of you, until you liked him again.

Jordan stumbled in the door, carrying pillows, boxes of toothpaste, bent metal spoons. His hair was matted with sweat. He grimaced.

"I can't stay long," Jordan said.
forte

"Why?" I said.
mezzo-forte

"I'm grounded," Jordan said.
forte

"What did you do?" I said.

mezzo-forte

"My sister found the dead flies I was keeping in the freezer," Jordan said.

forte

He dumped everything in the entryway.

"And then the dead frogs," Jordan said.

forte

He wiped his hands on his jeans.

"Anyway, I told my parents I kidnapped Grandpa Dykhouse," Jordan said.

forte

"You what?" I shouted.

fortissimo

"Relax, Calculator," Jordan said. "I knew they wouldn't

forte

believe me. Last night we drove all over town, checking different spots for Grandpa Dykhouse. We must have driven past this place like five times. Anyway, I got bored, so I stuck my face between their seats and said, 'Uh, by the way, I kidnapped Grandpa Dykhouse.' After I told them, they just yelled at me and said it wasn't funny. 'Grandpa Dykhouse going missing is a very serious thing, Jordan.' Whenever I say anything, they think I'm just trying to bug them. I tell them all sorts of things they would want to know, but they always ignore me."

Jordan tossed a pillow at Grandpa Rose.

"Grown-ups never care about kids' stories," Jordan grumbled. "They never listened to Grandpa Dykhouse
forte
either. Whatever he said, they would ignore it, or laugh it off, or tell him he didn't know what he was talking about." He dug through his pockets, searching for something. "They think what happens to us doesn't matter, like we're too young or too old to be important. But what happens to us is important. What happens to us are the most important things."

Grandpa Dykhouse hobbled in the door with the wooden bucket from the well, water swashing in the bucket.
piano
His jeans had dirt at the knees. His jaw was lined with stubble. He looked 300% happier than the night before.

"That was the worst night of sleep I've ever had," Grandpa Dykhouse said.
mezzo-forte

"Did you see any ghosts?" Jordan said.
forte

"No," Grandpa Dykhouse said.
mezzo-forte

"I brought the scissors you asked for," Jordan said.
forte

"Hey, that reminds me, when was the last time you got your allowance?" Grandpa Dykhouse said.
mezzo-forte

He nodded toward a scrap of paper hanging from a nail in the wall.

"Because I need some things from the pharmacy too," Grandpa Dykhouse said.
mezzo-forte

Jordan frowned, craning toward the list, squinting, mouthing words.

"Creams? Ointments? Lozenges? Pills? What do you need all of this stuff for?" Jordan said.
forte

Grandpa Dykhouse set the bucket on the fireplace, *mezzo-piano* straightened his glasses.

"You know how you kids get things like hangnails, dandruff, pimples?" Grandpa Dykhouse said. He leaned in, making a face like someone about to get to the freaki-
mezzo-forte
est part of a campfire story. "Well, old people have things like that, but a hundred times worse."

Jordan looked horrified.

"Alright, I'll get you whatever you want, just keep the details to yourself," Jordan said.
forte

Jordan tore the list from the nail.
mezzo-piano

"Anyway, listen, don't wander too far from here.

Everybody's on the lookout for you. My parents have been passing around photos," Jordan said.

forte

"We can stay busy here. Monte has a new project," Grandpa Dykhouse said.

mezzo-forte

"Monte?" Jordan said.

forte

"Mr. Rose," Grandpa Dykhouse said.

mezzo-forte

Grandpa Dykhouse shoved a pile of paper at Jordan. Pages torn from moldy manuals, mildewy handbooks. Someone had scrawled pencil across the pages.

"What is this?" Jordan said.

forte

"Monte's memories," Grandpa Dykhouse said. "When-

mezzo-forte

ever he can remember something, he tells me the memory, and then I compile the memories here."

"We're low on paper. Bring some, will you?" Grandpa Rose muttered, fumbling with a can of peas.

piano

"I've always wanted to write a book," Grandpa Dyk-house said. "When I was a kid, I wanted to write a book on

mezzo-forte

the history of our town. But Monte's story is better than history. It's like a crime novel. I love books like that, about the underworld."

"Underworld? You mean where dead people live?" Jordan said.

forte

"No, you know, the underworld. Bootleggers, kidnappers, assassins. The criminal underworld," Grandpa Dykhouse said. His glasses had slid down his nose when

mezzo-forte

he had bent toward the pages. He eyed us over the thick silver frame. "I've had to take some liberties with the story. Some of the memories from when he was younger are quite vivid, but most of the memories from when he was older have completely deteriorated. And then there are memories he remembers one way, and then later remembers a different way altogether."

I squatted above the pages. It was like music—with a memory, there was an original performance, when the memory was composed. But afterward, even if you had notes about the original performance—pictures, diaries, mementos—every performance of the memory was somewhat different. The memory was never quite the same.

"Is there anything about the heirlooms?" I said.

forte

"Nothing yet about where the heirlooms were hidden," Grandpa Dykhouse said.
mezzo-forte

"What are these heirlooms, anyway? A bunch of silverware or something?" Jordan said.
forte

"Monte said one of the heirlooms is a golden hammer," Grandpa Dykhouse said.
mezzo-forte

"A golden hammer?" Jordan said.
forte

"In Michigan, in the past, there was a tradition that if you built your own house—dug your own basement, laid your own plumbing, wired your own electric, everything—the governor would award you a golden hammer. Only the head was gold. The rest was wood. I've never seen one, only heard the stories," Grandpa Dykhouse said.
mezzo-forte

"Pipe by pipe. Brick by brick. Shingle by shingle. That's how he built this house," Grandpa Rose muttered.
piano

Dogs barked. Something clopped. Zeke peeked in the window.
forte *fortissimo*

"Hey," Zeke said.
mezzo-forte

"Who's this?" Grandpa Rose muttered.
piano

"Zeke. My locker partner. You met him last night, remember?" I said.
mezzo-forte

Grandpa Rose mumbled, confused again.

Grandpa Dykhouse *piano* shoved the sleeves of his sweater to his elbows.

"Alright, time to wash up, Monte," Grandpa Dykhouse said. Grandpa Dykhouse helped Grandpa Rose stand, *forte* then led the way to the bathroom, lugging the bucket. I heard water sploshing as Grandpa Dykhouse washed Grandpa Rose's face. *mezzo-piano*

Zeke hopped through the window with a jangling duffel bag. His wolfdogs *mezzo-piano* scrambled through the doorway. He barked at the wolfdogs, *mezzo-forte* and the wolfdogs flopped across the floor. *forte*

"Did you just bark, Boylover?" Jordan said.

Zeke frowned, *forte* then barked at Jordan.

"What a freak," *forte* Jordan muttered.

Jordan wasn't wrong. *piano* But all of us were freaks. I was a misfit^brainy, Zeke was a misfit^weird, Jordan was a misfit^mean. We were all misfits of some power.

Zeke emptied the duffel bag along the staircase. A stolen horn. A stolen oboe. Half of a stolen clarinet. Then— in a range of sizes—eleven pairs of stolen high-tops.

Jordan was gaping at Zeke.

"What?" Zeke said. "If you get to stash your grand-
forte
fathers here, I get to stash some goods here too."

"Are those Mark Huff's high-tops?" Jordan said.
mezzo-forte
"That blue pair? They were. Do you want to buy
them?" Zeke said.
mezzo-piano
"I have enough problems with Flatface already," Jordan said. "I can't even imagine what he would do if he
piano
caught me wearing his shoes."

●

Zeke unfolded the blueprint against the fireplace. The
ghosthouse had been drawn on it in white lines—the front
of the ghosthouse, the side of the ghosthouse, the back of
the ghosthouse—but so you could see through the walls
in some places, like the house itself was a ghost. Notes
had been added in the margins, signed with my great-
grandfather's initials.

"There's extra space under the floorboards in the bathroom, and in the kitchen, and in this room here. There's
a door in the side of the staircase, which somebody

wallpapered. There's a crawlspace under the porch. There's the cellar, which somebody locked," Zeke said.

"A waste of time," Jordan said.
forte

"What?" Zeke said.
forte

"There isn't any treasure," Jordan said.
forte

"When we're rich, we'll buy you a brain," Zeke said.
forte

Zeke got the crowbar from the shed. We tore apart the floorboards in the bathroom, found empty space below. We tore apart the floorboards in the kitchen, found empty space below. We stomped upstairs to the room Zeke had
forte
marked on the blueprint, tore apart the floorboards there. We found a bent nail, the handle of a screwdriver, a nest made of torn bits of paper. We didn't find any heirlooms.

Strips of maroon wallpaper hung from the walls, like bark peeling from a tree.

"This must have been a bedroom," I said.
mezzo-piano

"Once," Zeke said.
mezzo-forte

We stomped downstairs. The grandfathers had van-
forte
ished. Jordan was sitting cross-legged on the fireplace, eating a can of peas.

"Didn't you say you were grounded?" I said.

forte

"So?" Jordan said.

fermata

Both sides of the staircase were wallpapered with a faded pattern of bluish vines. Zeke studied the blueprint, paced along the staircase running his fingers across the wallpaper, found the edges of the door buried there. I took my knife, cut into the wall, sawed the outline of the

mezzo-forte

door. We tore the wallpaper from the handle. Jordan was

mezzo-piano

watching us, had stopped chewing.

"Ready?" Zeke said.

piano

We gripped the handle. Zeke nodded. We heaved.

The door budged, stopped.

"Weak!" Jordan called.

forte

We gripped the handle with both hands. Zeke nodded again. We heaved.

The door shot open, black dust flew at our faces, a broom clunked to the floor.

forte

Jordan was dying laughing.

fortissimo

"The heirloom was a broom?" Jordan laughed, knuck-

forte

ling tears from his eyes.

We dug through the room under the staircase. Aside

from empty barrels, mildewed curtains, and another broom, the room was empty.

"Let's try the crawlspace," Zeke muttered.

piano

We wiped the dust from our faces. Zeke got the lantern. We hopped through the window onto the porch. Grandpa Rose was perched on a stool there, surrounded by a circle of white hair. Grandpa Dykhouse was standing behind the stool, snipping hair with metal scissors. Jor-

mezzo-piano

dan wandered onto the porch, through the doorway, his hands on his hips.

"King Gunga, you can cut hair?" Jordan said.

forte

Grandpa Dykhouse was the sort of grandfather who had a totally silent laugh.

"We never spent money on barbershops, when your mom was younger. Once a month, it was me who cut her hair. She hated it, but it was fun for me," Grandpa Dyk-house said.

forte

Grandpa Rose muttered something about poorhouses,

piano

confused still.

We rounded the porch, studied the blueprint, tore at the wall of weeds. We found the entrance to the crawlspace. Jordan wandered around the porch. He frowned. He sniffed.

mezzo-piano

"Boylover, are you wearing perfume?" Jordan said.

forte

"One squirt," Zeke said.

forte

"Listen, just keep your hands to yourself. You try to kiss me, I'll drown you in the well," Jordan said.

forte

"Kiss?" Zeke said.

fermata

"Isn't that what you do? Kiss boys?" Jordan said.

forte

"Only ones I think are cute, and only boys who like boys too," Zeke said.

forte

"Little Isaac doesn't like boys," Jordan said.

forte

"He pretends he doesn't," Zeke said.

forte

"Little Isaac hates you for kissing him," Jordan said.

forte

Zeke lit a match, cupped a hand around the flame, lit

mezzo-piano

the lantern. Sunlight flashed across the silver mermaids on his arms. He crawled into the crawlspace, dragging the lantern.

"And who says I'm not cute?" Jordan muttered.

mezzo-piano

I crawled into the crawlspace. Brown weeds and monster cobwebs were lit by the light of the lantern. Farther ahead, the soles of Zeke's high-tops. I could hear

Grandpa Dykhouse pacing the porch above, Grandpa Rose
piano
murmuring.
pianissimo

Zeke tossed a rusted can. The can clattered into a
piano
patch of weeds.

"Nothing?" I said.
forte

"Let's try the cellar," Zeke muttered.
pianissimo

We crawled from the crawlspace, wiping cobwebs
from our high-tops.

Zeke got the hatchet from the duffel bag. We took
turns hacking apart the cellar door. Jordan just watched,
despite that out of the three of us he was the only one with
actual muscles. He had his teeth bared, kept poking the
tip of his tongue through the gap in his teeth. Whenever
the hatchet struck the door, the lock rattled on its chain.
forte   *glissando*

"Calculator, what would you use the treasure for, if
the treasure wasn't fake?" Jordan said.
forte

"My brother," I said.
forte

"Brother?" Zeke said.
forte

I told them about my brother the tree.

Jordan squinted, leaning forward to peer at me like at
a bizarre creature in a museum display.

"Don't you think that's sort of weird to just tell to people?" Jordan said.

forte

Zeke glanced at me, then glared at Jordan.

"What's so weird about that?" Zeke said.

forte

"You really don't think there's anything weird about
that?" Jordan said.

forte

Zeke swung the hatchet, sending wood splinters flying. The blade was stuck in the door. Zeke jerked on the
handle, ripped the hatchet out again.

mezzo-forte

"No. I can relate to it, actually. That same thing almost
happened to me," Zeke said.

forte

"A miscarriage?" I said.

forte

Zeke took his shirt and wiped the sweat from his face,
chin to hairline. "No," Zeke said, talking through the fab-

mezzo-piano

ric. His tone had changed, like now he was talking only
to me. "But I am still really lucky to exist. My dad didn't
want my mom to have me." His shirt dropped. His face
had left blotches of sweat along the hem. He gripped the
hatchet, grimaced, swung again. "This was before they
were married. My dad had the money even. He gave her
the money and made her swear to abort me. Then he left

116

for boot camp, to become a soldier. My mom used the money to buy a crib. She wanted to have me."

"I like soldiers normally, but, sorry, your dad's evil," Jordan said.

forte
"Evil?" Zeke said.

forte
"You must really hate him," Jordan said.

forte
"Just for that?" Zeke said, frowning.

forte
"Yup, killing an unborn baby, you'd have to be a monster to do something like that," Jordan said, folding his
forte
arms together and nodding.

Zeke shook his head. "My dad, other soldiers, they're paid to kill people every day. How can killing babies be wrong, but you let them grow up, and you pay our soldiers to kill them, and then it's right?" Zeke said.

forte
Jordan shrugged. "Those aren't our kids. Those are just the grown-up kids of other countries," Jordan said.

forte
"Those countries are like you, or me, or him," Zeke said, pointing with the hatchet, grip suddenly majorly
forte
tremolo. "Maybe none of the other countries are friends with them, but that doesn't mean that bullying them isn't wrong."

Jordan grinned—poking the tip of his tongue through the gap in his teeth again—then said, "The only thing I *forte* like about you is how easy you are to rile up." He pointed at the cellar. "Now that you've got some adrenaline, would you hit that with some muscle, and finish this already?"

Zeke scowled. His cheeks were flushed. He planted his high-tops, gripped the hatchet so tight his knuckles went white, then swung.

The hatchet split through the door.

fortissimo

"Finally!" Jordan said.

forte

We kicked the planks out. We wriggled through the

fortissimo

hole into the cellar. In the dusty light there, we found dirt, cobwebs, and a pair of crumpled socks.

Zeke chewed a lip.

"A waste of time," Zeke muttered.

piano

●

Grandpa Rose's hair was less messy than before. Grandpa Dykhouse was snipping at the beard now.

piano

"Listen, King Gunga, maybe he wants to keep the beard," Jordan said.

forte

"He acts like the beard bothers him," Grandpa Dykhouse said.

forte
Grandpa Rose muttered something about housebreakers, confused still. *piano* The sun was vanishing into the meadow beyond the ghosthouse. The shadows of the birch trees, the stone well, the ghosthouse, stretched across the grass. Loons hooted on a pond somewhere. I *piano* stunk of sweat.

Zeke threw the blueprint into the grass.

"We'll never find the heirlooms without the map," Zeke muttered.

piano
"There isn't any map," Jordan muttered.

piano
"The curse of being a memory factory," Grandpa Rose muttered.

piano
Even Jordan looked upset, like some part of him had believed in the heirlooms all along.

"Prison," Grandpa Rose said. His fingers twitched, *mezzo-piano* like the fingers of someone dreaming. "In prison usually nobody knows it's your birthday. On my eighty-third birthday, a doctor tested me. The doctor said my mind was failing. The doctor said my memories were fading.

The doctor said happy birthday. Even I hadn't known. I had forgotten. My cellmate was a younger kid with skin made of tattoos. An arm of stingrays, an arm of jellyfish. A chest with a diagram of a ship. The kid kept a needle, bottles of ink, hidden under his bed. My mind was failing. My memories were fading. There were things I needed to remember. That night, while the kid was sleeping, I tattooed myself with ink and the needle."

Grandpa Rose wrung his hands.

"Where the tattoos would be impossible to miss," Grandpa Rose said.

piano

Grandpa Rose blinked, tilted his head, blinked again.

"What were the things I needed to remember?" Grandpa Rose said.

pianissimo

I kicked the porch.

forte

"It's a fake memory!" I shouted. "I kidnap you, I hide

forte

you here, I lie to my mom, I lie to everyone, and all for nothing! You said the tattoos were the map to the heirlooms! And the tattoos don't exist! Which means we don't have a map! Which means we can't find the heirlooms! If the heirlooms even exist!"

120

Grandpa Rose looked at me like someone watching a storm through a window.

"There were things I needed to remember," Grandpa Rose muttered.

The scissors *pianissimo* snipped. Clumps of matted white hair drifted from the *pianissimo* scissors to the porch. Patches of skin surfaced where before there had been beard. A pair of wrinkles surfaced. A blemish. A letter. A number. More numbers.

The scissors stopped. Grandpa Dykhouse squinted. The breeze caught another clump of snipped hair, blew it away, revealed another number. Jordan was making stuttering noises. Zeke was making yelping noises. My *piano* mouth was moving, but noises weren't *forte* coming out. We gaped at Grandpa Rose.

It wasn't a fake memory.

He had tattoos on his cheeks.

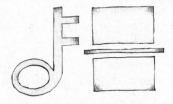

KEY OF C, KEY OF G, KEY OF E

Grandpa Rose's cheeks were tattooed with shaky bluish writing. One cheek said PAWPAW ISLAND THERE BOTTLED SHIPS BONES FROM BOW NINE PACES INLAND under a symbol of a key. One cheek said X18471913 under a symbol of a box.

My brain said 18,471,913 = prime.

"I tattooed myself while the kid was sleeping," Grandpa Rose said.

forte
Grandpa Rose peered into the cloudy mirror above the sink, poking his cheeks with his fingers. We stood around him, in the light of the lantern, staring at the

tattoos. Grandpa Dykhouse was gripping the whiskery scissors he had used to trim the beard to stubble, the foamy razor he had used to shave the stubble to skin.

Grandpa Rose poked the symbol of the key.

"We're looking for a key," Grandpa Rose said.

forte

"A key to what?" I said.

forte

Grandpa Rose poked the symbol of the box.

"A trunk. A dark trunk. A dark trunk with a brass lock," Grandpa Rose said.

forte

"The heirlooms are in a trunk?" I said.

forte

"I remember a dark trunk with a brass lock," Grandpa Rose said.

forte

"So we need to find the key and then the trunk?" I said.

forte

"Yes," Grandpa Rose said.

forte

"What's PAWPAW ISLAND?" Jordan said.

forte

"I don't remember," Grandpa Rose said.

mezzo-forte

"THERE BOTTLED SHIPS?" Zeke said. "BONES FROM BOW?"

forte

"I don't remember," Grandpa Rose said.

mezzo-piano

"NINE PACES INLAND starting where exactly?" I said.

forte

"I don't remember," Grandpa Rose said.

piano

"Couldn't the tattoos have been more specific?" I shouted.
fortissimo

"Calculator, relax, do you know how much being tattooed hurts?" Jordan said.
forte

"You can't write itemized instructions if you're writing on your skin," Zeke said.
forte

They seemed awestruck that Grandpa Rose had actually tattooed himself. I hadn't thought about how much that would have hurt. Especially on his face.

"Every word would have mattered," Grandpa Dykhouse whispered.
mezzo-piano

I touched the tattoo, X18471913, under the symbol of the box. Some large primes are so massively powerful that using them is illegal—you can use them to unlock government codes, or computer programs, or other things you aren't supposed to. That's what 18,471,913 was like. An illegal prime. One number that could unlock everything.

Grandpa Rose was mumbling to himself again,
pianissimo
hunched over his cane.

"If you want to find these heirlooms, you'll need to learn

everything about Monte's life that you can," Grandpa Dyk-house said. "I'll keep logging his memories. I'll make note of
_{forte}
every name, every word, every number. The meaning of the tattoos might become plain once you understand his roots."

"King Gunga is unstoppable in librarian mode," Jor-dan bragged.
_{forte}

"We still don't know if the heirlooms are worth any-thing," Zeke said.
_{forte}

"Why would he have tattooed himself if there wasn't anything worth coming back for?" I said.
_{forte}

Zeke uncapped a silver marker. He wrote PAWPAW ISLAND THERE BOTTLED SHIPS BONES FROM BOW NINE PACES INLAND between drawings of a mermaid leaping toward his elbow and a mermaid swimming toward his wrist.

"Aren't you worried that your arms won't look as pretty now, Boylover?" Jordan said.
_{forte}

"If you write something on your skin, it sinks in even-tually and becomes a part of you," Zeke said.
_{forte}

Jordan pointed at Grandpa Rose.

"That didn't work with those tattoos," Jordan said.
_{forte}

●

We split in the woods, each heading home through a different thicket of darkened trees. Once I was alone, I tightened the straps of my backpack and ran home at a breakneck tempo, taking shortcuts between garages and through backyards. The wind crept behind me from house to house, chimes jingling in the key of C, unlatched *pianissimo* doors knocking in the key of G, the lids of garbage cans *piano* thudding and clattering in the key of E. Pairs of eyes, pairs *forte* *fortissimo* of pairs of eyes, blinked in the trees. I felt nervous[hunted]. My house was dark except for a single window.

As I rounded my house, I took my violin from my backpack and plucked notes at my brother.

SORRY, IN A HURRY, GOODNIGHT FOR NOW! my song said.

I tucked my violin into my backpack and hopped the railing onto the deck.

With the wind in his branches my brother said, SOMEONE'S LAUNDRY HAS BLOWN INTO OUR YARD AND GOTTEN STUCK ON MY LIMBS.

I stopped. I spun around. I dropped my backpack and hopped the railing again and ran across the grass and the dancing shadows to my brother the tree. A sheet was caught halfway in his branches. The sheet snapped with the wind, like the sail of a boat. I yanked the sheet down *mezzo-piano* and ran into Emma Dirge's backyard and pinned the sheet to the line there.

I FEEL BETTER, THANK YOU, GOODNIGHT, my brother's song said.

I hopped the railing again and grabbed my backpack and shoved through the door.

●

Our house smelled like chemicals. The windows were gleaming. The wood of the piano was darker, less dusty than it had been, and its keys were white as bones. My mom was humming to herself and mopping the floor. *mezzo-piano* Where she was stepping, the floor was marked with footprints, like the blueprint of a dance. When she was a kid she was a dancer, and she still moves like one. Dancing is her music, her math, the language she speaks. She has books of dance choreography, ballet scores written in symbols only dancers understand. It's like the x's and o's on the locker room's chalkboard, the x's and o's that only the Isaacs and other basketball players understand, the x's and o's that tell them how to score.

"Where were you?" my mom said.
mezzo-forte

"Outside," I said.
forte

"Your dad called while you were out," my mom said.
mezzo-forte

I wrenched off my high-tops, then crossed the kitchen, stepping from footprint to footprint.

"Why are you cleaning everything?" I said.
forte

"We're doing a showing of the house tomorrow," my mom said.
mezzo-forte

I froze.

Here was what could happen, from bad to worst. Bad was "a showing"—this meant that families that wanted to buy a house would come visit ours. Worse was "an offer"—after a showing, if a family liked our house, they could make an offer of however much money they were willing to pay. Worst was "a closing"—if my parents agreed to the offer, everyone would sign official paperwork, and that's when we would have to leave the house and my brother forever.

A showing didn't mean things were hopeless. But

things hadn't been this bad since my mom had planted the FOR SALE sign in our yard.

"Hey, kiddo, you look pale. Do you feel okay?" my mom said.

forte

"I feel normal, I feel great, I feel 100%," I said. I

mezzo-forte

unfroze. I ran to my room and shut my door and dumped

forte

all of my clothes onto the floor, socks and jeans and sweat-shirts and jackets, like a pile of boys who had vanished. I bent the window blinds. I took my knife and climbed

mezzo-piano

onto my bed and scraped paint from the walls. I wanted

piano

my room to look messy. I wanted my room to look unliv-able. I wanted whoever came through the house for that showing to think, I wouldn't want to live here.

IF YOU FIND THIS

I haven't told you everything that's happened yet, but for now I have to move these notes somewhere different. It's not safe to keep them in my dresser, or anywhere at my house, after what happened in the smugglers' tunnels—Jordan says anyone who's after Zeke might be after us. So I'm moving these notes to the graveyard, behind the tomb with the stone boy, to an empty urn near the grave of ZACCONE. Before, my mom probably was the only one who would have found these notes, but now just about anyone could.

If you're a kid reading this, don't think you would

fall in love with me if you met me. Maybe you think you would, but you wouldn't. Not even 1%. My eyes are freakishly large, and my shoulders are stained with brown freckles, and my tooth is chipped from falling out of a tree. Here's the truth—no one loves a boy who takes violin lessons. Here's the truth—no one loves a boy who memorizes square roots.

Whoever you are reading this, I'm going to ask you a riddle. If you solve the riddle, I'll give you the gold lighter of a high schooler as a prize. But I won't tell it to you yet—I'll tell it to you later.

FROM THE NOTES OF
GRANDPA ROSE

*H*ere, this here, is something he remembers: He learned to swim wearing stolen pants. Whether anybody believes him doesn't matter, but as a thirteen-year-old already he could grow hair all over his chest. And now, just imagine, the clothesline springing, the clothespins flying, as this hairy bare-chested boy made off with a pair of trousers. Laughing, probably, as he leapt the fence. Those trousers, they were clean when he stole them, and never clean again. He hid them at the lake, when he wasn't swimming: just wadded them together, then crammed them under a rock. The day after he stole them, that's when they began to smell, and every day after that the odor got worse still. Monte was alone out there: just him, and the trees, and the dunes, and the water. If he had drowned, nobody ever would have known. Every day he made himself swim farther. He would swim from the clearer waters along the beach, through murky stretches of amber and sapphire and jade as the sand dropped off beneath him, out to where the water turned black. Then just float there, offshore, rising and falling with the waves. Generally, that's where he was when the men came: As he bobbed with the waves, wooden motorboats would streak past, manned by men in fedoras, headed for the dunes. After dropping anchor, the men would unload their cargo from the boats onto the sand. The men were smugglers, worked for the gangsters in Chicago. Their cargo? Sometimes it was crates. Sometimes it was bodies. Liquor the gangsters had brewed, people the gangsters had killed: things to sell, things to hide. Here, this here, is something he remembers: He was awfully curious about those smugglers. In town, people traded rumors about the smugglers constantly, with hushed, anxious tones, as if trading rumors about bloodthirsty monsters that lurked just beyond the town limits. The smugglers had built a labyrinth of tunnels under the dunes, would store their cargo there. Sometimes he would sneak after them into the trees, but when they ducked through the entrance to the tunnels he was always too afraid to follow them inside.

After sunset, Monte would amble back into town, barefoot down the dirt streets. The village was changing: Electric lamps flickered in kitchen windows, where oil lamps had once shone; at the feed store, the pharmacy, tinny voices hollered from radios, mingling like ghosts with the voices of customers; automobiles blew through town, coupes and roadsters and sedans, on steel wheels with balloon tires. Picture him, those same green eyes, but fatter cheeks, much thicker hair, a less prominent nose. A boy, stepping over dropped apples that are dust now, stumbling over fallen bricks that are dust now, crossing paths with stray cats that are long dead. Dragging his hands along strangers' fences, with fingers still pruney from the lake. If he was late, he ran home. He had been forbidden from swimming, which was why he'd had to teach himself to swim, out at the dunes, secretly, wearing stolen pants. His mother had drowned. His father built cabinets. In houses with mothers, the cabinets held fancy teacups and fancy saucers. His house didn't have a mother. In his house, the cabinet held family heirlooms: the ivory revolver, the bellows clock, the golden hammer, the music box. His father often slept in a chair across from the cabinet, guarding the heirlooms from thieves. Remember, these days the heirlooms are worth a fortune, but even those days the heirlooms were worth some money.

He had been forbidden from touching the heirlooms. He would touch the heirlooms anyway. He has memories, memories of sneaking the heirlooms from the cabinet as his father slumbered across the room. If his hair was still damp, he would towel his hair with a curtain, quietly, then tiptoe past the fireplace to the cabinet. He didn't sneak the heirlooms from the cabinet only to annoy his father. There was something that genuinely awed him about those heirlooms, about holding something that valuable in his hands. His great-grandfather had won the revolver during a duel with a ship's captain: The hilt was made of a creamy ivory, smooth to the touch, and the barrel was textured with engravings. His grandfather had been presented the clock after pulling a jeweler's daughter from a burning house: The clock wasn't the type that was wound, within the clock was a bellows, that's what ran the clock, air moving through the bellows, as if the clock were breathing. His father had been awarded the hammer. The music box had been made in Italy, for a famed composer, somewhere centuries back in his family tree. Monte always examined the heirlooms in that exact very order, saving the music box for last. He liked to savor it. Even then, when he came to the music box, he would stall before playing it: would disassemble the music box, then reassemble the music box, carefully inspecting each piece. Flick the clasp up and down. Breathe in the delicate musk of the polished wood. Finally, though, when there were no other ways to stall, he would allow himself to wind the crank. Then hold his breath, and stand very stilly. And listen to its tune. Invariably, that's when his father would blink awake, when that music began playing: His father would scold him for touching the heirlooms, and ruffle his hair, and yawn and stretch and clap and then march into the kitchen to light the oven for their supper. Put those back where they belong, his father would holler.

Fact is, aside from the heirlooms, the only things they owned were boots and tools. They were truly poor. They never had money for anything. Consequently, their routine never changed. Every day his father was away doing carpentry. Every night his father fixed beef, carrots, and potatoes for supper. After the plates were rinsed, his father would doze off again by the fire, and the house would fall silent. They didn't have a radio. Televisions didn't exist yet, or stereos, or video games, or mobile phones. There were no dishwashers to thrum, no coffeemakers to ding. Some families owned electric fans, which at least could have made a whirring sound, but they didn't have any. They had no radiators to ping and creak. Monte hated being there, in all that quiet. Sometimes he got so bored he would stick his hands onto the block of ice in the icebox, just to feel something. He felt as if he was going to be trapped in that house his whole life. He swore, if he ever got away, he was never coming back.

Weekends, time he could have spent with his father, he snuck away instead. If his father wanted help clearing gutters? He would sneak away to the dunes. If his father wanted help mending shingles? He would sneak away to the dunes. If his father wanted to toss around a baseball, kick around a football? He would sneak away to the dunes. All those *afternoons he could have spent with his father, instead he spent swimming in the lake where his mother had drowned. He liked doing it because he knew it was the wrong thing to do. Afterward, though, he always felt guilty. When eventually he would slink back home, his father was never angry, only disappointed. Even then, Monte understood that the patience that man possessed was simply astonishing. But his father believed in him. His father was always trying to get him to do his homework, eat all his carrots. Such great things, his father would proclaim, squeezing his shoulders. Someday you're going to do such great things. But Monte didn't like doing good things. He liked bad things. He was a troublemaker. He looted coins from his father's coat pockets to buy rock candy and slingshot pellets. He swiped pies, trampled flowers, chased dogs, smashed windows. He hid bicycles from their owners, spun street signs crooked. He used words even sailors wouldn't. He loved almost being caught, getaways that left him breathless, getting shouted at from afar. It wasn't that he missed his mother. People liked to say that was why he was a troublemaker, but that wasn't why he was a troublemaker. Whether anybody believed him didn't matter.*

Everybody agreed though that the biggest troublemaker in the whole village was a girl named Ana Sharon. Fact is, she was quickly becoming a local legend. Ana accidentally or intentionally had started a fire in the schoolhouse, accidentally or intentionally had shot a horse. Ana wore boys' boots and boys' hats with her dresses, wore her hair like a flapper, sang vulgar songs. He has a memory of watching her tumble through the street having a fistfight with a one-eyed boy. Monte secretly loved her, but secretly hated her, too. What Monte hated was being outdone at troublemaking.

And maybe that's why as a seventeen-year-old he started burying bodies for the smugglers: Because working for the smugglers meant trouble that even she couldn't outdo.

SKELETONS OF CHILDREN

The next day during lunch Jordan was sitting alone at a table next to Mark Huff's.

"Stand back up, Calculator," Jordan said. *forte* "You're not eating here."

"But you have no one else to eat with," I said. *mezzo-forte*

"Just because everyone hates me lately doesn't mean everyone's going to hate me forever," Jordan said. "If I *forte* start eating with you, though, that will be the end of me."

I looked around from table to table. I didn't know where else to sit. I stood back up.

"Also, I'm signing up for your treasure hunt," Jordan

said. "I'll help you look for your grandpa's treasure, but
_{forte}
when we find it, I get a third of it."

"I thought you were afraid even to be seen with me?"
I said.
_{mezzo-forte}
"I'm doing it for Grandpa Dykhouse," Jordan said.
_{forte}
"He never wanted to be dead before. He used to have
something to live for. His sailboat. But after he retired he
had to sell his sailboat to pay for my Grandma Dykhouse's
hospital bills, and after my Grandma Dykhouse died
he had to sell his house to pay for his own hospital bills,
and then my parents got a room for him at the rest home,
because neither of them wanted him living with us."

Someone at Mark Huff's table threw a wrapper at Jordan's head.

"I hate you too," he shouted at them. Then to me he
_{fermata}
muttered, "I'm going to buy my grandpa a boat."
_{mezzo-piano}

●

As per usual, I ate lunch in a bathroom stall.

From inside the stall, chewing my carrots, I could
hear the quivery faint crooning voices of kids in the choir
_{pianissimo}
room rehearsing, cycling from chorus to verse to bridge.

Sometimes I felt like I was the only one who noticed the music the world was playing—the only one who heard the song of the drainpipes, and the bedsprings, and the wheelbarrows, and the spilled marbles, and the flagpoles during windstorms, and the bleachers applauding, and the teakettles rumbling, and the lightbulbs humming, and the sticks cracking underfoot. I wished everyone understood—I somehow wanted to share it—there was music, not just noise, but music, there, every sound a note in some chord, even silence only another rest. I got lost in that music, sometimes, that everything was playing together. I could get totally overwhelmed with feelings— just listening to echoes of the choir singing, and paper

pianissimo

towel crinkling between someone's fingers, and a leaking

piano

faucet dripping water. Our town was my favorite song.

pianissimo

Leaving the bathroom, I spotted Little Isaac and Big Isaac hurrying along the hallway. I ducked into the bathroom and peeked from the doorway. The Isaacs bounced past. "Marcus, Marcus, Marcus!" they chanted, wrapping their arms around Mark Huff. Mark Huff laughed, then

forte

mezzo-piano

started telling them a story. I waited until Mark Huff had
piano
led them away.

When I walked into math class, someone had drawn a pair of faces on the chalkboard. The first face had a straight line for a mouth, with crooked teeth hanging there. The second face had a squiggly line for a unibrow. Underneath the drawings, the chalkboard said,

2 EYEBROWS = 1 BRAIN

1 EYEBROW = 0 BRAINS

Everyone laughed, except the Geluso twins. Crooked
forte
Teeth muttered, "Nobody's teeth are that crooked." The
piano
Unibrow crumpled homework and threw it at Jordan.
forte
"What?" Jordan said, turning around, laughing. "I didn't
forte   *piano*
draw it." That only made everyone laugh more. Then the
forte
math teacher carried in a stack of quizzes and erased the drawings and made everyone solve problems at the chalkboard.

●

Zeke was waiting for me after school, clutching a fistful of thief money. Today's high-tops were metallic gold, with thick gold soles. While we walked to our locker, I told Zeke what Jordan had drawn on the chalkboard during math class.

"I truly hate that kid," Zeke said.
mezzo-forte

"Jordan?" I said.
mezzo-forte

"What's so difficult about using somebody's actual name?" Zeke said.
crescendo

In band class, everyone had learned new terms. Crescendo means "play louder"—so if you were playing mezzo-forte, you would play forte, then fortissimo. Decrescendo means "play softer"—so if you were playing mezzo-piano, you would play piano, then pianissimo.

"If we're trying to learn about your grandfather's life, we should talk to everybody who knew him. But there's a problem. Which is that basically everybody who would have known him now lives in the graveyard," Zeke said.
mezzo-forte

"You mean is dead," I said.
mezzo-forte

"So I scheduled a seance with Kayley Schreiber," Zeke said.
forte

"The homeschooler?" I said.
glissando

The homeschooler was our age, but homeschooled,

obviously. She knew about voodoo, wrote fortunes for kids on slips of paper. Writing fortunes would have been just weird, except that the fortunes she wrote were never wrong, which was weird^{spooky}. Sometimes the fortunes were warnings, like POP QUIZ TODAY or DON'T RIDE THE BUS WALK HOME, but sometimes the fortunes had only a black circle—like a giant decimal point or a filled whole note—which meant death was coming for you. In third grade, she gave the Gelusos the black spot, and that night a tree fell during a storm, crushing their doghouse and killing their dog. In fifth grade, she gave Peter Burke the black spot, and that night he choked to death on a fish bone while his babysitter was sleeping. It's not the black spot that does the killing—the black spot only warns you of what's already coming.

My brother was still young, but that was the sort of thing he might become after he died—some trees became paper, became sheet music or graphing paper or fortune-teller fortunes. He might become something useful, but he might become someone's black spot.

"Tonight?" I said.
forte

"They may be dead, but they can still answer our questions," Zeke said.
forte

●

We rounded the corner.

Our locker was open. Our locker was empty.

Someone had written FREAK and FREAK and FREAK inside the locker with black marker. On the floor of the locker, where Zeke's gold backpack had been, someone had written NO MORE PIGGY BANK. My backpack was missing. All of my homework.

Zeke was so pale he looked ≈ dead.

"Did you give our combination to the Isaacs again?" Zeke whispered.
pianissimo

"I swear I didn't," I said.

"But then how...?" Zeke whispered.
piano

We just stood there, gaping at the empty locker.
pianissimo

"You had so, so, so much money," I said.

Zeke stared at the few crumpled dollars in his fist.
piano

"I've been saving money to visit my dad," Zeke whispered.
pianissimo

Maybe Zeke's dad works in the Upper Peninsula too,

I thought, but Zeke said, "My dad is a soldier still. When
I was younger, he fought in Iraq, and afterward got stationed in Arabia. He would leave for Arabia, then come
home again, then leave for Arabia. That was our life. Back
and forth. Back and forth. Back and forth. Then one time
he didn't come back. He got stationed at some base in
Italy, and got a house there, and started a new family. Now
that's where he lives, even when he's on leave. It was like
he forgot who he was." Zeke rubbed a finger over a FREAK.
"My dad had three kids with his new wife, so I have three
little brothers there now I've never even met."

"And now you'll never get to?" I said.

"I'll still get to," Zeke said. "The Isaacs don't want my
money. They want something I stole from them. They'll
try to trade my money for what I stole."

A kid with a piccolo came galloping down the hallway,
looking > hyper, shouting, "Fire in the parking lot, fire in
the parking lot!"

We ran to the parking lot with everyone who wasn't
on buses already—Emma Dirge, the Geluso twins, the
kid with the piccolo. Mr. Tim was there already, hosing

147

the garbage bin with a fire extinguisher. The Geluso twins booed him for putting out the fire.

fermata

"Can't imagine what's in there to light," Mr. Tim muttered. "The bin was just emptied this afternoon."

mezzo-piano

Mr. Tim used the handle of his broom to fish something out from the garbage bin—the charred remains of a gold backpack. Ashes tumbled out, caught in the wind. I spotted a couple of half-burned dollars in the whirlwind of ash, floating off into the parking lot.

"At least it wasn't a kid," Mr. Tim said.

forte

Now Zeke was so pale he looked = dead.

"They burned my money," Zeke whispered.

piano

Mr. Tim fished out another backpack—a black one— mine. Bits of half-burned homework went floating off into the parking lot after the bits of half-burned dollars.

"Nothing to worry about," Mr. Tim said. "Only a cou-

forte

ple of backpacks."

●

My mom's car was parked at the curb, across from the buses. She was wearing her uniform, plus her name tag, plus a gray jacket with black buttons. She had a bit of something leafy stuck between her teeth. A stack of flyers had spilled across the dashboard, all with the same picture of Grandpa Rose.

"Don't forget that there's a showing today. Do you want to come along to the rest home for a while? We aren't allowed at the house during the showing," my mom said.
forte

"I'm going to a friend's house," I said.
forte

"What friend?" my mom said.
forte

"I need a new backpack," I said.
forte

"What happened to yours?" my mom said.
forte

Sometimes your mom will give you this look where you can tell she's thinking about who you used to be. She wants you to be the you you were when you were younger, the smaller one with no secrets, but you can't help getting older, you're getting bigger every day. That was the look my mom gave me now.

"Nicholas, we can't afford another backpack," my mom said.
forte

I had to get home before the showing started. I shouted goodbye and flew onto the bus and dropped into
forte
a seat just as Mr. Carl shifted the bus into gear.

When I got home, a black station wagon was parked in the driveway.

The showing was already happening.

The kids in my brain shouted, "Don't peek in, don't sneak in, you'll get in trouble!" but as per usual I couldn't help ignoring.

I tried my bedroom window, which was locked. I ran around the house. My brother was talking to a salamander with golden speckles. The dirt was drier, the grass was deader than before. It still hadn't rained. I poured a bucket of water onto my brother's roots. Then I peeked through the kitchen window.

In the kitchen, a woman in a polka-dot dress was burping a baby in polka-dot overalls. A man in a black sweater was laughing at someone's joke, the laughter muted by the window. The agent my parents had hired was showing the family our stove, yoyoing the door of the oven.

I propped the bucket against the house.

I dropped through the bathroom window.

I crouched in the bathtub, where I had landed, and listened. Then I noticed the bathroom.

My towel had vanished. My toothbrush was missing from the sink. The shelf above the bathtub was empty—my mom had hidden our soaps, our razors, our shampoos. It looked like we had already moved out.

The door to the oven slammed in the kitchen. I could hear voices. My own house, *forte* and I had to sneak around *mezzo-piano, piano, mezzo-forte* like a thief. I slid from the bathtub onto the floor. I tested my high-tops. I took a breath.

I crept through the bathroom, my high-tops squeaking against the tiles. I bolted through the kitchen, where the *pianissimo* woman in the polka-dot dress was peering under the sink, my high-tops scuffing against the wood. I crept through *pianissimo* the hallway, my high-tops padding against the carpet. I *pianissimo* shoved a lock of hair out of my eyes and took a breath again and ducked into my bedroom.

A kid in a blazer was sitting on my bed. An elementary schooler, a third grader, maybe. I had never seen him before. His nose was crusted with snot.

"Who are you?" the kid said.

forte
"Your worst nightmare," I said.

mezzo-piano
"Do you live here?" the kid said.

forte
"Yes," I said.

mezzo-piano
"I like your room," the kid said.

forte
"You do not," I said.

mezzo-piano
"I do too. I like this whole house. It has neat windows," the kid said.

forte
"You hate this house," I said.

mezzo-piano
"My mom thinks it's too small—"

"It is," I said.

mezzo-piano
"—but my dad thinks it's perfect."

I dug through my closet for my knife. The kid stared at me like he was afraid^{uncertain}. I belted my knife to my leg.

"Here's what they won't tell your parents," I hissed.
piano
"We have ghosts in our attic, and monsters in our woods, and the skeletons of children bricked into our walls."

The kid stared at me like he was more scared than before even.

But as I dropped through the window, the kid shouted,
forte
"I think ghosts are neat too!"

●

That night at the ghosthouse, Grandpa Rose and Grandpa Dykhouse sat at the top of the staircase, chewing handfuls of raspberries. Grandpa Rose was talking, something *piano* about someone getting shot over gambling debts. Grandpa Dykhouse was scribbling notes about the memory with the stub of a pencil, his glasses hooked to his sweater. The lantern flickered between them, each of the steps darker and darker toward where the staircase turned into floor. New supplies lay dumped in piles there at the bottom— reams of paper, a plastic bag from the pharmacy, scattered library books, some bent cans of peaches.

I was perched on the fireplace, fiddling with the broken music box. Zeke was sprawled across the floor, his head propped on a wolfdog. Jordan was peeing from the porch.

"Shouldn't we start on PAWPAW ISLAND?" Jordan shouted.

forte
"Theoretically," Zeke shouted. "But I can't find anything about a PAWPAW ISLAND. I looked at my map of the lakes, at the index of the islands, but there wasn't a

PAWPAW. The index went from Parry Island to Pelee Island with nothing between."

"So now what?" Jordan shouted.
forte

"We may have to search the islands one by one," Zeke shouted.
forte

"Do you know how many islands there are in Michigan?" Jordan shouted.
forte

"34,981," I said.
mezzo-piano

"He meant approximately, but, yes," Zeke muttered.
mezzo-piano

"Prime number," I said.
mezzo-piano

"Like, a lot of islands," Jordan shouted.
forte

Jordan stepped over a wolfdog back into the ghost-house.

"We'll all be grandfathers before we've searched every one," Jordan said.
forte

Jordan sawed open a can of peas. Zeke frowned at a
mezzo-forte
water stain on the ceiling, running his fingers over his stubby bristles of buzzed hair. I wound the music box, the music box making the same sound it always made, click click click click click, trying to play its music with
piano piano piano piano piano
whatever parts it had left. Grandpa Rose was telling a
piano

154

story about someone with a lisp double-crossing someone with a toupee, while Grandpa Dykhouse scribbled
notes.

"I've been trying to solve the other clue, about the
trunk, X18471913," I said. "X is the twenty-fourth letter of
forte
the alphabet, so the clue could mean 2418471913, like a
phone number—241-847-1913—but when I tried calling
it, it didn't ring, just made a beeping sound instead."

"What's the language where letters mean numbers?"
Zeke said. "Like I means one, V means five, X means ten.
forte
Maybe the X means ten, so the clue means 1018471913."

"I tried that number too," I said. "Or another theory is
forte
the X represents a multiplication sign, which would mean
we're supposed to multiply something by 18,471,913." I
wound the music box again. "Or another theory is the X
represents a decimal point, which would make the number .18471913, which is approximately equal to a ratio
of 2,309/12,500, which you can't simplify any further
because 2,309 is a prime number."

Jordan threw the empty can at me.

"You're so smart that you're dumb," Jordan said.
forte

155

Jordan squatted.

"Here's what you're missing," Jordan said. "Are you ready, Calculator?" He jabbed me with a finger. "The x *forte* doesn't mean anything! The numbers are the clue! The x marks the spot!" He held his arms out, like someone after a performance awaiting a shower of bouquets.

Zeke shook his head.

"You're so dumb that you're dumb," Zeke muttered.

piano

I looked around from person to person. I was eleven, and Zeke was thirteen, and Jordan was thirteen, and Grandpa Rose was eighty-nine, and Grandpa Dykhouse was seventy-three. All of us were primes. All of us had Big Events coming. If we were going to find the heirlooms, this was the year.

Grandpa Rose was describing a memory about a tun- *pianissimo* nel collapsing and marooning someone underground.

"We don't even know what the heirlooms are worth," Zeke said. "A gun, a clock, a hammer, how valuable can *mezzo-piano* they be?"

"I don't know," I said. "But they better be worth at *mezzo-forte* least as much as a house."

156

"And a boat," Jordan said. "A house and a boat."

Zeke didn't even bother saying anything about a flight to Italy.

●

"We're late for the seance," Zeke grunted, rousing the wolfdogs.

"See you, King Gunga, we're off for some treasure hunting," Jordan called.

"You're coming?" Zeke gaped.

"Calculator didn't tell you? I'm hunting for the treasure now too. A third of that treasure's mine," Jordan cackled, wriggling into a sweatshirt.

As the others headed for the porch, bickering, Grandpa Rose waved me over to the staircase.

Climbing the steps, I suddenly thought of another theory.

"Hey, Grandpa Rose, you can't read music, can you?" I said.

"Kid, I'm hardly smart enough to read a magazine," Grandpa Rose said.

The x clue could have meant a sequence of ghost

notes—on sheet music, ghost notes look just like normal notes, except ghost notes have x's where normal notes would have heads. During performances, ghost notes get played almost totally silently—so that the notes are still there, but barely there at all—like notes hovering somewhere between the realms of living sounds and dead silence.

But how could ghost notes lead to a hidden trunk? What were you supposed to play them on? Where were you supposed to play them?

Anyway, if Grandpa Rose couldn't even read music, that must not have been the answer.

Just then, I noticed how anxious Grandpa Rose looked. He had his jacket buttoned to his chin. His fingers were streaked with raspberry. He wouldn't even look at me.

"Kid, I have to tell you something embarrassing, and somewhat disgraceful," Grandpa Rose said. He fiddled with a button. He quit fiddling. *forte* "The truth is that, lately, I've been having trouble remembering your Grandma Rose's face." He hesitated, and hung his head. "Okay, truthfully, I haven't been able to picture her face for some time now. Not at all. Believe me, that's been the worst part about the last few years. Worse than anything." He knit his hands together, like someone begging for some money. "Tomorrow, will you bring me a photo of her face?"

"We don't have any," I said.

"You don't have any?" *forte* Grandpa Rose said, hunching forward, frowning. *forte*

"My mom says Grandma Rose never let any photos of herself be taken. I was three months old when she died. I can't remember her face either," I said.

forte Grandpa Rose stared off toward the fireplace, still frowning.

"So, you don't even know what you're missing," Grandpa Rose murmured.

piano In the gold light of the lantern, the tattoos on his cheeks looked almost black. He blinked. He turned back toward me, and smiled, rapping his knuckles against my chest.

"You're lucky," Grandpa Rose said.
forte

I flew down the staircase, shot through the doorway out onto the porch.

"Finally finally finally, let's go!" Jordan said.
forte

Grandpa Dykhouse peeked out through the doorway, the lenses of his glasses smudged with spiraled fingerprints.

"Have you kids ever heard of holmgangs?" Grandpa Dykhouse said.
forte

We stopped on the steps.

"Wait," Jordan said, squinting at Grandpa Dykhouse.
forte
"I know that look. You're in librarian mode, aren't you? You're going to make us listen to some boring fact!"

"Do you want help looking for the heirlooms or not?" Grandpa Dykhouse said.
forte

"Okay, but this had better be mind-blowing, and don't add any extra details," Jordan said.
forte

"I can guarantee that you'll like it, because it's about fighting," Grandpa Dykhouse said.
forte

"Alright!" Jordan said, folding his arms together and
forte
nodding.

Grandpa Dykhouse leaned against the doorway, moonlight gleaming on his head.

"A holmgang was a duel," Grandpa Dykhouse said. "A
forte
duel that you had on an island. If you didn't like someone, or if you got into a quarrel, you would meet on an island with your pistols and your seconds. Then you would duel until somebody was dead."

"What's a second?" Zeke said.
forte
"A second was a friend you would bring along, to make sure the fight was fair," Grandpa Dykhouse said.

"Could the seconds fight each other?" Zeke said.
forte

forte
"Sometimes the seconds had to," Grandpa Dykhouse said. "The Scandinavian settlers who built this town,
forte
they would have holmgangs all of the time. Somebody would fall in love with somebody's wife, and then—holmgang—they would row to an island and shoot each other. A roof would collapse and kill somebody's kids, and then—holmgang—whoever's kids had been killed would challenge the roofer, and they would row to an island and shoot each other."

Zeke murmured something about the Isaacs. I didn't
piano

161

know then that this murmur was noteworthy, but it's noteworthy, 100%.

"Anyway, I keep thinking. Those skeletons are everywhere on the islands. Maybe that's where Monte hid the key. Maybe BONES FROM BOW means the bones of a dueler?" Grandpa Dykhouse said.
forte

"Let's ask!" Jordan said, but Grandpa Dykhouse said,
forte   *forte*
"I've tried already. Monte won't say anything, except, 'Who are you? What are you doing here? Get out of my house!'"

"Sorry," I said.
mezzo-piano
"It's not your fault," Grandpa Dykhouse said.
piano
Grandpa Dykhouse stepped into the ghosthouse, shivering, and waving goodnight.

"It's not even Monte's," Grandpa Dykhouse said.
pianissimo

●

We slipped through a meadow of chirring mosquitoes
forte
and trilling crickets, tightroped a tree across a creek of
forte
droning frogs, crossed an unpaved sandy road to a dead-
fortissimo
end neighborhood of one-story cottages. The wolfdogs kept bumping into each other, sniffing at the road.

"Why did you draw those pictures of the Gelusos today?" I said.

forte

"I didn't," Jordan said.

forte

"The Gelusos thought you did," I said.

forte

"Anything mean anybody does at that school, everybody assumes it was me. 'The Ballad Of Dirge And Keen,' I never wrote that either," Jordan said.

forte

Zeke laughed, like someone disappointed by a magician's trick.

piano

"Laugh if you want. But I'm not lying. Half of the things I'm blamed for I never did," Jordan muttered.

piano

Zeke ducked through a curtain of hanging ivy, unlatched the gate of a stone cottage. The gate tocked shut behind us. The wolfdogs huffed, then flopped onto the road, resting their snouts on their paws, staring at the gate, looking moody about getting left behind. Zeke led us along a path of stones.

piano

piano

"This will be my first and hopefully last ever seance," Jordan said.

forte

No one said anything.

"Do you believe in ghosts, Boylover?" Jordan said.

forte

"Really, after you've experienced something personally, you can't help but believe in it," Zeke said.
forte

"You're saying you've seen a ghost?" Jordan said.
forte

"Well, maybe not ghosts exactly, but related phenomena, definitely," Zeke said.
forte

"I don't know what that means," Jordan said.
forte

"Okay. Here. So, an example is, my dad is missing a hand," Zeke said.
forte

"You're lying. Like, how, from war?" Jordan said.
forte

"A spider bit him," Zeke said.
forte

"A spider bit him. Then, what? The hand just fell off? You can't lose a hand to a spider, that's completely impossible," Jordan said.
forte

"Not for this kind," Zeke said.
forte

"What kind?" Jordan said.
forte

"A violin spider. It bit his hand, and the skin on his hand turned necrotic, and so the doctors had to cut off the hand. Some people call the spiders fiddlebacks," Zeke said.
forte

"Necrotic?" Jordan said.
forte

"Dead. Necrotic. It means the skin on the hand was dead, even though the hand was still alive," Zeke said.
forte

Jordan pretended to puke, disgusted^delighted.

"Anyway, have you heard of phantom limbs?" Zeke said. "If your hand gets cut off, afterward sometimes you'll

forte

feel the missing hand. You'll feel it tingling, or cramping, or hurting, like it's still there. You'll feel something pinching it. And my dad always said the worst part is that you can't fix it. Because it's not actually there. Nothing's actually pinching it. So you can't fix it, you have to keep feeling it, until the pinching stops on its own."

Jordan stopped dead on the path.

"I really hate to agree with you, but now that you say it, this creepy thing happens to me sometimes," Jordan said.

forte

"In kindergarten, I used to have this sort of mullet. You know, where your hair is short in front and long in back? But, the creepy thing is, even now that my hair is normal, sometimes I still feel something bobbing around back there!"

Zeke buried his face in his hands.

"It's phantom limbs, not phantom haircuts," Zeke said.

forte

"I swear, sometimes I get this ghost mullet!" Jordan said.

forte

Jordan was still rambling about mullets. Zeke knocked
forte   *fortissimo*
on the door. I was peeking through an unlit window.

A shape appeared there, behind the lace curtain, drifting toward the door.

Zeke tugged my sweatshirt.

"You've never met Kayley Schreiber before?" Zeke
whispered.
piano
"Never even seen her," I whispered.
piano
"Did you know she speaks binary?" Zeke whispered.
piano
Binary is a language computers speak. Instead of
letters, it's zeros and ones. Like 01100010011100100110
11110111010001101000011001010101110010. That's what
you would say if you wanted to say "brother." I didn't
know much about the homeschooler except that she lived
with her grandmother and fed birds from her hands.

"No, why?" I whispered.
piano

●

Kayley Schreiber had bushy eyebrows, blotchy cheeks,
and a freakishly large mouth. She was eating celery and

wearing a shirt the size of a dress. I calculated the odds that she would have had any friends at a school like ours, which were about 0%.

"My earring's missing," Kayley said, pinching her earlobe, frowning.
mezzo-forte

A skull earring, the shape of a keyhole, hung from her other earlobe.

"What can be lost can be found," her grandmother murmured, her voice all singsong, as she sprinkled herbs into a pot of bubbling stew.
piano

mezzo-piano
Kayley led us along a wallpapered hallway, through a wooden door, and into a backyard of chirping bats. A treehouse had been built in the branches of a huge cedar
pianissimo
tree. Planks of wood had been hammered into the trunk. We scaled the tree from step to step, like the lines of a staff, the planks rough under my fingers.

"Do you hate homeschool?" Jordan said.
forte
"Today I read a book about the history of dressmaking. Then I collected different birds' nests to study their architecture. I love homeschool," Kayley said.
forte

"Is your accent fake?" Jordan said.

forte

"We used to live in the Keys, where voodoo is hugely popular," Kayley said.

forte

"Were you born weird?" Jordan said.

forte

"You can't help your obsessions," Kayley said.

forte

Jordan started to ask another question. Zeke hit Jordan. Jordan hit Zeke. We sat cross-legged. I memorized the treehouse. Dead leaves strewn across the floor. Voodoo signs chalked across the ceiling. A spiral shell on a weathered table. Bouquets of dried wildflowers. A deck of warped tarot cards. Hanging from a nail, drawn in charcoal on brown paper, a map of the smugglers' tunnels out at the dunes.

"Money?" Kayley said.

fermata

Zeke stared at his last few crumpled dollars. He chewed a lip. He handed over the money. Then he crossed his fingers, like a gambler banking on the jackpot.

"Before I summon the spirit, I'll read your palms," Kayley said.

forte

She held Jordan's hands, studying the lines.

"I don't believe in ghosts," Jordan said.

forte

"A hundred years ago people didn't believe in germs, but germs killed people anyway," Kayley said.

forte

She held Zeke's hands, studying the lines.

"Sorry, I didn't know he was coming," Zeke muttered.

mezzo-forte

"Heard that, Boylover," Jordan said.

forte

"I should charge extra," Kayley muttered.

mezzo-forte

"Heard that too," Jordan said.

forte

She held my hands. The charcoal map of the smugglers' tunnels flickered with the wind.

piano

"Do you speak binary?" I whispered.

mezzo-piano

She nodded, tracing the lines in my palms with the tip of her finger. I wanted her to hold my hands forever. I had never met anyone else who spoke a language made of numbers.

●

Kayley clapped, like SHALL WE BEGIN? She shoved aside the

mezzo-forte

table, pinched a stump of chalk between her fingers. With the hem of her shirt she erased a symbol from the floor.

"A treehouse is the best place for voodoo, when you're a beginner, because of its size," Kayley said. She rested

forte

her fists on her hips, nodding thoughtfully, like she

couldn't help agreeing with herself. "In a normal build-ing, with multiple rooms and layered walls, it's tough to pinpoint the heart of the structure. But a treehouse is one room! The heart of the structure is the center of the floor."

She bent over the floorboards, tucking her hair behind her ears, and drew intersecting ovals with swooping lines of chalk.

"Different seances summon different elements. A matter of voice and form. The medium's question," Kay-ley said. She flared her nostrils, and pursed her lips, con-
_{forte}
centrating. "This symbol I'm drawing summons just the voice of the spirit. The symbols that would summon the form of the spirit are way more complex."

She drew a spiral shell within the ovals.

"You can't just summon a spirit anywhere anytime. A spirit haunts a certain building. Namely, wherever that spirit died," Kayley said. She paused, glancing up at us.
_{forte}
Her eyebrows rose suddenly, vanishing under her bangs. "This treehouse is haunted by the spirit of its maker, who fell while building it. But through that spirit we can talk

to the others in the underworld. I'll summon its voice into the depths of the shell."

She tossed the chalk. She cradled the shell. She sat cross-legged on the symbol, holding an ear to the shell, shutting her eyes. The shell was pale pink, her fingernails a darker purple.

"You may now ask the question," Kayley murmured. *piano*

Zeke nudged me.

"We need to know anything anyone there knows about my grandfather, who was born here in town, and whose name is Monte Rose," I said. *forte*

She gripped the shell. Her eyes darted under her eyelids. Bats arced past the windows. The wind shook the *piano* tree. The floorboards creaked. The charcoal map of the *decrescendo* smugglers' tunnels flapped on its nail. *pianissimo*

The noise died.

"Monte Rose?" Kayley said. *mezzo-forte*

"Yes?" I said. *forte*

She set the shell on the table. She looked uneasy^puzzled. *piano* She frowned.

"I'm sorry," Kayley said. *mezzo-forte*

"For what?" I said.
forte

"The dead won't help you," Kayley said.
mezzo-forte

"What did they say?" I said.
forte

She erased the symbol from the floor.

"That he gave them no rest," Kayley said.
piano

●

Zeke hopped from the tree, landing with a whump.
piano

"What does that mean?" Zeke muttered.
mezzo-piano

Jordan hopped from the tree, landing with a whomp.
piano

"Do you believe in ghosts, Calculator?" Jordan said.
mezzo-piano

"Maybe not in the ghosts of the dead," I whispered.
mezzo-piano

"What then?" Jordan said.
mezzo-piano

I thought of my brother the tree.

"I don't think it's things that used to be that haunt us, but things that could have been," I whispered.
mezzo-piano

As I hopped from the planks, I saw a glint of metal in the grass. A skull earring. The metal hook a question mark with a skull for a dot. I could have set it on the door, but I didn't. I pocketed the earring, and ducked the ivy, and bolted after the others into the trees.

THE THIEF

The next day was a Saturday. I peed. I ate a bowl of cereal like sludge. I read a story in the news- paper about someone's tractors getting stolen. I spit toothpaste and gargled mouthwash. I peed again. I went into my backyard to talk to my brother the tree.

mezzo-piano

mezzo-forte *mezzo-forte* *piano*

BROTHER WILL YOU ASK THE BIRDS YOU SPEAK TO WHETHER THEY ONCE SAW OUR GRANDPA ROSE HIDING A KEY ON AN ISLAND MANY YEARS AGO? my song said.

THE BIRDS IN THESE WOODS ARE YOUNGER EVEN THAN YOU OR ME, my brother's song said. WHEN OUR GRANDFATHER

WAS HERE IT WAS NOT THESE BIRDS WHO WOULD HAVE SEEN HIM. IT WAS THEIR GREAT-GREAT-GREAT-GRANDFATHERS.

My mom was bent over the sink in the kitchen window, leafing through phone books, calling hospitals and homeless shelters to ask about Grandpa Rose. A pair of hummingbirds hovered around my brother, near where my dad had scarred the bark. I plucked more notes into my violin.

THEN WILL YOU ASK THE TREES YOU SPEAK TO WHETHER THEY KNOW THE MEANING OF X18471913? my song said.

I waited while my brother spoke to the other trees in the woods. Some of them had trunks as thick as three or five people—they were older than our house, older than our village, even.

With the wind in his branches my brother said, THE TREES SAY THAT IS A QUESTION FOR THE STONES.

My mom leaned through the kitchen window.

"Someone's at the door," my mom shouted.

forte
I calculated the odds it wasn't Zeke, which were about 0%. No one else would be willing to be seen standing at my door.

But when I ran around my house, it wasn't Zeke.

Jordan stood on my stoop, his hands on his knees, bent over panting. His cheeks hollowing when he inhaled, billowing when he exhaled. The armpits of his shirt wet with sweat.

"I was just downtown," Jordan panted.
_{piano}
He waved toward downtown.

"I saw Boylover. At the antique shop. Trying to sell your grandpa's music box," Jordan panted.
_{mezzo-piano}
He waved toward the ghosthouse.

"He stole it," Jordan panted.
_{mezzo-forte}
My bow dropped into the grass. My violin dropped into the grass. I was dumbfounded^{betrayed}.

"We have to get it back!" I said.
_{forte}
Jordan stood up, wiping sweat from his cheeks.

"What's this 'we'? I only tag along for treasure hunting. With anything else, you're on your own," Jordan said.
_{forte}
He crossed into Emma Dirge's yard, then walked down Emma Dirge's driveway, so he wouldn't have to be seen walking down from mine.

●

I ran to the ghosthouse to tell Grandpa Rose, but as I rounded the bend in the road, Zeke and his wolfdogs came slipping from the woods.

"Hey," Zeke said.
forte

When your locker partner has betrayed you by stealing your only living grandfather's only worldly possession, what's right and what's wrong isn't a matter of fact. It's a matter of belief. And, at that moment, I believed the logical thing was to tackle the thief.

So I ran at Zeke.

"Whoa whoa whoa...!" Zeke shouted.
forte

I tackled Zeke into the road. We rolled across the painted lines, our bodies leapfrogging.

"Where's the music box?" I shouted.
fortissimo

"What are you talking about?" Zeke shouted. He
fortissimo
tried to shove me off. His wolfdogs snarled, crouching to
forte
pounce. "It's at the ghosthouse!"

"Jordan saw you trying to sell it!" I shouted.
forte

A truck whipped around the bend, dead leaves scattering in its wake. As the truck blared its horn, we scrambled
fermata

out of the road into the woods, then watched the truck blow past the spot where we had been.

Zeke's wolfdogs were still growling. My elbows were tingling where my skin had been peeled raw by the gravel.
piano

"I had to know whether the heirlooms were actually worth anything or whether we were wasting our time," Zeke said. "My grandfather was friends with the woman
forte
who owns the antique shop, before he died, and she helps me with things sometimes. So I took the music box there to find out what it was worth. But afterward I returned it. It's in the ghosthouse again."

"Show me," I said.
mezzo-forte
We hiked up the hill, through sunny ferns, shadowed boulders, the rotting white trunks of fallen birch trees. Grandpa Rose was smoking on the porch of the ghosthouse, feeding raspberries to birds. Grandpa Dykhouse was reading the endnote of some book. My elbows were bleeding.

"Boys," Grandpa Rose nodded.

"Hungry?" Grandpa Dykhouse said.
forte
We shook our heads, then hopped through the living
forte
room window.

I unlocked Grandpa Rose's suitcase. The music box was inside, tucked between pairs of socks with gold toes.

"See?" Zeke said. "I didn't steal it. I only steal from
fermata
kids who hate me. They steal my happiness, so I steal stuff from them."

By now my fingers knew every hooked gouge and jagged scrape on the bottom of the music box. There wasn't even a single new scuff or nick. I popped the lid. The same parts were there, on the inside, as always. Nothing was missing that hadn't been missing all along. Someone had even cleaned the dust from the hinges.

"Did you learn anything about the heirlooms?" I said.
forte
"When the owner saw the music box, she said she would have to take out a loan if she was going to buy it. It was priceless, she said. A handful of these music boxes still exist, but none that works," Zeke said. "But then she
forte
wound it. And when she saw it was broken, everything changed. Broken, it's worth the same as the others. A couple hundred dollars, tops."

I stuffed the music box back into the suitcase.

"What about the other heirlooms?" I said.
forte

"The hammer, the clock, and the revolver, she said a lot, a fortune, and nearly priceless," Zeke said. "Probably. In that order. Provided they aren't broken."^forte

●

That night at the ghosthouse I told Jordan what Zeke had said.

Jordan only laughed.

"Now I wish I would have tagged along,"^forte Jordan said. "I would pay anything to have seen that look on his face^mezzo-forte when you tackled him."

A NUMBER IN THE UPPER
PENINSULA

My mom handed me the phone. I could hear television noises. My dad always called from *mezzo-piano* my uncle's living room—that's where my dad was sleeping now, when my dad wasn't working at the repair shop.

"Cold there?" my dad said.
forte

"Sort of," I said.
mezzo-forte

"Cold here," my dad said.
forte

Neither of us said anything for a while. My mom walked past with flowers for the piano. She was wearing a black cardigan over a gray shirt.

"School alright?" my dad said.

forte

He sounded tired. I could hear the workweek in his voice. He doesn't know anything about music, doesn't know anything about math. Whatever language I speak, my dad speaks something different. Still, we had to try. Even if we couldn't understand each other, there seemed to be something important about just getting to hear each other's voices.

I stared through the window at my brother the tree.

"School's okay," I said.

mezzo-piano

I waited for him to say it, before he hung up, but he didn't say it.

COULD HAVE SAVED LIVES, COULD HAVE BROKEN HEARTS

For my whole life, all of my teachers have been telling my parents the same thing. My violin teacher says I could compose symphonies. My math teachers say I could design supercomputers. My science teachers say I could become a brain surgeon, a nuclear physicist, a spaceship engineer. With my brain, they say, I could become anything.

"I've never taught a kid like him," they say. "When he grows up, he can become anything, whatever he wants."

mezzo-forte, mezzo-piano, forte

It's the worst thing about my life. Because if I can

become anything—if I can become anything that I choose—then whatever I become will be my fault.

What if I tried to compose symphonies but ended up becoming a band director instead? Then everyone I've ever known will say, "He could have been a brain surgeon. He could have saved lives. What a waste—spending all day teaching kids how to empty spit valves."

But what if I tried to become a brain surgeon and ended up becoming a foot doctor instead? Then everyone I've ever known will say, "He could have composed symphonies. He could have broken hearts with his music. What a waste—looking all day at people's feet."

Any other kid, if he became a band director or a foot doctor, his parents would be proud of him. It's not easy to become a band director. It's not easy to become a foot doctor. It takes a lot of work to become those things. But if I became either of those things, my teachers would be disappointed. Whatever I become, my teachers will be disappointed. "He could have become anything," they'll say. "And this is all that he became."

Grandpa Rose and I are the same that way. That night, as we sat together on the porch of the ghosthouse, Grandpa Rose pressed his fingertips to his tattoos, I touched the earring in my pocket, and we were both thinking about the same thing. Grandpa Rose doesn't know who he is—doesn't remember who he was anymore. I don't know who I am—don't even know how to choose what to try to be.

If I truly could become anything, I would want to become normal. I would want to be like Mark Huff, who can talk to other kids in a normal way about normal things, and who can dribble a soccer ball between the trees in his yard all day and have fun and keep laughing, and who can become a foot doctor, and no one will blame him for it.

EMPTY BOXES

The next three days were days of shaking heads.

We sat on wooden chairs in the library while a librarian with gray eyes searched the catalog for books about PAWPAW ISLAND.

"Isn't PAWPAW also the name for a grandfather?" Jordan whispered.
pianissimo

"Do you mean as a nickname or something?" Zeke whispered.
pianissimo

"Isn't PAWPAW also the name of a tree?" I whispered.
pianissimo

The librarian spun on his chair, shaking his head at us.

"Nothing," the librarian said.
forte

We stood on swaying docks at the wharf while sailors in black waders sprayed fish guts from the decks of their *mezzo-forte* boats.

"Does anyone here collect BOTTLED SHIPS?" I shouted. *forte*

The sailors shook their heads.

"Has anyone heard of PAWPAW ISLAND?" I shouted. *forte*

The sailors shook their heads again.

We waited on a bench across from the antique shop while Zeke and the owner gestured at each other inside.

"Listen, Calculator, I've been thinking. What do we need Boylover for? Why don't we split those heirlooms two ways instead of three?" Jordan whispered as the *piano* owner waved goodbye.

I shook my head.

"What did she say?" I shouted as Zeke trotted to the *forte* bench.

Zeke shook his head.

"NINE PACES INLAND, BOTTLED SHIPS, PAWPAW ISLAND, she can't crack it," Zeke said as we stood from the bench. *forte*

Jordan shook his head.

We cut through the graveyard, shuffling across graves overgrown with weeds, above coffins of bones, or the empty coffins buried there for people whose bodies were never found.

There was one place we knew we should have tried looking. But going there was basically suicide. None of us had even dared to speak its name.

My mom bought me a cheap backpack with money we didn't have. Every morning she wandered the neighborhood, wrapped in a jacket, searching for some sign of Grandpa Rose. My brother drooped. The rain didn't come. I watered his roots, brushed the leaves of other trees from his branches. Every night I sat scrawling PAW-PAW ISLAND THERE BOTTLED SHIPS BONES FROM BOW NINE PACES INLAND = ? on a notepad, chewing the insides of my cheeks, switching my lamp, off on, off on, off on, off on, off on. The equation made me feel angry^{imprisoned}. I hated the equation, for being difficult, for being impossible, for being everything. I hated myself, for being beaten by the equation. I threw my pen, left a hole in the wall.

At school, in the cafeteria, the Gelusos recounted a story to a table of kids, interrupting each other, waving their arms.

"Last night, this was," The Unibrow said.

piano

"Cutting through the meadow," Crooked Teeth said.

mezzo-piano

"Freaky things were happening in the ghosthouse," The Unibrow said.

piano

"Lights floating around," Crooked Teeth said.

mezzo-piano

"Singing. Laughing," The Unibrow said.

piano

"Worse than laughing. We heard hooting," Crooked Teeth said.

mezzo-piano

"The ghosts were hooting," The Unibrow said.

piano

"Nothing's as evil as a hoot," Crooked Teeth said.

mezzo-piano

Then Mark Huff carried a tray to the table, dark turkey and green beans and mashed potatoes, and everyone made fun of Mark Huff for getting tripped out the attic window.

Every evening, when we got to the ghosthouse, we found the grandfathers in a different room. The first night, Grandpa Rose and Grandpa Dykhouse had carved a chessboard in the floor of the entryway, were using tools

from the shed as pieces. The second night, Grandpa Rose was singing jazz numbers in the kitchen, Grandpa Dyk-
mezzo-forte
house coaxing him to remember the words. The third
mezzo-forte
night, Grandpa Rose was dancing along the hallway with an imaginary partner while Grandpa Dykhouse bravoed
forte
and encored. Afterward we built a fire in the fireplace,
fermata
sat hunched under blankets, ate canned peas and hunks of bread. Embers snapped from log to log. Grandpa
piano
Rose was feeling talkative. While he taught me chess, we quizzed him about the ancestors of kids we knew.

"Huff," Jordan said.
forte

"Samuel Huff supervised the carton plant, hosted poker games there after hours," Grandpa Rose said.
mezzo-forte

"Geluso," Jordan said.
forte

"Busoni Geluso worked fishing salmon, had a fat face, tiny hands, skin as rough as a brick's," Grandpa Rose said.
mezzo-forte

"Dirge," Jordan said.
forte

"Vern Dirge had the loudest sneeze in the state of Michigan," Grandpa Rose said.
mezzo-forte

"Keen," Jordan said.
forte

"Jan Keen was a sleepwalker, wandered the streets in pajamas," Grandpa Rose said.

mezzo-forte

Jordan was dying laughing.

fortissimo

"How can he remember the names of people who have been dead for fifty years, but he can't remember ours?" Zeke muttered.

piano

While Grandpa Dykhouse and Jordan played chess, Grandpa Dykhouse talked about sailboats. Even though he called us kids, he never talked to us like we were kids, but instead just people. I liked that he would tell us anything.

"Every summer we would sail across Lake Michigan, under the bridge at Mackinac, through the locks to Lake Superior. Pitch a tent in the forest. Roast marshmallows over a fire," Grandpa Dykhouse said. "Like Saint-Amour,

forte

I should have taken a vow to kill myself on my sixtieth birthday. Just when things seemed perfect—I had retired, Holly had retired, for the first time since high school we had all of this time to spend together—then we lost everything, and I lost Holly." He scooped a spoonful of peas, the spoon rattling against the can. "We were happy

piano

when we were sixty. We should have left then, together, so we could have left happy."

"Yes, okay, Mom and Dad hardly ever visited you, but, still, they were trying to take care of you. The rest home was just the best they could do," Jordan said, squinting at

forte

the chessboard.

"And if they ever find me, they'll take me back there, and they'll never let me die," Grandpa Dykhouse said,

mezzo-forte

setting aside the can. "They'll feed me pills, and hook me to machines that will keep me alive for another ten, twenty, thirty years, until all I can do is blink and breathe and get meals pumped into me through a tube."

"What's wrong with the rest home?" Zeke said. "My

mezzo-piano

grandpa loved it there. When we would try to bring him home for holidays, he wouldn't want to leave. The nurses called him Mr. Smiley."

"The fumes of gold cyanide," Grandpa Dykhouse said.

piano

His eyes were > his normal eyes. Twice as big, maybe. He took a pawn with a pawn. "That's what we should have done."

191

Jordan pointed at the pawn. His gap-tooth surfaced with his grin.

"King Gunga, you've fallen straight into my trap!" Jordan cackled, doubling over himself, drumming his fists
forte   *forte*
on the floor.

Grandpa Rose stirred the embers with a charred stick,
                          pianissimo
laughing. His tattoos were covered with stubble again
pianissimo
already, thick gray and white hair. The rate that he grew a beard at was just freakish. This didn't make sense, but for some reason seeing the tattoos starting to disappear like that worried me—made me feel like we had been given a chance to find the heirlooms, and that our chance was fading, and fading, and fading, and soon would vanish forever.

Leaving the ghosthouse, we yanked on sweatshirts and argued with each other about the notes Grandpa Dyk-
                    forte
house had made of Grandpa Rose's memories. Rippled clouds drifted over the moon. The weeds already were wet with dew. I had gotten desperate enough to consider going to the place we had never considered going before.

"The smugglers' tunnels?" Jordan said.
                          sforzando

In band class, everyone had learned new terms. Sforzando means "play this with sudden force." Staccato means "play this sharp and choppy," means "let none of these notes touch."

We stopped at the stone well, the empty bucket swaying creaking in the wind.

staccato

"He worked for the smugglers. Maybe there are clues in the tunnels. Papers, artifacts, something," I said.

forte

Jordan waved his hands at me, stepping backward.

"You're out of your mind, thinking about going there," Jordan said.

forte

Zeke hung his head, then nodded.

"Tomorrow, after school, let's try it," Zeke said.

forte

Kids our age were strictly forbidden from going into those tunnels, on pain of death.

●

I woke that night to the sound of thunder rumbling in the sky, rain lashing at the window. My breath fogged the

mezzo-forte

forte

glass. I watched trees buckling, snapped limbs bouncing across the backyard. The rain had come, but way too much.

I kicked into my high-tops and grabbed my raincoat and ran to the backyard, slipping across puddles, stumbling. Water hammered the hood of the raincoat. Light-

staccato

ning flashed white across the woods. My brother was pitching from side to side, like someone about to collapse. I dropped to his roots, pressed my back into his bark, propped his trunk with my body. Wind slammed the trees. I dug my high-tops into the mud. I dug my fingers into the mud. Wind slammed the trees again. I would have let it break my backbone before my brother. Thunder blasted. Snapped limbs somersaulted and cartwheeled

fortissimo

through the woods. The rain's tempo was breathless. I couldn't speak without music, and my brother wasn't speaking, was way too afraid. We just sat there together, quietly, through the storm.

●

In the morning the trees were still dripping rainwater.

pianissimo

The deck was littered with branches, muddled leaves, small round berries. Birds pecked at the berries, flew away again. I was eating cinnamon oatmeal from a cracked bowl.

"Did Grandpa Rose ever work?" I said.

mezzo-piano
My mom carried a plate of eggs to the table.

"He never had normal jobs. He was never home. When he was, he would just follow around Grandma Rose," my mom said. "He wasn't a deadbeat or anything. *mezzo-piano* He would fold laundry for her, help her cook, move furniture around, this wall to that wall, that wall to this wall, wherever she pointed next. They were wild about each other. When she came into the room, he would break into this goofy smile, like seeing her face made him, just, overflow. But, of course, then a week later he would disappear."

She dipped toast in the yolk of the eggs. She blew some hair out of her eyes. She chewed a bite.

"Once, at sunrise, before school, we took a walk in the woods," my mom said. "I still remember how, that *mezzo-piano* morning, whenever we heard a songbird, he would say, 'Finch,' or 'Cardinal,' or 'Whippoorwill.' Then he would sing back. He knew all the birds' songs. Note for note. Perfectly. I remember thinking, my father shouldn't have been a crook! My father should have become a ranger, become a biologist, worked at a museum! I was outraged and amazed, simultaneously, by this secret talent. Maybe we took walks other mornings. I don't remember. He tried to teach me the birds' songs. I couldn't sing them. But I still remember which sang which. He did teach me that."

She forked a bite of eggs. I had stopped chewing. I had never heard Grandpa Rose singing birds' songs. He had probably forgotten.

A bird landed on the deck, twittering. I swallowed a mouthful of oatmeal. My mom pointed at the bird with her fork, still looking at her plate.

glissando

"Sparrow," my mom said.

piano

●

In math class, I was solving problems about the golden number. The golden number is a ratio that's majorly powerful. If there is a blueprint to the universe, it's the architect's favorite number. It's the shape of everything. It manifests in the order of trees' branches, the curve of shells' spirals, the scales of pinecones, the seeds of sunflowers, the dimensions of bones, the bodies of galaxies, the trajectory of falcons, the ancestry of honeybees. It's been used in the design of books, of symphonies, of the tombs of pharaohs. Its first nine digits are 1.61803398, which is approximately equal to a ratio of 809/500, which you can't simplify any further because 809 is a prime number.

Jordan slid a note onto my desk.

"From the homeschooler," Jordan muttered, *pianissimo* pretending to fix his high-tops.

I gaped at the note.

"The black spot?" I whispered.

"I don't know," Jordan *piano* muttered. Then the math teacher spotted him and called *pianissimo* him to the chalkboard to solve a problem for the class. *forte*

I got a nervous *uncertain* feeling. If I had been given the black spot, that would mean death was coming for me. I shoved a lock of hair out of my eyes. I took a breath. I unfolded the note.

It wasn't the black spot. It was binary. It said,

01100011011101010111010001100101

I translated it. It meant "cute"? I didn't understand. What was "cute"? Normally the fortunes were warnings. How was "cute" a warning?

I met Zeke at our locker after school.

"I need to stop for my knife before we head to the tunnels," I said.

forte

"I have to round up my dogs. Won't take long. I'll meet you at your house," Zeke said.

forte

Zeke was rooting through crumpled schoolwork on the floor of our locker. His dictionary was on the shelf. I had thought the dictionary had been burned in the garbage bin with our backpacks, but it was back again, like a ghost of itself, its cover as tattered and stained as always.

"How did your dictionary survive the garbage bin?" I said.

forte

"It was never in it. When the Isaacs broke into our locker, the dictionary was at my house," Zeke said. "Nothing could have been luckier. I need those words in it."

forte

Zeke shut the locker, trotted off toward the door.

forte

"I've been thinking about what Grandpa Dykhouse said," Zeke shouted, glancing backward. "Those holmgangs, those duels, that might be the only way to settle things with the Isaacs."

forte

I imagined Zeke waving a pistol.

"The only way?" I murmured.

Leaving school, I saw the Geluso twins perched on *piano* tables in the cafeteria, reading a magazine with the Isaacs. A kid with dreadlocks walked past humming "The Ballad Of Dirge And Keen." Emma Dirge and Leah Keen walked *piano* out of the bathroom. The kid pretended to be humming something else.

●

When I got home, a black station wagon was parked in the driveway.

There was another showing.

I peeked through the kitchen window. A couple without children was sniffing our wallpaper. Both with black hair, both wearing grayish suits. The agent was opening and closing our cabinets, running through the usual ostinato.

I dropped through the bathroom window. I crept to the door, listening.

"Big big big backyard!" the agent said, standing at the *crescendo* window.

The woman frowned at the glass.

"We would have to remove those trees to build the pool," the woman whined.
forte

"Don't forget the lake is practically next door, Ms. York," the agent said.
forte

"Dead fish rot in that water," the woman said.
forte

"Ms. York, a pool sounds heavenly," the agent said.
forte

It was a new worst. If this couple made an offer—if this couple made a closing—we wouldn't just be leaving my brother. After we had gone, this couple would chop him down, would hack him apart.

●

Zeke stood at the bottom of the driveway clutching an unlit lantern. Today's high-tops were a shiny black, with black straps. Zeke barked at the wolfdogs. They galloped into the road from where they had treed a squirrel.
forte

"If you had something that could save Jordan, would you save him?" Zeke said.
piano

"What do you mean save him?" I said.
forte

"I mean nobody would hate him anymore," Zeke said.
piano

"Yes, I would save him," I said.
forte

I belted my knife to my leg.

"Wouldn't you?" I said.
forte

●

We walked to Jordan's house, past the ghosthouse, to the wharf almost. Jordan's house had gray shutters and a gray van in the driveway. Music throbbed, muffled through a
mezzo-forte
second-story window. Zeke knocked on the door.
forte

Jordan's mom answered, with dark pits at her eyes, plus maroon stains on her sweatshirt.

"Genevieve!" Jordan's mom shouted.
fortissimo

"We want Jordan," Zeke said.
forte

"Oh. Sorry. You didn't look his type," Jordan's mom said.
forte

A girl wearing neon elbow pads and neon knee pads ran to the door. She was younger than us—probably some sort of elementary schooler. She had twice the number of Jordan's freckles, but her hair was only half red, was half gold too.

"Will you fetch Jordan?" Jordan's mom said.
mezzo-forte

Genevieve bolted upstairs.

"You kids wait here," Jordan's mom muttered, shut-
mezzo-piano
ting the door.

●

A window scraped open. Jordan peeked out. He wasn't
mezzo-forte
wearing a shirt.

"What?" Jordan said.
forte

"We're going to the smugglers' tunnels," I said.
forte

"Enjoy," Jordan said.
forte

"You're not coming?" I said.
forte

"I'm grounded," Jordan said.
forte

"Again?" I said.
forte

"Somehow my sister's dollhouse got sawed in half,"
Jordan said.
forte

"Somehow?" I said.
forte

Jordan scratched his shoulders.

"Anyway, I wouldn't come along even if I weren't
grounded. The smugglers' tunnels are my brother's territory. Save me some heirlooms, if you find the treasure,"
Jordan said.
forte

"You don't get your share of them unless you're there
when we find them," Zeke said.
forte

Jordan frowned. Jordan sighed. Jordan swore[unwritable].
piano   *piano*

"Let me get a sweatshirt," Jordan muttered.
piano

Jordan tossed out a sweatshirt, which fluttered past the kitchen window and onto the wood chips. He snaked backward, hung from his bedroom window—his high-tops kicking above the kitchen window—then dropped.

Jordan's mom was bent in the refrigerator, rummaging. Jordan wriggled into his sweatshirt as we ran into the trees, headed toward the wharf. A molehill caved under my high-tops, making me stumble. At the farm where the Gelusos lived, their lone cow was mooing, and their lambs were bleating, and their turkeys were ticking at acorns in the grass.
fermata
staccato   *pianissimo*

"Ty, my brother, is just like Grandpa Dykhouse, although they haven't spoken to each other for three years," Jordan said. "They're both obsessed with history, especially the history of the lake. I try to care, I try and I try, but I can't. I hate memorizing things that already happened."
mezzo-forte

"Grandpa Dykhouse seems happier, now that he has the memory project," I said.
mezzo-forte

"Maybe, but that's temporary," Jordan said. "Your grandpa's memories won't stay long. When the memories
mezzo-forte

vanish, the project's finished, and King Gunga's sad again. No, what he needs is a boat."

Running past the wharf, we saw the Isaacs and Mark Huff perched on a sailboat, their arms hanging over the railing, their legs dangling between the bars. The Isaacs were sipping from ceramic mugs, pretending they didn't see us. Mark Huff was tossing cubes of sugar to gulls bobbing on the lake below.

"Do you ever wish you could be Mark Huff?" I said.

mezzo-forte

"I hate Mark Huff," Jordan said.

mezzo-forte

"You do not," Zeke said.

mezzo-forte

"And you can still want to be someone that you hate," I said, frowning.

mezzo-forte

"Nobody would want to be that Flatface," Jordan said,

sforzando

shoving the sleeves of his sweatshirt to his elbows. "His mom moved to Florida to live with some home-wrecker she met at a concert. Now she works at a record store by the ocean. She mails him postcards that say, 'Be good, eat your vegetables, birthday presents coming soon,' but she never mails the birthday presents, she always forgets. I was there the day he heard that she had left. His dad had told him that she was visiting his grandparents. For a month, that's what he had thought. After he heard where she actually was, he told me he wanted to jump off the pier and drown on the rocks. Instead we went into the street and played soccer until it got dark."

Mark Huff was laughing, dropping sugar to the gulls.

pianissimo

"Ty says everybody's stomach has this gray pod, and when you grow up it swells up and splits open and spills this thick gray slime into your stomach that makes you crazy and obsessed with something weird or illegal or just totally freakish, like how Mark's mom ran away with the home-wrecker from the concert, or how the Gelusos' dad names his motorcycles, or how the Gelusos' mom thinks about jigsaw puzzles like nonstop," Jordan said.

mezzo-forte

"What's Ty's thing?" I said.

mezzo-forte

"Torturing middle schoolers," Jordan said.

mezzo-forte

We crashed into the woods, scattering hissing rac-

forte   *forte*

coons, leaping gray mushroom caps growing from the craggy trunks of fallen elm trees, heading to the dunes. Wind flurried through, shaking leftover rainwater from

mezzo-piano

the leaves above.

"If I could be anyone, I would be Ty," Jordan said.

mezzo-piano

"I've never met anybody I like more than myself," Zeke said.

mezzo-piano

"Nobody?" Jordan said.

mezzo-piano

"I would miss me, if I wasn't," Zeke said.

piano

●

There was only one way in and out of the tunnels, in a shady nook on the backside of a giant dune. A thorny raspberry thicket had overgrown the entrance, where tilting wooden beams kept the tunnels propped. Nearby, a ∞ had been notched into the bark of an ash tree—one of the symbols the high schoolers used to mark their territory. The wind had died. All of the birdsong had gone quiet. Jordan tugged the sleeves of his sweatshirt over his hands and shoved through the thicket. We followed, ducking into the darkness.

Something snapped and crackled and a lit match

mezzo-forte   *mezzo-piano*

flared between Zeke's fingertips. Sand from above trickled through cracks between the wooden beams of the ceiling. The tunnels smelled like Grandpa Rose—like stale cigarettes and unwashed clothing. Zeke bent over the lantern, lighting it, the flame gleaming across the silver mermaids on his arms. Outside the entrance, beyond the thicket, the wolfdogs were whining. Zeke barked at them, and then they went quiet.

Zeke unfolded a piece of paper pocked with burn marks.

"I brought a map," Zeke said.

"Wasn't that the homeschooler's?" Jordan said.

"I didn't steal it," Zeke said. "Kayley wanted a blueprint of the ghosthouse, and we needed a map of the tunnels, so I swapped the blueprint for the map."

"What did she want a blueprint of the ghosthouse for?" I said.

"I didn't ask," Zeke said.

Jordan took the lantern. Zeke held the map to the light. In faded charcoal, the map was marked with different rooms—LOVERS HAUNT, THE OPIUM DEN, FAR FAR HIDEAWAY—connected by different tunnels.

Zeke pointed at the room named THE BOTTOMLESS PIT. Underneath, someone had drawn a row of dead faces with all exed-out eyes.

"I've heard rumors about THE BOTTOMLESS PIT," Zeke muttered.
piano

"Rumors?" Jordan said.
piano

They crept into the tunnels, whispering.
pianissimo

The kids in my brain were shouting, "These tunnels
forte
could collapse!" shouting, "A high schooler might catch
fortissimo
you!" shouting, "Run home, run home, run home!" but I
crescendo
shoved a lock of hair out of my eyes and crept after the
others.

●

We hiked through a maze of tunnels, room to room, the
rooms all empty. THE FIREWORKS PARLOR empty aside from
boxes of fireworks and scorch marks across the wooden
beams. THE GRAFFITI CHAMBER empty aside from boxes of
spray-paint and neon messages across the wooden beams.
WIDOWS LAMENT empty aside from spiders and an over-
turned rocking chair.

"We may have walked over the heirlooms already, if
the trunk is buried here," I whispered.
piano

We headed to THE BOTTOMLESS PIT.

•

After countless forks and bends in the tunnels, we still hadn't found THE BOTTOMLESS PIT. We passed a pair of black rubber boots, then another pair of black rubber boots, and then still another pair of black rubber boots. They may have been the same pair. The lantern swung on its hinges, throwing light from wall to wall. The tunnel snaked through tilting wooden beams. Something was yowling or wailing. We passed a pair of boots.

pianissimo
"Are we going in circles?" Jordan said.

piano
Sand from above trickled onto our hair. Zeke stopped, chewing a lip and squinting at the map.

"Do you know where we are?" Jordan said.

piano
Zeke spun the map 90°, 270°, 180°, like someone wrestling with the wheel of a sinking ship. Jordan hung the lantern from a nail.

"Do you know how to read a map?" Jordan hissed.
piano

"I'm reading it!" Zeke hissed.
piano

"Give it here," Jordan hissed.
piano

Jordan snatched the map. Zeke snatched the map.
mezzo-piano   *mezzo-forte*

Jordan snatched the map. It slipped from their hands,
forte
swooped past the lantern, arced toward the ground beyond
the light. Jordan lunged into the darkness, grabbing for it.

He tipped.

His arms flailed.

He dropped over the edge of the pit, screaming.
decrescendo

●

THE BOTTOMLESS PIT was a room with a hole for a floor. I
stood near the edge of the pit, clutching the lantern. Zeke
lay at the edge of the pit, peering into the darkness.

"Jordan?" Zeke hissed.
piano
The pit was silent.

"I never heard him land," I whispered.

"Maybe he's still falling," Zeke whispered.
piano
Sand from above trickled into the pit.
piano
"We're going to need some rope," I said.
piano
We ran back, winding uphill, curving downhill, guess-
ing which tunnels to take. At a fork in the tunnels, we
stopped, trying to remember which tunnel led above-
ground.

White flashlight beams swept across us. We squinted,

shielding our eyes with our hands. Silhouettes hovered at the end of the tunnel.

"It's that thief!" a silhouette shouted.

forte

Zeke yelped. The silhouettes pounded toward us, the

forte

beams of their flashlights chopping back and forth. Zeke bolted into the tunnel, turned into a silhouette himself, vanished into the darkness.

"You better run, freak!" a silhouette shouted.

forte

The silhouettes turned into high schoolers in black hoodies. I dropped the lantern. Someone grabbed me by my shirt.

"Bring that one in, Isaac!" a high schooler shouted.

forte

The high schoolers skidded through the fork, turned

forte

into silhouettes again, bolted after Zeke. The kid who had grabbed me was an Isaac, then. He was the biggest Isaac I had ever seen. His jaw was shaped like the bottom of a box.

"You snuck into the wrong place," Biggest Isaac said,

forte

wheezing.

piano

His voice was boomy, monotone. His hoodie said HILL 61 (prime). In high school, instead of your first name, hoodies have your last name. I tried to slip out of my shirt. He grabbed me by my hair.

"We're going to FAR FAR HIDEAWAY, once I've caught my breath," Biggest Isaac said, wheezing.

forte _pianissimo_

"My friend needs help!" I said.

forte

"Any other day I would have caught your friend myself," Biggest Isaac said, wheezing, "but today at tryouts we had

forte _decrescendo_

to run about fifty suicides thanks to Coach Q. And that after a few hundred down-and-back layups. And that after the three smokes I had between school and tryouts. So, I'm lucky you didn't run. Although, really, kid, you should have run."

Then Biggest Isaac took me into his arms like a bundle of firewood and carried me away.

●

FAR FAR HIDEAWAY was the size of three or five bedrooms. Hammocks had been hammered into the rafters, each hammock sagging with swaying bodies. The ground was littered with the stumps of dying candles, making the kids flicker gold.

"Ty, we've caught a trespasser," Biggest Isaac shouted.

forte

A hand rose out of the farthest hammock, its knuckles furry with reddish hair, its fingers snapping like COME

forte

CLOSER. Biggest Isaac shoved me ahead. I stumbled past snoring bodies, stepping between candles. A trio of girls

piano

in homecoming hoodies stared at me from a creaking

pianissimo

hammock, clutching black bottles. Root beer was made from roots. Birch beer was made from sap. Spruce beer was made from twigs. What they were drinking, it was water, and sugar, and trees.

Ty had swung himself sitting, planting his boots on the floor, twirling a scuffed golden lighter from knuckle to knuckle. He had a gap in his teeth like Jordan's, and the same messy hair, but his eyes were twice as dark. His forehead was marked with a white scar the shape of a saxophone. Jordan had said the scar was from their dad.

"He was with the thief kid," Biggest Isaac said.

forte

Ty knocked a cigarette from a pack, then lit the cig-

staccato

arette. He puffed it a few times so the tip went gold, then dark, then gold, then dark. His hoodie said ODOM 67 (prime).

"How old are you?" Ty said.
forte

"Eleven," I said.
glissando

"You were caught trespassing in high school territory. Worse yet, you were caught in the company of that kid with the buzzed head, who's a known thief," Ty said. "The
forte
customary punishment for trespassing is getting tossed into THE BOTTOMLESS PIT."

My hands trembled.

"Why were you trespassing?" Ty said.
forte

"We were trying to find artifacts from the smugglers," I said.
mezzo-forte

"Artifacts?" Ty snorted, spewing curling spirals of
forte
smoke at me. He shook his head, impatiently, and then leaned forward, candlelight glinting in his eyes. "It's been years since the smugglers used these tunnels. By the time I found this place, looters had carted away everything. The moonshine. The pistols. The metal for scrap." He waved his cigarette at the room. "Everything but ceiling beams and empty boxes."

My knees trembled.

"So there's nothing?" I said.
mezzo-piano

214

Ty leaned so close to my face I could smell the ketchup on his breath.

"Nothing," Ty said.

fermata

Ty twirled the lighter from knuckle to knuckle. Ty stared at me. Ty nodded.

Then Biggest Isaac dragged me screaming into the

fortissimo

tunnels.

●

Biggest Isaac tossed me into the pit.

I slid along the pit's walls, bounced off something that

piano   *forte*

sounded wooden, and hit the sand at the bottom.

piano

"Goodbye, kid," Biggest Isaac shouted.

forte

Biggest Isaac stamped off into the tunnels. I wiped

mezzo-piano

sand from my face. Ty stood in the oval of light flickering above, like someone peering into the depths of a well. I felt afraid^gallows. I couldn't see myself. I fumbled for my knife, but the knife dropped somewhere onto the sand.

Ty tugged his hood over his head, like an executioner, then pointed into the pit.

"Here's what I'll leave you with," Ty shouted.

forte

Something was grinding through the sand in the pit.

piano

"This village was founded by settlers from Scandinavia. The settlers shored their boats on the beach just beyond these tunnels, and they built some lopsided houses, which couldn't keep out the wind, or the dust, or the maggots, and they built some weedy farms, which grew about a vegetable apiece. By winter all of the settlers were sick with cholera or smallpox. Most of them died. But, in winter the ground freezes. You can't dig a grave. So, that first winter, instead of burying their dead in the village, the settlers dragged the bodies to these dunes. That's where they buried them. In the sand," Ty shouted.

forte

Something was grinding through the sand at my feet.

forte

"But windy days, the sand would blow, the dunes would shift, and the bodies would surface—an arm sticking from a dune here, a head sticking from a dune there—and the settlers would have to bury their dead again. They buried them deeper, and deeper, and deeper, and still, on windy days, the bodies would surface," Ty shouted.

forte

Something was rising from the sand.

"That's what's in the sand above us, below us, around

us. That's what the sand is, now. Bits of hair. Bits of bone," Ty shouted.

forte

Something bumped me.

I screamed.

fortissimo

Something grabbed my shirt.

"Relax, Calculator," Jordan muttered.

piano

The truth is that, even after I heard it was Jordan's voice, I screamed a bit longer.

forte

"I got knocked out, for a while, I think," Jordan moaned.

piano

Ty had heard the voice. Ty gaped into the pit.

"Jordan?" Ty said.

forte

"Hello, brother," Jordan said.

piano

"Why are you in THE BOTTOMLESS PIT?" Ty said.

forte

"I tripped," Jordan said.

piano

●

Ty couldn't stop laughing.

forte

"Let us out," Jordan said.

forte

"No," Ty laughed.

forte

"I'm your brother," Jordan said.

forte

Ty twirled the lighter from knuckle to knuckle. Sand trickled from between the wooden beams above him, twinkling sometimes. He opened, then closed, then opened his mouth again. His face was ticking like a metronome between opposite emotions.

"Do you remember, when we were younger, that weekend I went missing?" Ty said.

forte

I heard Jordan shift, somewhere in the darkness.

piano

"First grade. On your birthday. When you ran away," Jordan said.

mezzo-piano

Ty stepped toward the pit, the toes of his boots crossing the edge.

"First grade for you, fifth grade for me. I didn't run away. That's what I told Mom and Dad, but that isn't what happened," Ty said. "What happened is I found

forte

these tunnels. And, like you, I fell into THE BOTTOMLESS PIT. But, unlike you, I was alone." Ty squatted at the edge, coins and keys tinkling in the pockets of his jeans.

piano

"I spent three days here, in the pitch dark, in an empty pit, feeling sorry for myself. Crying. Barely moving. Asleep, awake, asleep, awake. It wasn't until the third morning that I stopped feeling sorry for myself and started thinking about what else was here with me." Ty twirled the lighter from knuckle to knuckle. "Don't ever feel sorry for yourself. It can kill you. And you're never totally alone." Ty frowned, rubbing his scar with his thumb. "When I got home, I lied to Mom and Dad. I told them I had run away. They grounded me for a month. If I had told them the truth, they wouldn't have grounded me. They would have felt sorry for me. But I didn't want them feeling sorry for me. I didn't want anybody feeling sorry for me ever again." Ty twirled the lighter from knuckle to knuckle. "If you want to understand why I toss trespassers into THE BOTTOMLESS PIT, you need to understand its true nature."

Ty smiled, his face a mask of light and shadow.

"It's not a prison," Ty hissed. "It's a riddle."

Ty twirled the lighter *forte* from knuckle to knuckle. Ty smiled into the pit. Ty stood.

"But knowing you, you would starve before you solved

it. So, since you're my brother, I'll give you the solution. Build yourself a staircase. Stack the crates," Ty said.

Ty tossed the lighter, the flame pinwheeling into the pit.

forte

There was a moment where the bottom of the pit was lit by the flame and we saw each other and the shapes of the crates surrounding us.

Then the lighter hit the ground and the pit was dark again.

Ty cackled, tramping off into the tunnels.

forte *piano*

"I hate how much he loved that," Jordan grumbled.

mezzo-piano

Jordan crawled around, bumping crates, bumping me again, feeling for the lighter. There was a scraping sound. There were clicking sounds. Jordan lit the lighter.

piano *mezzo-piano*

He squinted. His chin was bleeding. He was clutching a crumpled paper in his fist.

piano

He grinned.

"I caught the map," Jordan said.

mezzo-piano

He wiped blood from his chin. He blinked at the pit. Then his face changed.

"Calculator," Jordan whispered.

He pointed.

piano

Some crates were stamped THE SPIRIT OF LANGHORNE.

Some crates were stamped MADAM CRISTO.

Some crates were stamped PAWPAW.

MISSING MEN

P AWPAW isn't an island—PAWPAW is a ship," Jordan
said.
forte

"A ship?" Grandpa Dykhouse said.
forte

"Was a ship," Zeke said.
forte

Zeke unfurled a map over the porch, like someone
forte
unfurling a sheet over a bed.

"Is a shipwreck," Zeke said.
forte

We weighted the map's corners with the lantern and
our knees. Grandpa Rose hobbled into the circle of light,
hunched over his cane, wrapped in a blanket. Grandpa
Dykhouse squatted alongside the map.

"My map has a list of shipwrecks, with the number and the letter that matches the box in the grid where each ship sank," Zeke said. "But I had never thought to check the list of shipwrecks, until Jordan saw the ship's name on a crate."

forte

Zeke marked the map with a silver x next to a tiny brown island in Lake Michigan.

"The ship sank here, just along this island," Zeke said.

forte

"Which island?" Jordan said.

forte

"There isn't a name for it," Zeke said.

forte

"The island's unnamed?" I said.

forte

"Nobody bothers to name islands as small as that," Zeke said.

forte

Grandpa Dykhouse tapped the x with a thumb.

"So the key's there," Grandpa Dykhouse said.

mezzo-forte

"On that island somewhere," Zeke said. His jeans were torn from being chased through the tunnels. His

forte

shirt was sandy from hiding waiting for us in the dunes. He chewed a lip, measuring the distance between the island and our village with his fingers.

"Those crates probably weren't from the actual

PAWPAW," Grandpa Dykhouse said. "Smugglers sailing
mezzo-forte
illegal vessels often would mark their cargo with the
name of a legal vessel, to sneak their cargo in and out of
harbors."

"I have a memory," Grandpa Rose said, clenching
forte
and unclenching his fists, the blanket hanging from his
shoulders, "of your Grandma Rose scrubbing dirt from
potatoes, begging me to take a job. A job at a sawmill, a
job at a factory, a job anywhere. A job in town. Anything.
Begging. But I didn't. I was selfish. I liked being away. I
liked meeting strangers. I liked breaking laws, ducking
punches, cities with bars. When I was home, all I thought
about was everywhere else. When I was everywhere else,
all I thought about was home. She didn't mind, had never
minded, loved me for my troublemaking. But this, she
said, was different. A kid would need more than that, a
father around, some better life. I can remember her, whatever months pregnant, scrubbing dirt from potatoes.
I can see the curtains. I can see the flyswatter. I can see
the knuckles of her fingers, the color of her dress, the hair
against her neck. But I can't see her face. Ana, in every

224

memory, her face is missing." He wrapped himself into his blanket. "Kid, I want to see her face. Will you bring me a photo?"

"Sorry, but we don't have any, remember?" I said.

He had already forgotten. His whiskers glinted in the gold light of the lantern. The tattoos underneath had almost entirely disappeared. He swore^{unwritable}, then said, *forte* "I was the worst father I could have been. A nobody father. We have to find the heirlooms. One good thing."

Grandpa Dykhouse hooked his glasses to his sweater.

"Little sidenote?" Grandpa Dykhouse said. "We're out of peas."

"Bigger sidenote?" Jordan said. "Today the newspaper printed your photos. MISSING MEN: EDMOND DYKHOUSE AND MONTE ROSE. The rest home is offering a reward. Probably because my parents are talking about suing if the rest home doesn't find you."

"Biggest sidenote?" I said. "My house is still for sale. There have already been showings. After there's been a closing, it won't matter whether we find the heirlooms. Tomorrow we're digging for the key."

Jordan scratched his head, like he would during math class when something had stumped him.

"How are we getting to the island if we don't have a boat?" Jordan said.

forte

Zeke gathered the map.

"We'll steal one," Zeke said.

forte

FROM THE NOTES OF
GRANDPA ROSE

*T*he first time she told him she loved him, she shouted it from his roof. The second and third and fourth and fifth times she told him she loved him, she whispered it in his ears. She wore his boots and his hats everywhere, carved his name into strangers' fences, stole him fish from the smokehouse. Monte bought a dress, a light blue color, a loose cotton dress with round wooden buttons and a pair of ruffled pockets. Ana refused to wear anything else, ever.

There were other things she wanted him to buy her, but that dress was about the only thing he ever did. Instead? He used the money to buy himself a camera, and tobacco, and a deck of cards, and tins of pomade to slick his hair. Now, let's be clear: She knew how to take care of herself. At the age of seventeen, she was already irrefutably the strongest woman who had ever lived, and possibly the smartest. He was often unsure why she had chosen him exactly, but she had chosen him forever. She didn't care about the smugglers, didn't care how often she got to see him, as long as wherever he was he was hers. And he was.

He can remember that dress perfectly. But her face, her face is murky, all blurry, washed out. He can remember qualities: that the face was beautiful, or transfixing. Defiant somehow, like the face of a feral animal. Absolutely unique. But he can't remember features: can't see the size of the eyes, or the shape of the jaw, or the exact intricate configuration of that nose and that brow and those lips and those ears. Can't see the face. Just sees a blurred nothing, above her dress, as she thumbed through a stack of rumpled dollars, counting his money on the porch. She generally had to count his money for him. Fact is, once he ran out of fingers to count on, he wasn't much good with numbers.

Monte said the money was from a job at a factory. Everybody knew the money was from the smugglers. His father believed in him still anyway. His father was unwell, had become bedridden, couldn't work anymore, could walk but rarely did. Every day his father lay in the bedroom with the curtains drawn against the sun; every night his father lay in the bedroom with the lamps flickering against the dark; his father missed doing carpentry, terribly, and was dreadfully afraid of dying.

That face? Sure, that face, he remembers. Those drooping earlobes; that colossal nose, vast nostrils; woolly black eyebrows, grown wild like weeds after about a century of rain; those worn-out eyelids; the way those eyes looked at things, widely, kindly, as if waiting patiently for everything that seemed ugly in the world to reveal some hidden beauty. His father wore a knit cap in bed, had to drape himself with quilts to keep warm. Ana liked to sit in there on a stool and peel apples with a knife. Ana could put anybody at ease: She got his father to gossip about neighbors, to confess to a weakness for chocolate, to reminisce about building the house. She got his father, who never laughed, to not only laugh but even *snort. She adored his father, the snort especially. He's going to do such great things, his father always said, chatting with her. She would nod, pleased, seemed to think the same thing. Just like you did! she would say, throwing her arms out at the house. My greatest accomplishment, his father would brag, blushing. Quickly, his father would admit, I'm proud of every inch of this place. In the hallway, Monte would think, you built the worst house in the world. Monte liked to prowl the hallway, hiding, while his father chewed the apples. He avoided being in the room. Whenever he stood by the bedside, his father would clasp his wrists, and stare into his eyes, and ask him to swear to guard the heirlooms with his life. Swear, his father said. Okay, he said. He would try to sneak off, but his father would clasp his wrists tighter, and make him swear again. Someday your family might need that money, his father said. I don't even have a family, he said. Swear, his father said. Okay, okay, okay, he said. But you're not going to die, he said. Because he honestly believed his father never would.*

At sunset he would trek to the dunes and watch for the boats. Nights the boats came, the smugglers would splash ashore, the brims of their fedoras bent by the wind, their overcoats soaked with spindrift. Gruff wary men with waxed mustaches, velvety accents. They would make jokes without smiling, watching the dunes for police. Their eyes, they looked at things meanly, narrowly, as if waiting anxiously for everything that seemed safe in the world to reveal some hidden menace.

Fact is, though, the smugglers were actually quite friendly. Once they were sure the dunes were clear, the men would relax. Tugging canvas tarps from their cargo, they would gripe about the weather, babble about bets they had won or lost, parrot each other's speech, sing chanteys, chuckling. At seventeen, eighteen, nineteen, Monte was half the age of any of them. Genuinely, they liked having a local kid to talk to. They all were troublemakers, too, among the biggest in Chicago. They competed to amaze him, telling anecdotes about life there. The city was changing: skyscrapers leaping into the air, pavement leaping across the roads. Now films had sound.

The gangsters brewed the liquor, then paid the men to smuggle the bottles to speakeasies along the coast, each bottle marked with single or double or triple exes. Nights there weren't bodies, Monte would just help unload crates. But, most nights, there were bodies. Honestly, that's how many people the gangsters were killing those years; even in a city that size there wasn't anywhere to hide all the bodies. The gangsters were strangling rival bootleggers, shooting police officers, bombing the homes of politicians. These days bodies get dumped in Michoacan, by the narcos, but those days bodies got dumped in Michigan, by the bootleggers. The bottom of the lake wasn't deep enough. The middle of an island wasn't remote enough. The gangsters wanted the bodies buried where nobody would ever look. Along the coast, in the nobody towns. The smugglers got paid to sneak the bodies across the lake. Monte got paid to bury the bodies. His wages came in envelopes addressed to his alias, The Little Narentine. He never knew why the people had been killed. They could have been anybody. Now they were missing men. The smugglers bought him a clunky rusted truck; he drove the truck along the coast, nobody town to nobody town, burying the bodies where he had been told. Some of the bodies he had to bury in his own village.

He has a memory of a golden-toothed smuggler handing

him a slip of paper with a list of names, a name for each town, the name of whoever was buried there where he would have to bury the others.

He has memories of building bonfires on the beach with Ana, of licking petoskey stones together to bring out the honeycomb patterns of fossilized coral.

He has a memory from his nineteenth birthday of making promises again to his father.

And afterward of his father coughing spots of blood into a handkerchief.

And later that night of trekking to the dunes.

It was dusk. The boats had landed already. The smugglers were stacking crates along the shore. Moonshine, firewater, spirits. No bodies, that night. Monte stepped from the woods, chewing a stalk of beach grass. He remembers, lingering a moment, alone at the crest of the dunes, just watching the smugglers, admiring their grumpy camaraderie, enjoying their hoarse singing. Sucking flavor from the beach grass. Feeling very content. Then he saw others step from the woods, farther along the dunes—men gripping nightsticks, their coats pinned with stars. The beach grass dropped from his mouth.

The men, the police, surged down the dunes toward the smugglers. Monte stepped backward. He raised his hands to his mouth to holler a warning, when behind him somebody spoke his name. He spun around; a cop with a nightstick was standing there in the trees. Along the shoreline the smugglers were shouting. Some of the smugglers were crouched behind crates firing pistols at the police. Some of the smugglers were splashing for the boats. The cop said his name again, motioned at him to lie in the sand. Instead he slugged the cop in the mouth, tripped, stumbled sideways, staggered into the woods. He had never, never, never made trouble on this scale before. His shirt was torn. His knuckles were bleeding. He felt terrified, and panicked, and also happy. He was making another getaway. But this getaway he didn't want to make alone.

There was a blur of gates and birdbaths and flags and lamplit windows as he ran into town, then hopped the fence he was looking for. He threw a stone at a window. Ana dropped from the window into the road. He told her what had happened. He told her what had to happen. She didn't have to stop to think, had already decided, was nodding yes, yes, yes. They ran from her house to his house and jumped into the truck. But what about your dad, she said. No time, he said. Then he remembered the heirlooms.

He emptied the cabinet, pocketing the music box, then lugging the other heirlooms to the bathroom. He heard his father calling his name. He ignored his father, dragged the bathtub away from the window, popped the floorboards. He hid the other heirlooms there, then shoved the bathtub back over the floorboards again. The music box he wanted for himself. His father couldn't guard the heirlooms, ill as his father was; the other heirlooms were safer hidden under the floor. Would he have had time to say goodbye? Maybe, but he didn't take it. Upstairs came the sound of a muffled coughing. Downstairs came the sound of the door slamming. Monte jumped back into the truck, and Ana jumped back into the truck, and together they drove into the night, the stock markets crashing around them into all the seas of the world.

A NUMBER IN THE UPPER
PENINSULA

I worked some overtime this week," my dad said.
forte

I didn't know what to say, so I didn't say anything.

"That should make things easier, there, once the paycheck comes," my dad said.
forte

I heard television noises through the phone.
piano

I was starting to understand that he was calling from somewhere he couldn't come back from. No one could find jobs in our village anymore. He had no way home.

"School alright?" my dad said.
forte

I fingered the piano's keys, playing the ghost of a song, pressing each key so softly that it made no noise whatsoever.

"School's okay," I said.

mezzo-piano

I waited for him to say it, but it never came.

EQUATIONS

One of my theories is that, for everyone you know, there's a word or a phrase that, if you say it to them, it will destroy them. It's what Grandpa Dykhouse calls your True Name.

"It appears in countless stories worldwide," Grandpa Dykhouse said.

forte
"Brace yourselves! I know that look! King Gunga is about to enter librarian trance state level eleven and unleash his full power!" Jordan shouted.

forte
"Like the story of Rumpelstiltskin, when the queen can't save her baby until she learns the name of the

spirit," Grandpa Dykhouse said, ignoring Jordan. "The story of Tarandando. The story of Titteliture. Or stories of changelings—do you know what a changeling is? In some stories, spirits will sneak into a house to steal a newborn child. Then the spirits will leave behind a fake child that looks just like the one that was stolen. That's the changeling—the fake child. But here's the trick. The spirits can only steal a child that hasn't been named yet— the spirits don't have any power over a child that has been named."

mezzo-forte

"Or like the story of Mr. Mxyzptlk," Jordan added, but no one knew what he was talking about.

mezzo-piano

Grandpa Dykhouse says a spirit can be defeated if you know its True Name. But I've known for years that a person can be defeated the same way.

It's like the math.

Since first grade, I've had the same equations.

Nicholas Funes = Boy With Zero Friends.

Nicholas Funes = Boy Who No One Would Want To Kiss.

Nicholas Funes = Boy Whose Mother Wishes He

Had Never Grown Older, Whose Father Never Says I Love You.

My name is Nicholas Funes, but that isn't my True Name. To destroy me, you would only have to whisper into my ears, "You are friendless, unloved, unlovable, *pianissimo* unwanted." Then you'd have all the power over me that you could ever want.

A DUEL WITH THE ISAACS

In the morning I ran outside to talk to my brother. The wind had torn the last of the leaves from the other trees—all that was left were the birds' nests, made from the trees' twigs, tucked into the trees' branches, the nests that had been hidden there before the leaves had fallen. It was like suddenly you could see into the trees' heads, and the nests were the trees' thoughts, hanging there exposed. But my brother was a pine tree—he never lost his needles—so his nests stayed hidden. I loved that about him. You never knew what he was thinking until he said it aloud.

I plucked notes that meant, BROTHER WE ARE GETTING CLOSE TO FINDING THE HEIRLOOMS AND SAVING THE HOUSE SO THAT WE WILL NOT HAVE TO LEAVE YOU.

IF I COULD HELP I WOULD HELP, my brother's song said.

YOU DON'T HAVE TO. I'M THE OLDER ONE. THAT'S WHY I'M HERE, my song said.

BUT THEN WHY AM I HERE, WHAT DO I DO, I SHOULD BE HELPING SOMEHOW, my brother's song said.

My brother thrashed with the wind, flinging pine-
fermata
cones, throwing a tantrum. Younger brothers didn't like getting helped. Sometimes even when they needed it they didn't want it. A pair of squirrels scrabbled into a pine, screeching.
glissando
My brother quit thrashing.

DO YOU REMEMBER, WHEN WE WERE YOUNGER, THE MORN-ING OUR FATHER TOOK YOU AWAY CARRYING FISHING POLES AND TINFOIL LUNCHES? my brother's song said.

I didn't.

I REMEMBER, my brother's song said.

The sky was still starry.

I REMEMBER YOU LEAVING, my brother's song said.

I started to pluck more notes, but my brother spoke again.

I HATE BEING STUCK HERE, my brother's song said.

●

Before school, I went walking through the neighborhood with my mom, helping to search for Grandpa Rose. I usually avoided going, because helping to search for someone when you know exactly where that person is can be minorly nerve-racking, and also can make you feel horrible. We walked toward downtown, as far as the stone bridge, and then back home. My mom kept whistling, trying to mimic birds' songs—maybe trying to call the *staccato* birds, maybe trying to call Grandpa Rose. Her whistle was totally off-key. As we trudged up the driveway, she finally quit trying.

"You don't have any other memories of Grandpa Rose?" I said.
mezzo-forte
The door whooshed shut. My high-tops had tracked
forte
dirt clods into the house. My mom saw the dirt, opened the closet for a broom.

"I remember wanting a normal father. Somebody

who mowed the grass, chatted with neighbors, washed cars in the driveway. Came to dance recitals. Was home at night. Grandpa Rose wasn't. He was never home. When kids asked about him, I said that he was dead," my mom said. "Then, one day, Grandpa Rose appeared
mezzo-piano
at school at the fence. Wearing the same clothes, carrying the same suitcase, he always wore and carried. Like a mirage. He was away, hadn't been home now for months. We were on the swing set when he appeared. I remember my friends soaring past me, forward, backward. My swing had stopped. I hadn't noticed I had stopped kicking." She started sweeping the dirt. "I ran to the fence to
pianissimo
talk to him. He gave me something. A toy, a book, I don't remember. Afterward, my friends asked about who he was. I said he was an old neighbor."

She stopped sweeping.

"Isn't that awful?" my mom said.
mezzo-piano
The phone rang. My mom ran to her bedroom. I heard
fortissimo
a murmuring. I zipped my backpack. I scooped my house
piano   *forte*
key from the counter. Kids were lined at the bus stop already.

My mom danced into the kitchen with the broom.

"Somebody made an offer on the house!" my mom said.

forte

"Who?" I said.

sforzando

"Named the Yorks," my mom said.

forte

The couple in the suits.

I stared through the window. I imagined all of the trees chopped down. An empty pool where the trees had been before. My brother hacked apart, stacked against the fireplace.

"Did you say yes?" I said.

crescendo

"I'll call Dad next," my mom said.

decrescendo

●

Before school, Zeke sent a note to Little Isaac.

In band class, I overheard a pair of kids talking about me while they pieced together their flutes.

"It's kids like him," the girl muttered.

piano

"That make everybody think that band class is for losers?" the boy whispered.

pianissimo

"He's like a living breathing black spot on the orchestra's reputation," the girl muttered.

piano

As per usual, I ate lunch in a bathroom stall.

After lunch, Little Isaac sent a note to Zeke. The message said,

I ACCEPT YOUR DUEL

FREAK

JUST SAY WHEN AND WHERE

FISTS ONLY

I WIN, YOU GIVE US WHAT YOU STOLE

YOU WIN, YOU KEEP IT

BUT YOU WON'T

"You're actually going to duel?" I said.

mezzo-forte

"Tonight. At the island. A proper holmgang," Zeke
said.

forte

I gaped.

"You told the Isaacs about the island?" I said.

mezzo-forte

"Sorry. But I can't row out to an island by myself. The
duel had to be tonight," Zeke said.

forte

"How are we going to look for the heirlooms with the
Isaacs there?" I said.

mezzo-forte

"I'll tell the Isaacs to meet us later, to give us time,"
Zeke said.

forte

Zeke asked me to be his second.

"Does that mean that I would have to fight Big Isaac?" I said.

mezzo-forte

"I asked Jordan first, but he said that he wouldn't," Zeke said.

mezzo-forte

The kids in my brain shouted, "Don't say yes!" shouted,

forte *crescendo*

"Big Isaac will break your ribs!"

"Actually, Jordan said, 'Never, Boylover, never in a trillion years,'" Zeke said.

mezzo-piano

"I'll be your second," I said.

mezzo-piano

Zeke uncapped a silver marker. He wrote FRIEND on my arm. He trotted toward the bathroom. No one had ever called me a friend before.

A kid in a hooded coat walked past rapping "The Ballad Of Dirge And Keen." Leaving school, I saw Emma

piano

Dirge and Leah Keen sitting cross-legged in the gym, cheering as the Isaacs shot baskets from the keys.

fermata

●

I found Jordan out by the buses, under the flagpole, across from my parents' lopsided heart.

Jordan frowned at the FRIEND on my arm.

"Congratulations, Calculator," Jordan said.
forte

"You don't sound like you mean it," I said.
forte

"Enjoy it while it lasts," Jordan scowled.
forte

"Friends are like brothers. A forever thing. An infinity," I said.
forte

"Friends are temporary. Brothers are the forever," Jordan said.
forte

Zeke ducked through a crowd of backpacks, kids in bright jackets trudging to buses. I told Zeke what Jordan had said.

"Brothers are temporary. Friends are the forever," Zeke said, glaring at Jordan. "You just don't know how to be an actual friend."
forte

"Of the three of us, I'm the only one who's had any actual friends. I've had lots of them, I've lost all of them," Jordan said. "You only think brothers are temporary because you've never actually had one."
forte

"I have three brothers, and Nicholas had one—"

"Has," I said, "has one."
forte

"—so we know about brothers."

"Brothers and friends are the same," I said. "I think,
forte
once you've had them, you always have them, even if eventually they hate you or die or move to another country.
Either way they're a sort of infinity. Just, when you have
them, they're an infinity, and after they leave, they're an
infinitesimal."

"Infinitesimal?" Zeke said.
forte
"A number that's infinitely small," I said.
decrescendo
"And I've never seen either of you fight Mark Huff for
me, so don't tell me I'm the one who's temporary," Jordan
muttered.
glissando
Everyone else was already on the bus. Mr. Carl shut
forte
the door, pretending he was going to leave us behind, the
same trick he always tried to get kids to hurry up.

"Are we going to the wharf already?" Jordan said.
forte
"Meet me at your house—I'll bring what we'll need to
steal a boat," Zeke said.
forte
"Why can't we meet at your house?" Jordan said.
forte
"That place is totally off-limits—nobody's ever allowed
to go there," Zeke said.
forte

Zeke vanished toward downtown, without even a wave goodbye. The grooves between the sidewalk squares extended like ledger lines into the distance.

"Let's tail him," Jordan hissed.
piano

"Zeke?" I said.
piano

Mr. Carl cracked the door back open, peering out at us, pouting.
piano

"Aren't you dying to know where he lives?" Jordan said.
mezzo-piano

"I'm not going to follow him home!" I said.
mezzo-forte

"You're going to make me follow him alone?" Jordan said.
forte

Mr. Carl honked, like GET ON THE BUS, but we ditched the bus and flew after Zeke. Our high-tops smacked against the pavement. Our backpacks thudded against our backs. In band class, everyone had learned new terms. Allegro means "play quickly." Adagio means "play slowly." Caesura means "time stops here," means "everything is quiet."
fortissimo
allegro
adagio

●

Zeke stole a fistful of flowers from the grocer.

"Those flowers for Little Isaac?" Jordan muttered, laughing to himself.
mezzo-piano
piano

250

We followed at a distance, crouched low to the sidewalk. Zeke hurried into the graveyard, the flowers bobbing in his arms. Today's high-tops were a glassy silver, with emblems stamped onto the heels. Zeke paused, stepping off the path into the graves—tilting his head, like a dog hearing a distant whistle—then frowned, and trotted off through the gravestones. We ducked from mausoleum to mausoleum, VANLOON 1753–1823 to BRANDER 1811–1867 to XAVIER 1847–1913, using the tombs to hide from Zeke. A nest of doves was cooing from the branches of a hickory tree with hollow knots.^piano

Zeke laid the flowers on a hunched gravestone between tombs that said OBETTS and DEBOER. The OBETTS tomb (5 NOVEMBER 1931) had a man in a stone sweater and a stone helmet reaching for a stone football. The DEBOER tomb (1861) had a stone soldier strapped to a stone rifle tipping a stone cap at the sky. The gravestone between the tombs said HYO WAEGU SONG. Underneath the name was 05-21-97, like the combination to a locker that now no one could open.

Zeke stood over the flowers with his fingers knotted together behind his head.

"I told you to meet me later," Zeke said, still looking at
mezzo-piano
the gravestone.

We were peeking around the backside of a mausoleum
coated with tangled vines. Jordan looked at me, stunned.
I shrugged. Jordan jabbed a finger at me, scowling, like
I was the one who had given us away. I shook my head,
pointed at Jordan. Jordan rolled his eyes, mimed a laugh,
then kicked some leaves at me.
sforzando
We shuffled out from behind the mausoleum, both
pretending that we had meant to get caught.

"What kind of name is 'Hyo'?" Jordan said.
forte
"Korean," Zeke said.
mezzo-piano
"It sounds like something out of a cartoon," Jordan
said.
forte
Zeke shoved his hands into the pockets of his jeans.

"I'm half Korean," Zeke muttered.
mezzo-piano
"I'm half Italian," I said.
forte
Jordan didn't say anything.

"What are you?" I said.
forte
"Danish. Finnish. Swedish. Norwegian. Whatever,"
Jordan muttered.
mezzo-piano

252

Zeke squatted on the grave.

"I bring flowers for my grandfather on the twenty-first of every month," Zeke said.

piano

"What was he like?" I said.

piano

"Big," Zeke said.

piano

"Fat?" Jordan said.

fermata

"Big. Not fat. Big," Zeke said. He touched the grooves

sforzando

of the letters on the gravestone. "The rest home kept him alive for years and years and years, until he couldn't talk or move or anything. The only way you knew he could hear you was, if you asked, he would blink his eyes. My mom said it was time, when he died, but I wish the rest home could have kept him alive longer." He chewed a lip. He swiveled to face us. He pointed at the palm of his hand. "My dad's missing hand. That's what it's like for me. A phantom limb. He's gone, but you still feel him sometimes, in the place where he was."

caesura

Zeke said, "You were wrong, what you said before

forte

about ghosts. It's not what could have been that haunts us. It's what was."

Zeke said to meet at Jordan's house, then hurried off beyond some mossy tombs.

"Alright, Calculator, come on then," Jordan sighed.
mezzo-piano

We cut through the woods, passing beneath abandoned treehouses with rotted planks, passing abandoned outhouses topped with mewling cats, hopscotching stones
forte
across the creek. In the garage of a three-story house, high schoolers in hoodies and bandannas were stapling stream-
mezzo-forte
ers to a homecoming float on a flatbed trailer. A boom box sang garbled clips in major and minor keys.
fortissimo

When we got to Jordan's, Jordan's mom was measuring Genevieve with a yardstick from heel to shoulder.

"Do you have to do that in here?" Jordan grumbled.
mezzo-piano

I stopped and watched as Jordan's mom knelt on the carpet, counting numbers off from the yardstick. Gen-
mezzo-piano
evieve's arms were outstretched, hands rigid, fingers pointed toward opposite walls.

When I turned around, Jordan had vanished, suddenly, had just left me there alone. I felt uncomfortable^castaway.

Jordan's mom was staring at me. Genevieve was staring at me. I ran upstairs.

I passed a bedroom littered with muddy dresses, then passed a shut door that said TY in uneven letters, then found Jordan's bedroom. There was a bed with a faded quilt, a dresser with some missing drawers, a lamp, a chair, a desk, and not much else. A few sweatshirts hung from wire hangers, but otherwise the closet was totally empty. Jordan's backpack was slumped against the desk. Jordan was perched there, carving JORDAN into the wood of the desk with a knife.

piano

I wanted to know if we were friends, like how Zeke had written FRIEND onto my skin, but I didn't know how to ask, plus I thought we probably weren't.

"Do you hate me?" I said.

forte

"What?" Jordan said.

forte

"Do you hate me?" I said.

forte

"No, I don't hate you. Why are you just standing there? Would you sit down or something?" Jordan said.

forte

"So you like me?" I said.

forte

"I don't feel anything about you," Jordan said. "You're just a person that I know. Who says I have to feel something about everybody? I don't feel anything about anybody. Except for Grandpa Dykhouse. And maybe Ty."

forte

Jordan had photographs of his ex-friends taped to the walls, all of the kids who hated him—Jordan and the Geluso twins leaping from the pier, Jordan and Emma Dirge and Leah Keen hugging someone's dog, Jordan and Mark Huff and the Isaacs dressed as outlaws for a play, Jordan and Mark Huff building snow forts, Jordan and Mark Huff destroying sand castles, Jordan and Mark Huff poking at a campfire with sticks. I felt bad for him. He still loved all of the friends he had lost. I felt bad for myself, too. All of these kids had so many memories together, and I had never been there for anything.

"My sister has scoliosis. If you're wondering why my mom was measuring her shoulders, that's why, Calculator," Jordan said.

piano

I didn't say anything.

"Do you know what scoliosis is?" Jordan said. "It means the bone in her back is all curvy." He carved a

mezzo-piano

staccato

sharp zigzag shape into the wood of the desk. "Like that. Her backbone is shaped like a snake. What's wrong with her is on the inside, but you can see it on the outside. Her shoulders are tilted. The head of the snake forces one higher than the other. The first time she got x-rayed, her backbone was curved 19°. 19° is bad, but isn't that bad, because you don't have to wear a brace unless your backbone is more than 20°. Every month since then my dad has been taking her for checkup x-rays. You can see her backbone, in the x-rays, like the ghost of a snake charmer's snake rising out of some basket in her hips." He carved another jag into the zigzag. *sforzando* "Last month the ghost rose a little higher. This time when she got x-rayed, the snake was 23°. She's going to have to wear a brace now. She'll only have to wear it a few years, and even with the brace, she can still have sleepovers, play volleyball, go out on dates. But she says her life is over. No one is ever going to want to date a cyborg, she says. So every day after school she makes my mom measure her shoulders. She's hoping that maybe her shoulders will shift back to normal. That maybe her body will fix itself."

Someone clomped upstairs. Jordan stopped talking,
crescendo
watched the doorway. Something clumped in the hall-
piano
way. Zeke peeked into the room.

"What's that look for, Boylover?" Jordan said.
mezzo-forte
"What's your mom doing to your sister?" Zeke said.
mezzo-forte
Jordan frowned, hopping down off the desk.

"I tried to tell her, some people really like cyborgs,"
Jordan grumbled.
mezzo-piano

●

Zeke dragged in a lumpy duffel bag.

In the bag were a metal snorkeling mask with a pair
of flippers, a wooden snorkeling mask with zero flippers,
a pair of chipped trowels, a brass spyglass, and fireworks.

"Where did you get all of this?" Jordan said, rooting
forte
through the bag.

"Stole the fireworks. The rest was my grandfather's,"
Zeke said.
forte
"These were Yo-Yo's?" Jordan said, waving the spyglass.
forte
"His name was Hyo," Zeke said. "And he was an archi-
decrescendo
tect, which is just as important as a librarian."

"Why the fireworks?" I said.
forte

"For the duel. Since we don't have pistols," Zeke said,

forte

snatching the spyglass.

"Didn't the Isaacs say fists only?" I said.

forte

"Little Isaac doesn't make the rules," Zeke said, gath-

crescendo

ering up the bag. "If he wants a duel, he's going to have to risk taking a firework in the chest."

THE NAMELESS ISLAND

S wim to the rowboat, untie it, then row it back for
me," Zeke whispered.

pianissimo
"Why do we have to fetch it?" Jordan said.

piano
"If you swim in the lake under a full moon, the
drowned will drag you under," Zeke whispered.

piano
"So you're sending us instead?" Jordan hissed.

piano
"You don't believe in it, so the drowned will probably
leave you alone. If you don't believe in something, it has
less power over you," Zeke whispered.

piano
"So why don't you just stop believing in it and swim
with us?" Jordan said.

piano

"You can't help what you believe. I could pretend I didn't believe that if I swim in the lake under a full moon the drowned will drag me under, but I would still believe it," Zeke whispered.

We were *piano* crouched on the wharf, hiding under the shells of wooden boats that had been mounted on wooden cradles for repairs. The lighthouse hulked at the end of the pier, a beam of light swiveling in its head. The rowboat was tethered to the buoy where the lighthouse keeper kept it. I was afraid[prison] to steal the rowboat. We didn't know how to start a motorboat or work a sailboat, though, so the rowboat was the only boat we could steal.

"I call the metal snorkel," Jordan whispered.

"That's the one *mezzo-piano* with the flippers!" I hissed, but Jordan snatched the metal *allegro* snorkeling mask anyway.

We kicked our high-tops, peeled our socks, tossed our shirts at Zeke. Jordan tugged the metal snorkeling mask over his face, squeezing into the flippers. I tugged the wooden snorkeling mask over my face, biting the snorkel, sucking on the rubber. We leapt into the lake feetfirst.

The cold hit like an Isaac, knocking the breath from

me. Jordan shouted, probably swearing, muffled by the
mezzo-piano
snorkel. The water rippled like tree rings. A gull cawed
mezzo-forte   *forte*
from the shrouds of a sailboat. I blew a spout of water from
mezzo-forte
the snorkel, and Jordan blew a spout, and we swam away
mezzo-piano   *piano*
from the docks, through the anchored sailboats, imagining all of the drowned swimming beneath us, waiting for
us to reach deeper water before lunging up to grab fistfuls
of our hair and drag us under.

●

Jordan shimmied into the rowboat, flippers still kicking.
He hauled me into it, swearing[unwritable], water dripping
piano
from the nose of his mask. "Practically arctic," Jordan
muttered.
mezzo-piano
 "Did you see that?" I said. Mr. Carl and Mr. Tim were
piano
fishing from the pier, Mr. Carl chewing a glowing cigar,
Mr. Tim wearing a plaid jacket. "Since when are they
friends?"

 "Since always," Jordan said, tugging his mask to his
piano
neck.

 We each gripped an oar, rowing toward the wharf, the

oars rattling in the oarlocks. The rowboat thwacked into

piano

the dock. Zeke tossed the duffel bag into the boat.

forte

"This maybe isn't the best time to mention it, but do we even know where we're going to dig?" Jordan whispered.

piano

"PAWPAW ISLAND, THERE BOTTLED SHIPS, BONES FROM BOW, NINE PACES INLAND," Zeke whispered.

piano

"So, what, we'll find the island, look at some bottled ships, tie a bow on a bone, and then take nine steps?" Jordan whispered.

piano

"We have all night to solve it!" Zeke hissed.

piano

"It's a whole island!" Jordan hissed.

piano

Zeke stepped into the boat, lurched onto a seat.

"You're shaking the boat, Boylover," Jordan grumbled.

piano

"Call me Boylover again," Zeke said.

piano

"What?" Jordan said.

piano

"Call me Boylover again," Zeke said.

crescendo

"Boylover," Jordan said.

piano

"I meant don't call me Boylover," Zeke said. "My

sforzando

name is Zeke. And my grandfather's name was Hyo. Call me Boylover again and I'll feed you to my dogs."

"Boylover," Jordan said.

piano

Zeke bent over the duffel bag.

"After I fight the Isaacs, you might be next," Zeke muttered.

piano

"Scary, Boylover," Jordan said.

piano

We rowed to the mouth of the harbor. I was shivering from the wind. Mr. Carl and Mr. Tim were pounding on

forte

the door to the lighthouse, shouting the lighthouse keep-

forte

er's name.

"Did they see us?" I said.

piano

"Maybe they just need more bait," Jordan said.

piano

"You better row faster," Zeke said.

piano

●

The waves were whitecaps beyond the harbor. The lake was hazy with fog. Hooks and lures and screwdrivers clattered along the deck, from bow to stern to bow to

staccato

stern, the rowboat seesawing across the waves. Zeke was hunched across a compass and the map of the lakes. We rowed through the drifting fog, like people voyaging through a world of clouds.

I spotted something glowing. Ahead of the boat, a

light flickered above the water. The light flickered, vanished, flickered again in the fog.

"We aren't alone," Jordan *piano* hissed.

"What?" Zeke *piano* said.

"Something's *piano* there," I hissed.

Zeke raised the spyglass, peering at the light. The light swung about, a streak of gold. Zeke lowered the spyglass.

"What is that?" Zeke *piano* said.

"Probably the ghost of Grandpa Yo-Yo, a light that fat," Jordan said.

"What did *piano* you say?" Zeke said, whirling.

"Probably the ghost of Grandpa Yo-Yo—" *crescendo* Jordan said, *piano* but then all at once Zeke flipped his grip on the spyglass and leapt standing and swung the spyglass at Jordan, and Jordan tipped backward, clutching his forehead, dropping to the deck.

Jordan's oar swung in the water, unmanned, jerking the boat. "What do you want?" Zeke shouted, brandishing the spyglass like a cutlass, and *forte* staggering as the rowboat knocked through a wave. Jordan scrambled at Zeke, *forte* but Zeke kicked him in the chest and knocked him to the deck again. "You whiny, ignorant, gap-toothed runt." Zeke shook the spyglass, his hands all tendons and knuckles. "Is that it? You just want some nicknames of your own?" Zeke kicked Jordan again. "You ginger, you mutant, you goon, you worm." I wanted to help, but I didn't know who to help, and the rowboat had swung sideways, waves plowing into the hull. The rowboat lurched, tilted, teetered *forte* midair, then slammed flat, the fishing tackle clattering. *sforzando* We didn't have any life preservers. I fumbled at *staccato* the oars. "Exile, outcast, leper."

In the fog, the light vanished, flickered, vanished again. Jordan coughed. His ear was bleeding. His fore-head *piano* was bleeding. Zeke stood waiting, clutching the spyglass, panting, ready for an attack. But Jordan didn't *piano* attack. Instead, he crawled onto a seat. He bowed his head. He just sat there.

Zeke staggered. He had destroyed the fight in Jordan, somehow. Somewhere, in everything he had said, he had said Jordan's True Name.

Jordan swayed, on his seat, as the rowboat swayed. The metal mask hanging from his neck was still dripping.

"For a while my dad couldn't live with us, because he used to hit us," Jordan said, staring at some fishing sinkers on the deck of the boat. "Hardly ever, really, and afterward he was always sorry. But sometimes he would just get, like, wound up, and totally lose control." He hunched his shoulders. "I'm worried I'm becoming my dad. Already sometimes I feel like hurting people, not for any reason, just totally random people. I'll see Calculator, and suddenly for no reason at all I'll feel like punching his teeth out."

That answered that question. We weren't = friends. We weren't even ≈ friends. If he wanted to punch my teeth out, obviously we were ≠ friends.

"Or you," Jordan said, pointing at Zeke. "I'll see you, and totally randomly I'll feel like knocking your head into a wall." He frowned. "The meanness is like this snake inside me, and in the beginning it was tiny, but then it molted its skin and got bigger, and then it molted its skin again and got bigger again, and it keeps getting bigger, and if I could kill it I would kill it, but I can't, I can't stop its growing." He wiped blood from his ear. "But I never hit anybody. Sometimes I feel like hitting everybody, but I never hit anybody. When I say things, that isn't me being mean. That's me holding myself back."

Zeke dropped the spyglass. He didn't look like he wanted any power over Jordan anymore. He turned toward me.

"I'll row for now," Zeke murmured.

piano

The waves were dragging the rowboat toward the flickering light. Zeke stumbled to the oars as the rowboat pitched. My arms were > shuddery, not from the cold, but from the tiredness. I staggered to the seat across from Jordan's.

Jordan wouldn't look at me. His fists were clenched. Parts of him were fading in and out with the fog. I didn't know what to say, but I had to say something, so I started talking anyway.

"Even when you're eleven, there are already so many yous that you've been," I said, gripping the underside of

allegro

the seat as the wind thrashed my hair. "Sometimes I miss who I was when I was seven, when I was five, when I was three even. The ways they thought. The things they felt about my parents. The words they used that I don't use anymore. And I keep trying to bring all of those mes together, to be all of them at once. When I walk, I want to feel like all of us are walking, like a smaller me overlapping a smaller me overlapping a smaller me still. But I can't. Every day I lose some more of them. Already they're so faded that they're nearly gone."

This was the sort of Dangerous Idea that normally sent kids running away from me, but once I had started talking, I just couldn't stop.

"Do you know the thing about violins and fiddles?" I said. "They're these musical instruments. But they're actu-
_{allegro}
ally the same instrument. The difference is how you play it. If you play the instrument this way, it's a violin. If you play the instrument that way, it's a fiddle. That's the choice you have to make, as the musician, every time you play it. But you have to make the choice with yourself, too. You play yourself this way, you're a fiddle. But you play yourself that way, and then you're a violin, a completely different sound, something you never knew you could be."

Jordan's eyebrows scrunched together. Jordan glanced at me. Jordan let his fists relax.

"You're like zero years old and a hundred years old at the same time," Jordan said.

piano

"Sorry," I said.

piano

"Why are you sorry?" Jordan said.

piano

"I wanted to help you, but when I started talking, only weird ideas came out," I said.

piano

"Well. They were weird. But they helped," Jordan said.

piano

The light swelled to the size of a house, and then the rowboat slid into a clearing in the fog where the light shrunk to the size of a lantern. That's what the light had been all along—a lantern, hanging from the prow of a rowboat with paint peeling from its hull. A bearded man was fishing at the prow. He was wearing ragged pants, a ragged shirt, and a sort of hat that hadn't been stylish for at least a hundred years.

"Something about that man feels very wrong," Zeke whispered.

piano

The bearded man unhooked a lure from the weave of his pants where seven other lures were hanging. He knotted the lure to the line of the pole. He glanced at the rowboat.

"He saw us!" Zeke said, ducking.

piano

The bearded man shouted something that got lost in
pianissimo
the wind. We stumbled to Zeke's seat, grabbed the oars,
rowed together. The rowboat spun sideways, but the
waves were still dragging us toward the bearded man. His
rowboat reared with a wave, crashed back. A chain dan-
mezzo-piano
gled from his rowboat, its anchor somewhere underwater.
Our boat was aiming to plow sideways into his. As we
bobbed closer, I gripped my knife behind my back, ready
if he tried to board us.

"Are you boys lost?" the bearded man called. One eye
forte
was milky with white, like a fog had settled across the
color there. His beard was pointed like the endpin of
a cello, and his voice had a hollow twangy timbre. He
plucked a strip of raw meat from a brown paper wrapping,
hung the meat from the hook of the fishing pole.

Our rowboat knocked into his, swaying.
piano
"Is that meat?" Jordan said, frowning.
glissando
The bearded man cast the line. "Squirrel," the bearded
fermata
man said. "Shot on the island this morning. You boys
forte
aren't fishing, are you? This is my spot. You boys can't fish
here."

"We're leaving, we're leaving," Zeke said, leaning into
forte
the oars.

The bearded man reeled the line. "This spot's prime
staccato
fishing," the bearded man said. "Shipwrecks, you'll see,
forte
that's where the big fish live."

Zeke stopped rowing. The hull of our rowboat scraped
piano
against the hull of the bearded man's. "Shipwreck?" Zeke
said.
forte
"THE DANTES is the wreck under us now," the bearded

man said. He cast the line again, the meat still on the hook.
forte   *fermata*
"A laker, a cargo freighter, sunk by one of the November

storms." He pointed into the fog with the pole. "Onshore

there, there's another, named the PAWPAW."

Jordan's eyes were > his normal eyes. Twice as big,

maybe.

"You've seen the PAWPAW?" Jordan whispered.
mezzo-piano
Zeke grabbed my shirt.

"The PAWPAW went down on the island itself!" Zeke

whispered.
mezzo-forte
I was gaping at the bearded man.

"The odds of that were about 1%," I whispered.
mezzo-piano

272

"An old wood schooner, wrecked a century ago, almost," the bearded man said. "I like to camp there, some-
forte
times, when the weather's agreeable. Shot this squirrel there. You boys aren't camping, are you? That's my spot. You boys can't camp there." He lowered the pole, but Zeke said, "Wait, keep pointing!"
forte

Zeke leaned into the oars, our rowboat grating past
mezzo-piano
the bearded man's toward the island in the fog.

I shouted to the bearded man, "Can you see with that
forte
other eye?"

The bearded man squinted the white eye. "Not you, or my boat, or this lake," the bearded man shouted. He tugged
forte
at its lid. "This here is my eye for other things. For seeing the other worlds. The ruins. The spirits. Where the fish sleep."

The fog sucked the rowboat into itself.

"What a creep," Jordan muttered, laughing.
mezzo-piano   *piano*
Then a motor growled somewhere in the fog, and Jor-
sforzando
dan wasn't laughing anymore.

"That man didn't have a motor," I said.
piano

Zeke frowned.

"The Isaacs are early," Zeke muttered.
piano

273

A sailboat lit with electric lights slid from the fog, seven hooded kids on its deck—Little Isaac at the helm (ISAAC 17), Big Isaac at the railing (ISAAC 19), five Isaac wannabes slouching alongside (LUCAS 4, IAN 24, ETHAN 26, KEVIN 15, SCOTT 10), most of them evens, none of them primes. Little Isaac spun the wheel, and the sailboat swung, circling the rowboat, trapping us in the wake.

"Hey, it's Odom!" Big Isaac shouted. "And the freak's locker partner!" A Wannabe Isaac (SCOTT 10) ^{forte} spit at us, but the spit corkscrewed in the wind and hit another Wannabe Isaac (KEVIN 15) in the face. Little Isaac spun the wheel again, and the sailboat swung into the fog.

"Are you allowed to bring seven people to a duel?" Jordan said.

"Big Isaac is Little Isaac's second. The rest aren't allowed to do anything other than watch," Zeke said.

"Did you bring what you stole from the Isaacs? For if you lose?" I said.

Zeke ignored me, pretended he hadn't heard.

The rowboat ground onto a sandbar. We hopped over-
mezzo-piano
board into the shallows. Jordan lugged the rowboat by its
prow. Zeke hoisted the bag of fireworks above the waves,
wading toward the island. I splashed ashore, wriggling
piano
back into my shirt, yanking the collar to tug the wooden
mask through. The fog had vanished. The island was
forested.

"Like a rib cage," Zeke whispered.
pianissimo
"What?" I said.
piano
Zeke pointed. A rock bluff loomed farther along the
beach. Below the bluff, a shipwreck sat pinned to the
sand, half underwater, half abovewater, moonlight spik-
ing through the curved ribs of its hull.

"We've been misreading the tattoo this whole time!"
Zeke said. "The punctuation! It wasn't PAWPAW ISLAND,
piano
THERE BOTTLED SHIPS, BONES FROM BOW, NINE PACES INLAND!
It was PAWPAW ISLAND, THERE BOTTLED, SHIPS BONES, FROM
BOW NINE PACES INLAND!"

"SHIPS BONES?" Jordan said, but I knew what Zeke
piano

meant. My brother was still young, but this was the sort of thing he might become when he died. Some trees became the frames of ships. And afterward, after he had been wrecked, he would be bones like these. Rotten timber.

"The key's buried NINE PACES INLAND from the PAW-PAW!" Zeke said.

piano

"THERE BOTTLED," I whispered.

piano

The hooded silhouettes of Isaacs and Wannabe Isaacs were pounding along the beach, past the shipwreck, coming toward us.

"The Isaacs are coming," I hissed. "We can't dig while they're here."

piano

"You dig," Jordan said. "We'll duel."

"He can't dig," Zeke said. "He's my second."

piano

"I'll be your second, Skulltooth," Jordan said. "Let him dig."

piano

mezzo-piano

"'Skulltooth'? What's 'Skulltooth'? And since when will you be my second?" Zeke said.

mezzo-piano

"Listen. I hate normal names. I can't call you Zeke," Jordan said. "'Skulltooth' is a nickname masterpiece. It's

mezzo-piano

single-handedly the toughest and most totally prestigious nickname I've ever invented. I spent forever making it. How can't you like 'Skulltooth'?"

Zeke squinted.

"It will do," Zeke said.
mezzo-forte

Jordan thumped my back, saying, "If the lighthouse
mezzo-forte
man knows we stole his rowboat, he might already be sweeping the lake for us. We need to get that key and get out of here. Move fast."

I tore down the beach, just as the Isaacs and Wannabe Isaacs came stomping up, Big Isaac shouting, "Where's
forte
he headed?" and Jordan shouting, "What do you care,
forte
Trollhole?" and Big Isaac shouting, "Who are you calling
forte
Trollhole?"

I splashed alongside the shipwreck. Bats swooped
forte
away from the rotting hull. The beams creaked, the waves
glissando
battering the ship. I was standing at the SHIPS BONES, on
forte
the ISLAND of the PAWPAW shipwreck, where the key to the trunk had been THERE BOTTLED. I touched the bow of the ship. The paint rough, the wood glassy. Something skittered inside the shipwreck. Rats, or maybe opossums.
piano

I crossed from the shipwreck toward the bluff, NINE PACES INLAND, FROM THE BOW, counting my paces.

After nine paces, I was > halfway between the shipwreck and the bluff. I gripped my knife and dropped to the sand, digging. I listened for the clink of knife against bottle, but as I dug, I heard only the scratch of knife against sand, and once the chime of knife against stone. *piano*

I heard someone shouting. A pair of lighters flickered along the beach. I kept knifing at the sand, but wasn't finding anything, only sand and stones. I tossed my knife aside, started digging frantically with my fingers. Everything felt unbalanced. This wasn't the answer. I was still missing something. I felt my brain trying to solve an equation—rearranging variables, simplifying ratios, squaring roots. *piano* *pianissimo*

I stopped.

I shoved a lock of hair out of my eyes.

The numbers clicked into place, everything canceling everything.

1 Grandpa Rose footstep ≈ 1 1/2 Nicholas Funes footsteps.

9 paces for him ≈ 13 1/2 paces for me.

I was digging in the wrong spot.

Golden fireworks spiraled along the beach, throwing light onto the sand, the driftwood, the shapes of the duelers. I pushed myself standing, counted 4 1/2 paces, found myself at the rock bluff. Waves smashed against the rocks, lashing
forte *forte*
the bluff with water, drenching me. The trees above the bluff were shadows the shape of my brother. There was a hollow. Fireworks streaked fizzing from dueler to dueler, flashing
forte
against the beach, the tempo rapid-fire. I braced myself, a wave whirling against the rocks, spraying me. I wiped water
forte
from my face. I shoved my hand into the hollow. I felt the shape of something. A lip of rounded glass. The neck of a bottle. A misfired firework arced into the sky, exploding with a boom that shook the trees, raining golden light.
fortissimo

I wrestled the bottle from the hollow. The cork in the mouth of the bottle was jammed stuck. I shook the bottle, something metal clinking inside. The clink of key against
forte
bottle. Goosebumps flew along my spine, from tailbone to skull.

That's when a wave twice the size of the others tackled me.

●

I toppled underwater. My body slammed into the lakebed. I kicked abovewater, gasped, saw everyone lit by a dying *forte* firework, as the wave bashed into the rocks, surged at the *forte* lake again. I shouted for help, and then the wave sucked *forte* me back under.

The undertow dragged me through seaweed, across sand, into rocks. I fumbled with the bottle. The water roared like blaring trombones. I kicked, but the undertow *sforzando* wrenched me upward, downward, sideways, like a kid trying to break a cheap toy. My shirt thrashed with the current, like from some wind, the cloth leaping, plunging, twisting around me. I clawed at the sand, clutching the bottle with one hand. Underwater, even screaming fortissimo is screaming pianissimo. The undertow spun my body, left me clawing at nothing, then loose ridges of sand, a log slick with muck, then suddenly nothing again, in the dark, as my body ripped backward through the water. I couldn't fight the undertow without both hands. It was drown or drop the bottle. I imagined losing the key, losing the heirlooms, losing my brother. I couldn't drop the bottle. I imagined boats combing the lake for my body in the morning, my parents hunched over an empty coffin at the funeral, my teachers touching the coffin. I didn't want any of that. But I didn't have much air. Without both hands, fighting the undertow was hopeless.

I stopped screaming. I stopped kicking. Bubbles spilled from my lips, and then the bubbles stopped, and my chest was empty. I couldn't tell anymore if I was upside down or downside up. I was alone, and I was afraid, but I didn't feel sorry for myself. I chose this. I hugged the bottle and let the water carry me.

●

I bounced into a chain.

I groped at it, my fingers slipping along its links. I wrapped myself around it, yanked myself up it, hauled myself abovewater. I hung there, from the anchor of the shipwreck, gulping for air.

The truth *forte* is that, even when I had known it was only water, it had felt like the hands of drowned fishers, drowned sailors, drowned swimmers, dragging me under.

Using the shipwreck for handholds, I struggled toward

shore with the waves. My knuckles were cut from rocks.

The bottle hadn't broken.

I grabbed my knife, then tore down the beach, along

the tree line, pounding footprints into the sand. Wannabe

Isaacs were flying back toward where their sailboat was

anchored, their faces streaked black with smoke. Jordan

and Zeke had vanished. Our rowboat had been knocked

crooked. Waves surged onto shore, foamed away again,
crescendo *decrescendo*

trying to drag the boat into the lake. Farther along the

point, Little Isaac and Big Isaac were standing at the

tree line, throwing stones into the trees, kicking sand,

shouting. I stopped, watching the Isaacs. A stick cracked.
forte *mezzo-piano*

Branches snapped. Behind me, Jordan leapt from some
mezzo-forte

trees, grabbed my arms, hissed, "Move move move . . . !"
piano

We ran for the rowboat, trampling the paper shells of

fireworks, the stony shells of mussels. His lip was split,

his sweatshirt was torn, he was laughing. We splashed
piano *forte*

into the lake, dragging the rowboat. "What about Zeke?"

I whispered, but then Zeke shot out of the trees straight
piano

between the Isaacs and darted toward the lake, howling. *forte* The Isaacs spun and chased him. He snatched the duffel bag and stumbled into the shallows. I hauled him into the *forte* rowboat. Jordan heaved at the oars. The Isaacs tripped *piano* through the shallows, dove headfirst into the waves, swam for the boat. As the boat lurched away into deeper waters, the Isaacs finally stopped, treading water, slapping waves, shouting threats and curses.

pianissimo
Zeke dumped the duffel bag onto a seat.

"You got the key?" Zeke said.
forte
I waved the bottle.

Zeke yipped, all dimples, pumping his fists.
forte
"We are my heroes!" Zeke cheered.
forte
I shook the bottle over my head, making the clinking *forte* sound, celebrating.

"Did you win the duel?" I said.
forte
Jordan laughed and laughed, rowing us into the lake.
forte   *forte*
"Nobody won! Skulltooth shot Little Isaac in the foot—"

"—but before that Big Isaac started shooting fireworks too, at Jordan, a firework exploded exactly where

Jordan had been standing, I still don't know how Jordan isn't dead—"

"—then one of the other kids tackled Skulltooth—"

"—they were cheating! So I broke their armlock and yelled the duel was over and hid in the trees—"

"—but before that I had Little Isaac in a headlock, and Skulltooth drew a heart on Little Isaac's cheek—"

Zeke laughed, barked again, flopped onto a seat. His fingers were streaked black with smoke. A firework had burned a hole through the duffel bag.

●

We didn't have any trouble finding the wharf again. The wharf was where the trouble was.

As we rowed past the pier, the lighthouse keeper was waiting for us, squatting there with Mr. Carl and Mr. Tim. The lighthouse keeper shouted, pointing at the rowboat. Jordan kicked into the flippers and dove into the water, I grabbed the bottle and dove after, and we swam away from the lights of the docks, already vanishing into the dark of the water.

Zeke had said he was coming, but when we looked

back, Zeke was still there, bobbing with the rowboat. Too afraid of the drowned to swim away. To save himself.

We hid under a dock, gripping the edge, watching Mr. Carl and Mr. Tim haul the rowboat onto shore. The lighthouse keeper was hurrying from dock to dock, clutching his cap, frowning, searching for us.

"We better go," Jordan whispered.

pianissimo
My teeth were chattering. My body was shuddering.
piano
Mr. Carl and Mr. Tim pulled Zeke from the rowboat.

"He'll be okay?" I whispered.

piano
"He'll be fine. With Mr. Carl and Mr. Tim? Maybe they'll yell at him for stealing the boat, but that'll be the worst of it," Jordan whispered.

piano
The lighthouse keeper tromped past our dock. Zeke
forte
was nodding at something Mr. Carl and Mr. Tim had said.

"Okay," I whispered.

piano
We shimmied from the water onto the docks, bolted from the docks into the trees.

KEY OF X

I slumped against my house, clutching the bottle. Dead leaves blew through, rustling. I dripped water onto the grass. My brother was *piano* bending, was peering forward, was watching everything I was doing.

I broke the bottle against my house.

fortissimo
Fingering through the broken glass, I didn't find a key. I found a pair of keys. An iron key the length of a hand and a brass key the length of a finger. The bow of the iron key said X. The bow of the brass key said ROSE.

I stared at the X key. I stared at the ROSE key. Which was the key to the trunk? I already knew Grandpa Rose wouldn't remember.

I changed into a dry sweatshirt. I stepped into wool socks. I wrapped myself in a blanket.

I was eating a plate of leftovers, my hands trembling still from all of the rowing, when I heard a tapping at the door. *forte*

Kayley Schreiber stood there among the whirling moths. She was wearing unlaced boots, mismatched socks, a shirt the size of a dress. The blotches on her cheeks were different, had changed shapes like drifting clouds. She was clutching a book of keynote speeches. Staring at me, her expression kept wavering, like there was some new string inside of her that she was trying to tune, some feeling that wasn't quite yet at the right pitch. She handed me a folded note.

Before I could even speak, she shuffled into the darkness. I memorized the sound of her footsteps. I liked every sound she had ever made. *decrescendo*

I found a pencil. I drank some water. I sat at the table to translate the binary in the note.

But when I unfolded it, it wasn't binary.

I had been given the black spot.

FROM THE NOTES OF
GRANDPA ROSE

*T*he sentence was for eleven years. The charges included conspiracy, bootlegging, and assaulting an officer. The sentence could have been worse. The police didn't know about the bodies.

The prison was a squat tower in an inland city. Prisoner Thirty-Four, that was the name he was given there, the number sewn to the breast of his uniform. His cellmates included a murderer who snored, an arsonist who stuttered, and a seventy-nine-year-old bootlegger who was as toothless as a baby. Once a week, Ana drove the truck in from town to visit, brought baskets of homemade biscuits. Monte would share with the others, always: Since the bootlegger had trouble chewing, the murderer would carefully dampen a biscuit with water, then mash the biscuit with his fingers into bites the bootlegger could swallow. Their cell faced the sunrise, would flood with bright light every morning, waking everybody. One morning, though, the bootlegger never woke; the bootlegger had died, sometime during the night, curled into a humped ball. With stiff fingers the bootlegger was clutching a scrap of paper that read Arch Stanton. Nobody knew what the paper meant. Still, Monte considered the incident an omen. He wasn't wrong there; his father died the very next day. That week Ana brought a flower with the biscuits, and cried. The murderer, who was especially sensitive, cried some too after he heard, and the arsonist said shucks. Monte himself though didn't know what to do or say, so did and said exactly nothing.

Going to prison was like going to college. He learned about hijacking trucks, about printing counterfeits, about scamming bookies. He met prisoners who had come from other states, from other countries. He was promised various jobs after he had been freed.

The country was changing. The guards pored through comic books about superheroes, flipping past pictures with bright sound effects, kapows, zwaps, bloofs, fwaks, speech balloons that captured voices. The economy had collapsed and recovered, villages of shanties had been set up and torn down, farms had been deserted and bridges erected, all somewhere beyond his barred window. Prohibition had ended years ago: Selling liquor wasn't illegal anymore. But there were plenty of things that still were; there were always things to smuggle.

Here, this here, is something he remembers: a memory of leaving prison, pockets loaded with returned possessions, the day he became an ex-con. The sun flaring, the seagulls wheeling overhead, the truck waiting beyond the fence. She was humming a jingle. She was wearing that light blue dress. She drove the truck back to the village, winding through the trees along the lakeshore, honking at the children leaping from rope swings into the waves. Ana was renting a cottage across from the storehouse. The world was at war again. America wasn't, yet.

He shaved, bathed, ate three eggs. He drove her to the

orchard where she worked picking apples. Then he drove to the house his father had built.

The house looked the same. The roof was coated with leaves. A family was eating popcorn on the porch. The father had a pitted face. The mother wore a patterned dress, had a wooden leg attached to a knee stump, was gathering popcorn the children had spilled.

He had been told his father had died. But that was the moment he understood his father actually was dead; on the porch his father had built, strangers were eating popcorn.

He had sworn he hated his father. As a kid he had needed somebody to blame. The voice went like this: *Why didn't you drown, instead of my mother?* Seeing those strangers eating popcorn on the porch, though, all at once, all of that hate became love. He has a memory of that feeling. He didn't have to pretend to hate his father anymore. He didn't have to blame his father for anything. He was thirty-one years old.

Seated in the truck, still watching the family, he slipped the music box from his coat and wound the crank. That song had the power to wake his father from even the deepest slumber. But the crank wound down, and the music stopped playing, and his father was still dead. Monte did not like crying; after that he carried the music box with him everywhere, and never let himself listen to the song again.

Later that afternoon the family drove away wearing swimsuits and beach towels. Monte broke into the house. He dragged the bathtub away from the window, popped the floorboards. The other heirlooms were still there. The clock still ticking, the bellows still breathing. Monte carried the heirlooms to the truck. Still hanging from a hook in the shed he found the thick ring of iron keys the smugglers had given him. Monte carried the keys to the truck. He shut the window he had forced open. He hadn't bothered shoving the bathtub back where the bathtub belonged.

He broke into the house again a week before being married, sat in the kitchen, staring at nothing. He broke into the house again a day after becoming a father, sat on the fireplace, staring at nothing. He kept breaking into the house, between smuggling jobs, whenever he came home from troublemaking, just to sit there in the quiet and to stare at everything and to remember.

Rumors that the house is haunted—that the families that lived there were driven away by a ghost—may have begun then.

The bathtub moved, the chairs drifted, handprints formed in the fireplace's soot.

There was a ghost.

Monte.

THE BALLAD OF DIRGE AND KEEN

In the morning I scrubbed my face with soap at the sink in the bathroom. Brown and gold specks of sand still crusted my eyebrows, clung to the curves of my ears, from the night before. The keys were in my bedroom, hidden under my pillow.

"Before, you said you always just told other kids that Grandpa Rose was dead," I said.

My mom rubbed lotion into her arms, bent over the bottle, hair hanging over her face.

forte

"I did," my mom said.

mezzo-forte

"So when did you tell Dad that Grandpa Rose was actually alive? When you were my age? Or later?" I said.

"Dad found out the same way as everybody else," my mom said.

mezzo-forte

She squirted out another dollop of lotion.

"Grandpa Rose liked to act like a mobster, but he wasn't. He was harmless. A petty crook. Hired from job to job, loading and unloading boats, trafficking things for the actual mobsters," my mom said. "That second time he was arrested, he was fifty-nine. They were crossing the lake in a boat, counterfeit money belowdecks, probably worse, when they saw other boats coming. Police, official police boats, shooting toward their boat! Their boat was junk, couldn't outrun the police." She wiped lotion from between her fingers. "The other crooks started dumping the cargo overboard. Grandpa Rose didn't. What he did next, it was crazy, at his age. He threw himself overboard! Leapt, from the boat, into the lake! Wearing his shirt, his pants, his shoes, everything! Then he swam for an island. His heart could have stopped, he could have drowned, he probably almost did. After the other crooks had betrayed him, that's where the police found him, a few hours later. On the island, sitting on the beach, an old man in soaking clothes. He was too tired to run."

I stopped, clutching the soapy dripping towel, imagining Grandpa Rose. Bottling the keys, leaping from the deck, struggling against the waves. Splashing onto the island. Stumbling to the hollow. Collapsing onto the sand. His face wrinkled. Untattooed.

"The newspaper printed an article about the trial. Everybody heard the story," my mom said. "Before that, everybody at school believed my father was dead, which was bad enough. After that, everybody at school knew my father was a crook, which was even worse."

She capped the bottle.

"Oatmeal?" my mom said, smiling.

Before breakfast, I ran outside to talk to my brother the tree.

OUR MOTHER HAS BEEN COMING INTO THE BACKYARD MORE AND MORE, STANDING ON THE DECK, STARING AT ME, my brother's song said.

SHE MISSES DAD, my song said.

My brother was changing, growing older, his limbs thicker, his bark rougher. He had been wearing grasshopper shells on his branches, lately, porcupine quills at his roots. Tokens from his friends. I was proud of the life he had made for himself, here in these woods.

HAVE YOU FOUND THE HEIRLOOMS? my brother's song said.

NOT YET, my song said. BUT I WILL NOT STOP LOOKING, EVEN AFTER EVERYTHING WE OWN HAS BEEN PACKED INTO BOXES AND CARRIED ONTO TRUCKS AND DRIVEN AWAY AND THE LOCKS ON THE DOORS HAVE BEEN CHANGED AND THE NEW KEYS HAVE BEEN GIVEN TO THE NEW FAMILY AND I HAVE BEEN TAKEN AWAY TO A DIFFERENT HOUSE FOREVER, I WILL NOT STOP LOOKING, I WILL COME BACK FOR YOU.

PLEASE DON'T LEAVE ME, my brother's song said.

Somehow my brother understood how desperate things had gotten—was scared enough now to beg me for help.

I WILL NEVER STOP, my song said, but then my mom shouted for me, and I ran into the house.

forte

297

My mom was laying the phone in its cradle.

"We're going to close on the house!" my mom said.

I almost dropped the violin. I tried looking happy^{lucky} ^forte^, because that's how my mom looked. But the kids in my brain were shouting, "You're out of time, Nicholas, you're out of time!" ^fortissimo^ The truth was that after the closing the heirlooms would be worthless. I couldn't come back for my brother after the closing. The Yorks already would have chopped him down.

"That's great," I whispered.

I downed some juice. ^piano^ I bolted some toast, hardly even chewing, standing at the counter. I kicked into my high-tops, pocketed the x key, the ROSE key, the scrap of paper with the black spot. Then I grabbed my backpack and ran for the bus.

●

Zeke wasn't at school.

As per usual, I ate lunch in a bathroom stall.

In math class, I was working on problems about limits. Say you had a function, like $f(x) = 1/x$. When $x = 1$, $f(x) = 1$. When $x = 0.001$, $f(x) = 1,000$. When $x = 0.000000001$,

$f(x) = 1,000,000,000$. So as x approached zero, $f(x)$ approached infinity. But a person was also a sort of function. I was a function, and sometimes I felt there was some infinity my brain was approaching, like when my arms were saying things with my violin that there were no words for, or when my fingers were saying things with numbers.

x was a variable. X18471913 could have meant anything. A cross. A crossing. Crosswords, crossbones, crosstrees, crossroads, crossbeams. The trunk could be anywhere. Buried at a crosswalk. Buried at a railroad crossing. Buried on one of the thousands of islands in Lake Michigan.

From the desk, I eyed the classroom, unfolding and refolding the black spot, waiting for the lightbulbs to shatter, a bookcase to topple. The spirits had seen death coming. I didn't know how it would come for me, but it would come. A roof collapsing. A bus swerving. Poisoned meat.

I understood Grandpa Rose now. Why he had tattooed himself. Why he had struggled off to the ghosthouse alone. Why he was willing to live on canned peas, drink murky water with soggy leaves, wrack his brain all day for memories under a leaking roof, make a nest of crumpled blankets on a dirty wood floor, sleep in unwashed clothing, be woken by bats, kick away mice, suffer anything. If I had to die, I would die. Nothing could stop death now. But first I was going to save my brother. I was going to do one good thing.

●

"Did you see Skulltooth?" Jordan said.
piano
"He wasn't at school," I said.
piano
We thumped off the bus. Girls leaned through win-
forte
dows, jeering at Jordan. The band class and the choir
homophony
class had been practicing together lately. The band had learned that homophony means "play together, all at once, together make your chords." The choir had learned that falsetto means "sing in your highest shrillest voice," learned that creak means "sing in your lowest raspiest voice." Some girls had their faces painted already for the homecoming game, were wearing mesh jerseys, had tinsel braided into their hair.

The bus jolted away toward the next stop.

"I have the keys," I said.

forte

"I'm grounded again," Jordan said.

forte

"The odds of that were about 100%," I said.

forte

"Somehow my sister's shampoo got dumped in the trash," Jordan said.

forte

He knotted his high-tops.

"Then replaced with mud," Jordan said.

forte

He stood.

"Anyway, wait here, my mom has to at least think that I'm home," Jordan said.

forte

He walked into the house, shouted something to his mom (who was racking dishes in the kitchen), walked through the living room (the living room light flicked on, off), walked upstairs (the staircase light flicked on, off), walked into his bedroom (his bedroom light flicked on, off), then threw open the window and dropped to the ground.

He walked back to the road.

"What about Zeke?" I said.

forte

"He's at his house probably," Jordan said.

forte

"How are we going to find that?" I said.

forte

Jordan started walking, shoving the sleeves of his sweatshirt to his elbows.

Glancing backward, Jordan shouted, "You think yes-

forte

terday was the first time I've ever followed him?"

●

Zeke's house was tucked into the woods beyond the Gelusos' farmhouse. Its gutters overflowing with dead leaves, its windowsills greening with mold. Jordan knocked. A

forte

woman with cheekbones like Zeke's answered the door.

"Skulltooth around?" Jordan said.

forte

"What?" Zeke's mom said.

forte

"Zeke?" I said.

forte

Zeke's mom pointed at a door with a silver z painted on the doorknob. She shuffled into the kitchen, knotting

piano

her bathrobe. We heard a chair groan, then the clacking

pianissimo _piano_

of typewriter keys. Tufts of fur were clumped along the iron floor grates, the legs of an empty coatrack, the bottom of an umbrella stand spiked with dry umbrellas.

"Ezekiel isn't going anywhere until we solve this

problem with the other kids," Zeke's mom shouted. We didn't know what she was talking about—or if she was *mezzo-forte* even talking to us—so we didn't say anything.

Jordan twisted the doorknob with the silver z. The door swung onto a basement. I rubbed a thumb over the x key's x, over the ROSE key's ROSE. I creaked downstairs after Jordan. *piano*

Sunlight had puddled in spots on the floor, but otherwise the basement was dark. Something growled. A wolf- *pianissimo* dog loped into a puddle of sunlight, sniffing our hands.

"Skulltooth?" Jordan whispered. *piano*

Bedsprings squeaked. Zeke's voice drifted from the *pianissimo* darkness.

"My dad kept hunting gear down here, before he moved away," Zeke said. "After my mom sold everything, *piano* she let me move my room to the basement."

My eyes adjusted to the darkness, 23%, 47%, 71%, shapes appearing there. An unlit lamp. A sleeping wolf-dog. A mattress lumpy with twisted sheets. Piles of books—mermaids on their covers—topped with antique perfume bottles. Inside a blue bottle, a firefly blinked, then faded to nothing. Across the room, inside a green bottle, another firefly blinked back.

"How do you keep them alive?" I said.

<small>mezzo-piano</small>

I could see his silhouette on his mattress.

"Once a month you feed them flowers," Zeke said.

<small>mezzo-piano</small>

Jordan swore^{unwritable}, I didn't know why, but then my eyes adjusted <small>fermata</small> 100% and I saw Zeke's face. Zeke's eye was swollen. Zeke's lips were cracked and scabbed. Zeke's chest was more bruise than skin. If Jordan normally looked beat up, Zeke looked beat up^{beat up}.

"Did that happen at the lighthouse?" I whispered.

<small>mezzo-piano</small>

"No," Zeke muttered.

<small>mezzo-piano</small>

He coughed. He shoved himself sitting. I couldn't

<small>piano</small>

stop staring at his face.

"The lighthouse keeper lectured me awhile, then gave me a choice between a police record or a month of labor. So now I have to work at the lighthouse every weekend, scrubbing the rowboat with bleach. I didn't tell him your names, though. Although he's making me work an extra weekend for that," Zeke said.

<small>mezzo-piano</small>

He pointed at his bruises.

"It was after the lighthouse, walking home again, that the Isaacs jumped me. They said I have until the end of the week to give them what I stole. Otherwise they're going to pound me like this again," Zeke said.

mezzo-piano

"Are you going to give them what you stole?" I said.

mezzo-piano

"I can't. I would, now. But Jordan needs it," Zeke said.

mezzo-piano

"What do you mean, I need it?" Jordan said.

mezzo-forte

Zeke grunted, leaned toward a pile of books, set aside

mezzo-piano

a maroon bottle with a blinking firefly. The pile toppled as

mezzo-forte

he slid out the book at the base. It was the dictionary—its cover even more tattered and stained than ever.

Zeke flipped the cover. There were no words there. The dictionary had been hollowed with a knife, leaving a rectangular hole in the pages where the words had been. Hidden in the hole was a stack of paper bound with twine.

Zeke unbound the stack, flattening the papers.

"Little Isaac had them under his bed in a box marked ISAAC NOTES," Zeke said. "Notes from Little Isaac to Big

mezzo-piano

Isaac. Notes from Big Isaac to Little Isaac. Every note they ever wrote."

"Why were you in Little Isaac's bedroom?" I said.
mezzo-forte

"I snuck through a window one night while he was at basketball practice," Zeke said. "I wanted to see what his room was like. Also he had a pair of high-tops I wanted to
mezzo-piano
steal. I never found the high-tops, but I did find these."

The notes had been written on graphing paper, pre-algebra handouts, the flip sides of loose-leaf essays. Zeke handed Jordan a page of prealgebra. Jordan said, "Is this...?" and Zeke said, "Yes." Jordan said, "Impossi-
piano
ble..." and then didn't say anything. I stood with him to
piano   *piano*
look at the page.

Penciled among the numbers on the page was a title, THE BALLAD OF DIRGE AND KEEN. Underneath, with some lines crossed out and reworded, were the lyrics to the song. Half of the handwriting Little Isaac's. Half of the handwriting Big Isaac's.

"How do you know they wrote the song, though? Maybe they wrote this after they heard someone singing it," I said.
mezzo-piano

"Prealgebra was sixth grade," Jordan said. He pointed
piano

at the date on the homework. 09/29. "And this was writ-ten in the fall. Nobody was singing the song until winter. I remember it wasn't until after winter that everybody started hating me."

"I'm going to show it to Emma and Leah. I'm going to show it to everybody," Zeke said. "The Isaacs pretend that
mezzo-forte
they're the perfect friends, that they're only mean to kids like us, but their friends should know the truth."

"Do you know what the Isaacs will do to you if you do?" Jordan said. He stared at the page. He tossed it to the
mezzo-piano
floor. "I don't care if everybody hates me. This isn't worth those bruises. Give the Isaacs their notes."

"But everybody hates you for a song you never wrote—" Zeke said, but Jordan said, "Even if I never
mezzo-forte   *sforzando*
wrote it, I've given kids other reasons to hate me." "But—" Zeke said, but Jordan said, "Listen, I'm trying to help you,
mezzo-forte   *crescendo*
I'm trying to be your friend, so would you stop fighting me? If the notes are what they want, give them the notes."

Zeke stared. A firefly in a brown bottle blinked, then faded to nothing. Zeke nodded.

"Okay," Zeke said. He gathered the papers, bound
mezzo-piano
them with twine, and shoved them into the waist of his
jeans. Then he tugged a sweatshirt from a pile.

"Can you walk?" I said.
mezzo-forte
"More or less," Zeke said.
mezzo-forte
"Your mom said you aren't allowed to leave," I said.
mezzo-forte
"She always says that, which is why I'm always leaving," Zeke said.
forte

●

The wolfdogs stalked through the ferns ahead, scattering
clucking pheasants. The sun had set, the hillside was turn-
staccato
ing bluish in the dying light, and everything was transforming into silhouettes. I rubbed a thumb across the black
spot, the paper rough, the ink glassy. I hadn't told Zeke and
Jordan about the black spot, but I should have. Being close
to me put them at risk. If the roof of the ghosthouse collapsed, it wouldn't kill only me. It would kill them too.

At the ghosthouse, Grandpa Dykhouse was scribbling notes on the floor. Grandpa Rose looked clammy,
tired, like someone with a fever. He kept coughing into a
fist. He was sawing the lid from a can. Lately, when they
forte
mezzo-piano

played chess, they would bet each other cans of peaches. The loser had to eat the peas.

"We were outnumbered nine to one," Grandpa Rose was saying, spooning peaches from the can.

piano

Grandpa Dykhouse gaped at Zeke, dropping the pencil.

"Who hurt you?" Grandpa Dykhouse said.

forte

Zeke shrugged at Grandpa Dykhouse, looking at the floor.

"We have a problem," I said. I held the x key and the

forte

ROSE key, pinching them at their bows. "There were two keys in the bottle instead of one."

"No keys was a problem. Two keys isn't a problem," Grandpa Rose said, coughing again. He pointed at the

piano *forte*

ROSE key. "That's a skeleton key. That's the key to the trunk."

"Wouldn't the x key unlock the trunk, since the clue has an x?" I said.

forte

"No, that x key is way too big for the trunk," Grandpa Rose said.

piano

I felt the black spot. Death could come from inside of

you even. I might have had brain cancer already for years and never even known.

Jordan skimmed the notes Grandpa Dykhouse had been making.

"Anything about where the treasure is buried?" Jordan said.

forte

Grandpa Dykhouse shook his head.

"We have a key to nothing," Jordan muttered.

piano

Jordan flopped backward, grumbling. Zeke stood

piano

at the cupboards, hitting a fist against the wood. I felt <

piano

smart. The key was useless without the trunk.

Grandpa Rose had stopped chewing, was staring off toward the kitchen, cheeks bulging with a mouthful of peaches. I had learned by now that there was this certain look he would get when he was trying to remember Grandma Rose's face. This certain way of creasing his forehead, and squinting his eyes.

He set the can on the fireplace, suddenly, and swal-

forte

lowed the peaches. He leaned in, gripping my wrists with both hands. His eyes were bloodshot.

"Kid, don't lie to me, tell me the truth," Grandpa Rose said. "Do you think one good thing can make up for *forte* eighty-nine bad years?"

"Definitely," I said.
forte

Grandpa Rose frowned. He shook his head, angrily, like I had misheard him, or like I was wrong. He leaned closer, clutching my wrists in a death grip.

"But just one?" Grandpa Rose said, urgently, stressing *forte* each word.

I paused, to think, about whether I really believed. I glanced away. I glanced back.

"I'd count it," I said.
forte

Grandpa Rose stared at me, then nodded, and patted my hands.

I had never seen Grandpa Rose looking this desperate before. Seeing him that way scared me. He coughed *forte* again, wiped some syrup from the curls of hair around his mouth, reached for the peaches.

His tattoos, I suddenly realized, were completely gone, totally hidden again under beard.

Jordan was sprawled backward, staring bleakly at a water stain on the ceiling. Zeke was leaning against the cupboards, with his face pressed into the wood. We had come so far, and had gotten nowhere, all just going rondo. I didn't want to be around anyone. I didn't want to think about anything. All the feelings inside of me were going flat and sharp. I brought a fistful of the notes to the porch, sat cross-legged in the dark there with my back to the door.

I fanned the memories across the porch—pages and pages of "bodies" and "moonshine," "heirlooms" and "nightsticks," "petoskey" and "the nobody towns"—reading by the light of the lantern in the ghosthouse. Everything was connected but not connected. What our village had been, what our village had become. I had learned to swim in the same water where Grandpa Rose had learned to swim. Grandpa Dykhouse had sailed his sailboat across those same waves. Ships had been buried there. Little Isaac and Big Isaac wrote notes. Grandpa Rose had sung to birds. Grandpa Rose was a criminal. Kayley Schreiber had moved from Florida to Michigan, from peninsula to peninsula, from saltwater to freshwater, talked to spirits in a treehouse. Jordan's ancestors had come here from Scandinavia, Zeke's ancestors had come here from Korea, my ancestors had come here from Italy, from peninsulas to peninsula. The settlers had buried their dead in dunes, had dueled on islands to their deaths. My parents' initials were carved into their school, our school, my school. Mr. Carl and Mr. Tim were always alone together, Ms. Wilmore heard things no one else could, Ty said that everyone's stomach had a gray pod, Genevieve's backbone was the wrong shape but once had been perfect. The ghosthouse had been built by my great-grandfather—then the shingles had peeled from its roof, the wallpaper had peeled from its walls, its gutters had rusted, busted, collapsed, its floors had rotted, the slats of its porch had weakened from the sun and the rain and the years—had become a ghosthouse, somewhere no one could live. The Gelusos had lost their dog to a storm. The Yorks wanted to build a hole in the ground. The smugglers had dug a pit for moonshine.

Ty had fallen. Jordan had posed for photos with Mark Huff, had fought with Mark Huff on classroom floors. My dad called me from the Upper Peninsula, Mark Huff's mom sent him postcards from Florida, Mr. Wilmore was somewhere where he couldn't send anyone anything anymore. The music box was priceless but broken. Grandpa Rose's brain was priceless but broken. Every month Zeke stole flowers for his grandfather's grave. Every month Zeke fed flowers to his fireflies. My brother was a tree.

Owls whooped. Something cooed, fluttered, scrunched
mezzo-forte   *forte*   *mezzo-piano*   *piano*
through dead leaves. I reread a note about Grandpa Rose's father. Then I heard the wolfdogs baying.
fortissimo

Flashlight beams swung through the birch trees, illuminating a pair of boulders, a thicket of ferns, the stone well.

I ran to the door.

"Someone's coming!" I said.
forte

"Who?" Grandpa Dykhouse said.
mezzo-forte

"Everyone hide!" I said.
forte

Grandpa Rose hobbled to the staircase. Jordan scooped an armful of blankets, Zeke snatched the fire stick, they vaulted upstairs. Grandpa Dykhouse snuffed the lantern, started gathering empty cans. I ran for the notes I had been reading, raked the notes into a pile, but as I stood with the pages, *forte* a flashlight beam swept across me, blinding me.

"What are you doing here?" someone shouted.

Other flashlight beams swept across me. *forte* The Geluso twins stepped from the trees. Emma Dirge and Leah Keen, wearing matching jackets. Mark Huff, high-tops triple-knotted. Kayley Schreiber, wearing unlaced boots, mismatched socks, a shirt the size of a dress. Her blotches had changed shapes again. She was clutching a faded scroll. The blueprint to the ghosthouse.

"Who told you about the seance?" Mark Huff said, *forte* frowning.

"No one," I said.

I didn't know what to say. *forte* I thought of a lie. I unfolded the black spot.

"I came here hiding from this," I said.

The Geluso twins muttered something. *forte* Mark Huff murmured, *piano* "He's a goner," and Emma Dirge said, *mezzo-piano* "You *mezzo-forte*

315

got the black spot?" and Leah Keen spat, "That's what you get for hanging around with a jerk like Jordan Odom!"

forte

"Why aren't you at the homecoming game?" I said.

forte

The Geluso twins beamed.

"We've got something way better than that," Crooked Teeth said.

forte

"Mark Huff in an amazing rematch," The Unibrow said.

forte

"—him versus the ghost that tripped him—"

"—a few months ago he got totally humiliated—"

"—maybe you heard—"

"—a ghost tripped him out the attic window—"

"—so now we're going to summon the ghost—"

"—with that blueprint somehow—"

"—so he can trip the ghost back, and avenge himself, and reclaim his honor."

"Nicholas Funes, you are welcome to join us, provided you don't drop dead during the middle of the seance," Kayley said.

forte

Mascara shadowed her eyes. The skull earring hung

from her throat by a string. A stick of chalk was stuck in the pocket of her shirt.

"No flashlights from here," Kayley said.

forte

As the flashlights switched, on to off, on to off, on to off, the faces vanished. Mark Huff's face was the last to vanish. It looked, for the first time I had ever seen, scared.

I led everyone into the ghosthouse, which sounded empty, but wasn't empty at all.

●

"We must pinpoint the heart of the structure," Kayley said.

piano

She unfurled the blueprint, tracing the lines of the *piano* blueprint like she had traced the lines in my palms.

"In the room where the beams converge and diverge," Kayley whispered.

pianissimo

She paced from room to room, using the blueprint as a map. She drifted through the hallway. She drifted through the kitchen. She drifted through the entryway. The others stood whispering, in moonlight, in darkness. It felt weird*nightmare* *piano*, seeing strangers inside these rooms. I calculated the odds Grandpa Dykhouse had hidden in the bathtub, which were about 43%, and in the cabinets, which were about 17%, and in the space between the door and the wall, which were about 29%. The others had hidden upstairs, unless someone had doubled back.

Kayley paused at the bottom of the staircase, facing the fireplace. She crouched, her back hunched like the crook of a bassoon. She tossed the blueprint. She drew a pentagram on the floor with a stump of chalk. She chalked the outline of a body into the pentagram, with the head, the hands, the feet, at the star's five points.

"Here," Kayley said.

piano

Everyone circled the pentagram. I sat alongside Mark Huff. "I'm not sitting by the black spot!" Mark Huff hissed.

piano

Everyone scooted away from me, squeezing into a half circle across the pentagram, like people avoiding someone with a majorly contagious disease.

"Two spirits haunt this house," Kayley said.

piano

Kayley stuck the stick of chalk in the pocket of her shirt.

"One's soul haunts the staircase, the kitchen, the

cellar, often appearing as a hovering glow. One's soul haunts the porch, the bathroom, the fireplace, often appearing as a hovering mist," Kayley said.

piano
"Hovering glow?" Crooked Teeth said.

piano
"Hovering mist?" The Unibrow said.

piano
"Freaky," Leah Keen whispered.

fermata
I spotted something shadowy gliding along the railing upstairs. The Geluso twins were facing the staircase, but didn't seem to notice.

"Which shall we summon?" Kayley said.

piano
"I don't know," Mark Huff whispered.

piano
"Which tripped you?" Kayley said.

piano
"I never saw," Mark Huff whispered.

piano
"Make him fight them both!" the Geluso twins said.

homophony
"Maybe this wasn't such a good idea," Emma Dirge whimpered.

pianissimo
"The mist ghost, okay, the mist ghost!" Mark Huff whispered.

piano
Kayley pointed at the chalk symbol.

"Spit on the body," Kayley said.

forte
Mark Huff spit on the outline of the body.

"Stand on the star," Kayley said.
forte

Mark Huff stood on the pentagram. His eyes were >
his normal eyes. Twice as big, maybe. A hacking noise
forte
shook the staircase.

"What was that?" Mark Huff said.
glissando

"In requiem. In harmony. Tonight the stars align.
We summon the spirit's form. The soul uses your spit to
regain its body," Kayley said.
forte

Again the hacking noise. Emma Dirge and Leah
forte
Keen were hugging their flashlights. The Geluso twins
were clutching the earflaps of their hats like people gripping the sides of a roller coaster. Mark Huff crouched,
fists clenched together. Wind whaled against the house.
forte
Leaves skidded across the floor. The curtains snapped.
forte   *forte*
Again the hacking noise. The Gelusos shouted, "Get
fortissimo   *homophony*
ready, Mark!" Kayley shouted, "The spirit draws near!"
crescendo

Then, from upstairs, a vast white form exploded
across the railing, hanging above us and then fluttering at
forte
the pentagram, and everyone screamed, even me.
falsetto, creak

"A message from beyond!" Kayley shouted. She leapt
forte

for them as they swooped to the floor—graphing paper, prealgebra handouts, loose-leaf essays. It was the ISAAC NOTES.

But, from upstairs, more hacking, and a thudding *mezzo-forte* *forte* and a spewing sound, over and over and over, like a mon- *fortissimo* ster's growling, and as the Gelusos snatched fistfuls of floating paper Mark Huff shouted "What is that?" *piano* and Emma Dirge and Leah Keen huddled together fumbling *staccato* for their flashlights but Kayley shouted, "Lights will upset the spirits!" but Mark Huff had switched his flash- *sforzando* light too and their beams swung across the staircase and the bathroom and the ceiling and each other and some- thing kept spewing and the Gelusos were gaping and Emma Dirge was whimpering "Let's leave let's leave let's *fortissimo* leave!" and Leah Keen was whispering majorly illogical *allegro* things like "Don't—" and "Please—" and "Everybody—" *adagio* until the beams met at the fireplace, at the hearth, alight- ing, together, like a spotlight, onto Grandpa Dykhouse's shoes.

"Legs in the fireplace!" Mark Huff shouted.
forte

"Abandon ship!" the Geluso twins shouted.

homophony

Everyone bolted from the ghosthouse into the yard. The Geluso twins scattered into the trees. The others dodged yapping wolfdogs and flew after the Gelusos. I ran for the shed, *forte* to hide until everyone had vanished, but then something shoved me against the dead walnut tree.

"Once you've been given the black spot, nothing can stop what's coming for you," Kayley hissed, ISAAC NOTES crinkling between her arms. *piano* "But here," Kayley said, "for luck." *piano* *decrescendo* Then she kissed me, her lips to my eyebrow.

My eyebrow felt happy*jamboree*. My eyebrow had never had feelings before. My eyebrow wanted more feelings. "What if I need more luck than that?" I said.

She squinted. She stared at my eyebrow. *piano* Then she kissed me again, her lips to my lips.

Then, in my brain, only numbers—zeros and ones, zeros and ones, zeros and ones, 01101100011011101110 11001100101, a sort of symphony, all pianos and violins.

"That's all the luck I have for now," Kayley said. *pianissimo*

Before, Nicholas Funes = Boy Who No One Would Want To Kiss.

Now, Nicholas Funes = Boy Who Was Somehow Kissable.

It felt odd, having become this other thing.

"Please don't die, Nicholas Funes!" Kayley shouted, fly-
forte
ing into the trees. "I want to teach you to be a better kisser!"

●

In the ghosthouse, Grandpa Dykhouse was lighting the lantern.

"Everyone saw your shoes," I said.
mezzo-piano
"I'll hide somewhere foolproof next time," Grandpa Dykhouse muttered.
mezzo-piano
Grandpa Rose had puked during the seance. He was sick, was mumbling, wasn't himself. The blood had drained
pianissimo
from his face. He hobbled from the staircase toward the fireplace, using Jordan's shoulders as a cane.

"Who threw the ISAAC NOTES?" I said.
mezzo-piano
Jordan waved at Zeke.

"I tried to stop him," Jordan said.
mezzo-piano
I gestured at Zeke.

"You could have ended things with the Isaacs forever," I said.
mezzo-piano

Zeke chewed a lip, helping Grandpa Rose onto the hearth.

"There will always be Little Isaacs. There will always be Big Isaacs," Zeke said. "There will always be Isaacs."
mezzo-piano

caesura

"I knew what I had to do," Zeke said. "No Isaac will ever stop me from doing that."
piano

●

Numbers had been humming through my brain ever since the kiss, but it wasn't until Jordan and Zeke and I had left the ghosthouse and were hiking home through the swaying birches and the swaying pines and the swaying oaks that I hit the limit, my brain touched infinity, the numbers clicked into place, everything canceling everything, equation solved.

$X18471913 = ?$

I whispered to myself, "The stone boy."
piano

"What did you say?" Zeke said.
forte

"We're going back to the ghosthouse," I said.
piano

"Now?" Zeke said.
forte

"And we need to run," I said.
piano

324

We bolted to the ghosthouse, the wolfdogs galloping alongside. Grandpa Dykhouse was settling Grandpa Rose into a bed of crumpled wool blankets.

"I know where the heirlooms are," I said.

forte

"How?" Grandpa Dykhouse said.

forte

"You," I said.

forte

Jordan gaped.

"The librarian powers actually worked?" Jordan said.

forte

I rooted through the notes about Grandpa Rose's memories, flattening pages on the floor.

"Here" (pointing at "he started burying bodies for the smugglers") "and here" (pointing at "the name of whoever was buried there where he would have to bury the others") "and here" (pointing at "the thick ring of iron keys the smugglers had given him").

"What? What 'here'? I don't get it," Jordan said.

forte

"He buried the heirlooms where he buried the bodies! The same place! The graveyard!" I said.

forte

"The graveyard?" Jordan said, but Zeke said, "Makes

forte   *forte*

sense. Already hundreds of bodies there. Nobody would notice a few extra."

"And I know where they're buried," I said. "The tomb
of XAVIER. Born 1847. Dead 1913."

forte

"X18471913!" Grandpa Dykhouse whispered, and Jordan said, "We're going to need shovels."

piano

"It's not that sort of grave," I said. "What we'll need is

forte

a crowbar."

forte

HEIRLOOMS

S leet poured from the sky, making ghosts of the
trees and slush of the road. I huddled into myself
as we walked, hugging the crowbar to my chest,
my nose leaking snot. None of us had coats. Grandpa
Rose wasn't himself, didn't understand where we were
going.

"Take me back, take me back to that house," Grandpa
Rose begged.

"Quiet, Monte," Grandpa Dykhouse hissed.

Jordan and Zeke kept tight grips on Grandpa Rose,

leading him along. A black truck honked at us, its tires
forte
spinning in the sleet as it fishtailed across the bridge. The
mezzo-forte
wolfdogs barked until the taillights had vanished.
forte

When we got to the graveyard, we tried to boost
Grandpa Rose over the spiked fence, but he was too weak
to get over.

"Who are you people? Where are we going? Do you
know who you're dealing with?" Grandpa Rose shouted,
fortissimo
spittle flecking his shirt.

"Would you shut up!" I hissed, clapping a hand over
piano
his mouth.

I shoved the crowbar at Jordan, then led Grandpa
Rose along the fence to the gate, an iron archway with a
padlocked chain, with Grandpa Dykhouse hobbling after.
Jordan was at the gate already, bashing at the padlock,
the crowbar clanging against it again and again and again
fortissimo *fortissimo* *fortissimo*
like a song of Can't Get In. Zeke was crouched at the gate
with his wolfdogs, whispering into their ears. A van drove
pianissimo
past us, its tires swishing in the sleet, and parked at the
mezzo-piano
rest home, its headlights switching off.

"Hurry, boy, hurry!" Grandpa Dykhouse hissed at
piano
Jordan, staring at the van.

"My fingers are starting to freeze to the crowbar," Jordan muttered, swinging the crowbar at the padlock.
piano
The headlights of a car parked at the grocer switched
on. Zeke was chewing a lip. Jordan swung the crowbar at
the padlock again, and then, from the crowbar and the
padlock, rang a different song, a one-note song of Enter.
forte
The padlock dropped from the chain, and the chain
rattled through the bars of the gate and dropped into the
forte
sleet. Zeke shouldered the gate, and we stepped into the
graveyard, the wolfdogs galloping ahead.

●

At the mausoleum, Grandpa Rose was himself again.

"And this place," Grandpa Rose whispered. He wiped
piano
sleet from the face of the mausoleum, unburying letters,
first X , then X VI , then XAVIER. Underneath that,
1847–1913.

Zeke had scrambled onto the tomb with the stone
boy, was keeping a lookout as the wolfdogs prowled

through gravestones below. The mausoleum's padlock
> the gate's padlock, at least twice the size. Jordan was
cradling the crowbar, staring at the padlock, looking
defeated.

"There's no way we'll break this one," Jordan said.

"We won't have to," I said. _piano_

piano

I dug for the key in my pocket, felt the shape of the x
with my thumb.

"I see flashlights!" Zeke hissed.
piano

"Where?" Grandpa Dykhouse hissed.
piano

"Outside of the graveyard!" Zeke hissed.
piano

I jammed the x key into the padlock. As I twisted it, I
felt it scraping through the rust on the inside, unlocking
something that had been locked even longer than I had
been alive. The padlock popped open.
piano

I hauled the chain from the rings on the doors.

Jordan stepped past me, but I stopped him.

"After Grandpa Rose," I said.
piano

Grandpa Rose nodded, and frowned.

Then Grandpa Rose gripped the rings, shoved apart
the doors, and stepped inside.

The air in the mausoleum smelled rotten. Skeletons in tattered clothes were piled along the walls—a skull blindfolded with a wool scarf, a skull with a broken eye socket, a skull split by zigzag parallel cracks, a skeleton in a checkered suit jacket tangled together with skeletons in plain suit jackets, bones stuffed into boots flecked with dried concrete, bones stuffed into leather loafers, jaws with uneven teeth, jaws with silver teeth, jaws stuffed with moldy gags—all of the bodies Grandpa Rose had been paid to hide. Near my high-tops lay a loose hand of pale bones, wearing a dull wedding ring. I hadn't expected to be afraid of the bodies, but seeing them was different from hearing about them. Seeing them, I got cold^{deathbed}, like all of the warmth inside me had been sucked straight out.

Zeke stood in the doorway with his wolfdogs around him. "I don't like this place," Zeke whispered. Zeke wouldn't step inside. ^{piano}

"So many bodies," Grandpa Dykhouse whispered, staring at the skeletons, but Grandpa Rose whispered, ^{adagio} "Yes, this place, I remember being here!" ^{allegro}

XAVIER's casket sat in the center of the mausoleum. A dark trunk with a brass lock had been shoved against the foot of the casket. The lock was engraved, with cramped gold letters, ROSE.

My heartbeat beat faster, and faster, and faster, hit an uncountable tempo.

"The key," Grandpa Rose said.

piano

I dropped the ROSE key into Grandpa Rose's cupped hands.

I knelt at the trunk.

Grandpa Rose twisted the key and lifted the lid.

●

The trunk was almost empty.

No ivory revolver. No bellows clock. No golden hammer.

At the bottom were a faded photograph, a pair of leather notebooks, and a rusted metal cog.

I gaped at Grandpa Rose. Grandpa Rose gaped at the trunk.

"Are these the heirlooms?" I said.

piano

Grandpa Rose shook his head.

"I remember there being so much more," Grandpa Rose whispered.

piano

My heart had quit. I slumped against the trunk.

Grandpa Rose murmured something I couldn't under-*piano* stand. He shoved his shirtsleeves to the elbows, then reached into the trunk. He took the faded photograph, carefully pinching the curled edges. He grimaced, like someone about to either puke or cry.

"Do you know who this is?" Grandpa Rose said.

piano

It was a woman with tangled hair and an upturned nose, wearing a bluish dress, standing against some birch trees. She was holding a garden spade and a watering can.

"Who?" I said.

piano

"Your Grandma Rose," Grandpa Rose said.

piano

"But she never let anyone take her photo," I said.

piano

"She only ever let me take just this one," Grandpa Rose said.

piano

I sat back up. I took the photo. I stared at her face. I memorized the eyebrows, the jawline, every wrinkle, every freckle. No one would ever want to buy it, but there was nothing else like it. It was totally worthless and totally priceless. I couldn't stop staring.

"You were right," I whispered.
piano

"A picture? What about the treasure? Where are the revolver, the clock, the hammer?" Jordan said, but *forte* Grandpa Dykhouse grunted at him, like BE QUIET.
piano

"What about these?" I said. I took a leather notebook, *piano* flipping to a random page of misspelled words and underlined numbers.

"Nothing, useless, diaries I kept when I was away," Grandpa Rose said. He collapsed onto the casket, scratch-*piano* ing at his beard with both hands. In the moonlight, his face looked ancient. "Where are your heirlooms, kid? Kid, why aren't your heirlooms here?"

"What's this?" I said, touching the rusted metal cog, *piano* but Grandpa Rose shouted, "I don't know, Nicholas, I *forte* don't know!"

It was the only time he had ever used my name.

Then the wolfdogs snarled, and from the doorway *forte* Zeke said, "Do you remember when I mentioned those *forte* people with flashlights?"

I spun around.

"Why?" I said.

piano

"Because they're here," Zeke said.

forte

●

We stepped from the mausoleum—Grandpa Rose, Jordan, Zeke, and I. The four of us stood in the sleet, Grandpa Rose mumbling to himself and squinting at the flash-

piano

lights, Jordan's fingers swollen from breaking the padlock, Zeke's face purpled with bruises, me clutching my grandmother's photograph, the leather notebooks, the rusted metal cog.

I said once that I would ask you a riddle. Here is your riddle—what was bad, and what was worse, and what was worst of all?

Bad was this—a nurse at the rest home had spotted us sneaking into the graveyard.

Worse was this—I had zero heirlooms, or at least none worth any money, the money I needed to save my brother, the money I had promised Zeke could get him to his father, the money I had promised Jordan could get him a boat for his grandfather.

But worst was this—of those people with flashlights standing there, watching us walk out of a mausoleum we had broken into, in a graveyard we had broken into, with a grandfather who was supposed to be missing—one of those people was my mom.

AFTERMATH

The nurses peeked into the mausoleum to check whether we had broken anything, then chained the doors.

Grandpa Dykhouse was still inside. When Zeke had spotted the nurses headed for the mausoleum, Grandpa Dykhouse had said that he wasn't going back to the rest home, that he wouldn't live like that again. Then Grandpa Dykhouse had crawled into XAVIER's casket.

The next seven hours of his life were probably his scariest—hiding in a casket with XAVIER's bones, and then crawling out of the casket, but still trapped with skeletons piled from the floor to the ceiling.

Or maybe he wasn't scared. Maybe he had seen enough dying and death and dead that bones couldn't scare him anymore.

In the morning we snuck into the graveyard and unlocked the mausoleum. Grandpa Dykhouse was huddled shivering on the trunk.

"Where's Monte?" he said, his voice rasping.

"Rest home," I said. "Now even if they catch you, they can't send you back. Grandpa Rose is living in your room. The rest home is full again."

●

Grandpa Dykhouse spent his last months in the ghosthouse, playing chess with Jordan, building fires, reading books. His lungs flooded with phlegm from the weather, but he refused to live anywhere else.

It was winter, when all of Michigan turns white, everything like a ghost of itself—snow piled on the roads, on the roofs of houses, on the hoods of everyone's parkas. The lake's shallows had frozen, the waves dead now, ice—you could walk from the beach onto the water, even beyond the lighthouse across the frozen waves, before the ice met the black of the unfrozen water. It's freshwater, but most of the lake never freezes. The math tells it to freeze—the temperature drops to 19°, 13°, 2°, into the negatives—but the lake is the size of a sea. It's beyond the math of it.

During winter the lighthouse keeper kept his rowboat in a boathouse along the lighthouse. After having worked for the lighthouse keeper, Zeke knew where the boat was kept. He also knew when the lighthouse keeper napped, a fire crackling in his stove, drowning out the other noise.

Jordan was getting better with the crowbar—broke the padlock with a single swing.

We carried the rowboat to the dunes, hid the rowboat in the trees.

We ripped rafters from the attic of the ghosthouse, took hammers and nails from the shed.

Zeke stole everything else we needed—a white sail, a wooden rudder.

It took all winter to build it. Below us, high schoolers warmed the smugglers' tunnels with the heat from their cigarettes, the heat from their fireworks, the heat from their breath. On other lakes, anglers built icehouses, fished through holes sawed into the ice.

●

We never told anyone the truth about Grandpa Rose. We told my mom we had spotted him that night walking along the road, had run after him into the graveyard, had caught him breaking into the mausoleum. I felt bad^{criminal} for lying to her. But she never would have forgiven me if she had known the truth.

I wanted to tell her, "I spent so many days with him and while we were together we were friends." I wanted to tell her, "Even if he wasn't a good father, he was a better grandfather, because he came back for us and taught me chess and told me stories and had my eyes and slept on a floor in a house with no windows for night after night after night just to save you, and your house, and your son the tree."

My mom said I was a hero for finding Grandpa Rose. But I was < a hero. I had always been < a hero. I was a thief and a liar. I knew where skeletons were buried, the skeletons of missing people, and I hadn't said a word.

●

At school we turned into an us, a Nicholas + Jordan + Zeke.

We sat together in the cafeteria. Jordan and Zeke got detention together for drawing anti-Isaacs graffiti in the locker room. Zeke and I got detention together for setting loose hundreds of fireflies during a school dance. Jordan gave me a new nickname, one like Skulltooth—instead of Calculator, now I was Mastermind.

●

The Geluso twins didn't hate Jordan anymore. Mark Huff still hated Jordan, but he hated him < he had hated him before. Emma Dirge didn't. Leah Keen didn't. But they didn't hate the Isaacs, either. All of them had read what the Isaacs had written. But, even then, none of them hated the Isaacs.

There would always be Isaacs.

●

My mom took the Yorks' offer. Our FOR SALE sign went down.

But before the closing, the Yorks called my mom

again. They had found another house, an empty one owned by a bank. They liked it better. Bigger windows, newer floors. A pool in the backyard.

Our FOR SALE sign went up again.

●

Jordan's dad hit Genevieve one night during dinner—split her lip and made her cry.

"It had been months since he had hit any of us," Jordan said. "I thought it was over, but then the meanness
piano
just came back out."

I could see Jordan thinking, that meanness might come out again.

"You aren't the only one with a mean father," Zeke said.
forte
"At least your grandfathers weren't killers," I said.
forte
"Grandpa Rose wasn't a killer," Zeke said.
forte
"He hid the bodies," I said.
forte
Then Jordan was thinking, what if when I have kids I hit them too?, and Zeke was thinking, what if after I fall in love with a man someday I leave him and move to a new country and never come back again?, and I was thinking,

what if I become something like Grandpa Rose became, what if that's what happens when my pod splits open, what if I become a criminal?

Zeke uncapped his silver marker.

"We will not become our grandfathers. We will not become our fathers. We will take only their best parts, take none of their worst," Zeke said.

He made us swear it. He wrote it on our arms. *piano*

●

Kayley Schreiber taught me new things. With her hands she taught me THESE ARE YOUR HANDS. With her tongue she taught me THIS IS YOUR TONGUE. She would sit across from me, her knees touching my knees, and when our knees touched I would remember THESE ARE MY KNEES. I had forgotten I had them, until then. She gave me my hands, my tongue, my knees, everything that needed giving back.

●

Zeke already had sold enough instruments and backpacks and high-tops that he had the money he needed to fly himself to his father.

When he tried to buy a ticket, though, he couldn't. No

one would let a thirteen-year-old fly alone. At least not unless he had his mother's permission.

He did not have his mother's permission.

"Some things you can't have until you're older," Zeke said.

forte

Zeke wrote each of his brothers a letter. He drew a silver wolf over the seal of each envelope. He mailed each of the letters the same day.

●

After school, I would ride with my mom to the rest home. While she mopped floors, I sat with Grandpa Rose. None of him remained. He didn't remember where he was, didn't remember when he was, didn't remember who he was, even. He was dead, but kept living.

Every day I brought his leather notebooks and read from his diary aloud. "This is who you were," I would say, then read the memories he had written. Sometimes he

piano

would smile, like he remembered. But he didn't remember. I would show him the photograph of Grandma Rose, and he would stare at her the same way he stared at anyone now—like at a stranger.

In the notebooks, he wrote about having sold our

heirlooms, one after another, to pay for things he never needed. Hotel rooms, poker games, luxury cigarettes. That was the truth about the heirlooms. Even he had underestimated just how selfish he had been. Everything that had been ours—the ivory revolver, the bellows clock, the golden hammer—he had pawned while my mom was still a girl. He had spent everything on himself.

During breaks between mopping, my mom would perch on his bed with him, and listen to me read.

"So there really were heirlooms," my mom said, *forte* leafing through a notebook.

"Once," I said.

My mom *forte* laughed, shaking her head. She leaned in to adjust the *piano* cardigan Grandpa Rose was wearing— straightening the shoulders, smoothing the chest.

"Is that what you ran away looking for?" my mom said, creasing her eyebrows. *forte* "You'd be so embarrassed, if you knew you'd gone off searching for something that wasn't even there."

Grandpa Rose stared blankly at a murky patch of sunlight on the wall. My mom blew some hair out of her eyes, then reached for the photograph of Grandma Rose. She had bought a gold wooden picture frame for the photograph with money we didn't have.

"He always did love making trouble," my mom said. "At the very least, he got to cause one last giant uproar."
forte

What he liked most was to have his hands held. Sometimes, if you squeezed them, they would squeeze you back.

Afterward, Jordan and Zeke would come for me, and all of us would hike out to the dunes, where we would work on the boat.

●

In band class, everyone learned new terms. Everyone learned that grave means "play grimly." Everyone learned that vivo means "play lively." We played songs that were grave. We played songs that were vivo. Most of them, they were both.

●

When the trees grew leaves again, we hauled our boat down the dunes and into the water. Grandpa Dykhouse stood with us there, his glasses hooked to his sweater, his jeans rolled to his ankles, the skin of his feet as pale as the insides of apples from a winter without sun.

"It's a bit smaller than my old boat," Grandpa Dykhouse said.

forte

"It was the biggest we could get," Jordan said.

forte

"It's perfect," Grandpa Dykhouse said.

forte

Foamy waves slid onto the beach, to our ankles, then

piano

slid out again. The boat's sail was snapping in the wind.

piano   *piano*

The boat's rudder was knocking against the hull. With

piano

thick lines of white paint we had named the boat PAWPAW.

"Where will you go?" I said.

forte

"Somewhere I've never been," Grandpa Dykhouse said.

forte

"But you're coming back?" Jordan said.

forte

"I'll find you then," Grandpa Dykhouse said.

forte

Zeke gave Grandpa Dykhouse $3,889 (prime).

"Eat well," Zeke said.

forte

●

Letters with Italian stamps arrived at Zeke's mailbox—an envelope from a NICO, an envelope from a DINO. Then, weeks later, a crumpled envelope with dirty thumbprints from a GIORGIO.

The letters were written in a language he couldn't understand.

"I guess I'll have to steal some books about Italian," Zeke said.

forte

He carried the letters with him everywhere.

●

Grandpa Rose's blood pressure was 140/90, then 150/100, then 160/110. The math was telling him to die. But he was beyond the math of it.

I read his memories to him every day.

But, next to my brother, I planted an acorn.

Grandpa Rose's self had died already—that was the black spot that I had been given. When the next one came for me, Grandpa Rose's body would die too.

By then his tree would already be growing.

IF YOU FIND THIS

I'm going to keep these notes in the ghosthouse, under the floorboards, in a cardboard box. If you find these, you're standing where everything happened. And I want you to understand everything. I want you to understand that I am not dead. I want you to understand that I am alive. I want you to understand that I live somewhere not too far from where you're standing, in the house where I've always lived.

We are not losing our house. And we will not lose our house. Because, in the end, Grandpa Rose left us an heirloom—an heirloom Grandpa Rose had forgotten how to use.

It was after Grandpa Dykhouse had sailed away, after Jordan and Zeke and I had sat on the dunes chewing beach grass together, after I had walked home to be alone, that I spotted everything sitting there on my dresser. The passport with stamped pages. The rusted metal cog. The photograph of my grandmother. The broken music box. Everything Grandpa Rose had left us. Then I realized it was an equation.

I simplified it—subtracted the passport, subtracted the photograph.

I studied what was left.

Rusted metal cog + broken music box = ?

I put them together. I wound the music box. A song came tinkling out of it, grave, then vivo, then grave again.

Then I ran outside, leaping from the deck and tearing across the backyard, and the birds were shrieking and the wind was rattling through the leaves of the trees and *forte* the squirrels were crunching through the dead leaves *forte* below, and I shoved a lock of hair out of my eyes and *piano* dropped to my knees at my brother's roots and before my brother could even speak I wound the music box again and the song came tinkling out of it and I held it toward my brother, saying with it, again and again and again and again, LISTEN TO THIS SONG, BROTHER, LISTEN TO THIS SONG—THIS IS THE SONG THAT WILL SAVE YOU.

MY THANKS TO

BRIAN JACQUES, 1939–2011, "You're gonna carry that weight."

SERGEI PROKOFIEV, whose duck, even after being eaten, could be heard.

MARY CLIMIE, for the letter she mailed me seventeen years ago.

KRISTEN and KARA, AMANDA and ALEXANDRA, who are even better than brothers.

MOTHER, FATHER, for letting me run wild through the woods, for giving me knives and shovels, for not caring if I came home hands sticky with sap and hair caked with mud.

OTHER FATHER, OTHER MOTHER, for letting me run wild through the woods.

BRIAN HODGSON, for running wild with me through the woods.

CHRISTIAN PIERS, who discovered the skeletons under the dunes.

TRACY BARRETT, the original mastermind.

TONY EARLEY, who can teach something to even an alien from the crop circles.

LORRAINE LOPEZ, for all the hours and hours and hours she gave this.

NANCY REISMAN, one of the planet's preeminent readers.

HEATHER SELLERS, who swore this could happen.

SARAH BURNES, for battling the dragons.

BETHANY STROUT, for giving this misfit book a home.

DAVID FOSTER WALLACE, for everything.

SUFJAN STEVENS, for "Holland" especially.

CHARLES SCHULZ, whose children spoke numbers and notes.

And thanks, as always, to JACK RIDL, and his brother the star.

WHICH WORDS MEAN WHAT

forte means "play loudly"

piano means "play softly"

da capo means "return to the beginning," means
   "play the song again"

mezzo-forte means "play sort of loudly"

mezzo-piano means "play sort of softly"

glissando is when you suddenly leap between two
   notes

fortissimo means "play very loudly"

pianissimo means "play very softly"

fermata means "hold that note"

crescendo means "play louder"

decrescendo means "play softer"

sforzando means "play this with sudden force"

staccato means "play this sharp and choppy,"
    means "let none of these notes touch"

allegro means "play quickly"

adagio means "play slowly"

caesura means "time stops here," means "every-
    thing is quiet"

homophony means "play together, all at once,
    together make your chords"

falsetto means "sing in your highest shrillest
    voice"

creak means "sing in your lowest raspiest voice"

grave means "play grimly"

vivo means "play lively"

Matthew Baker

was born and lives in Michigan. He is thirty-one years old. (Prime.)